LOST IN REWIND

a novel by

TALI ALEXANDER

Editing by Kristen Clark Switzer & Lori Sabin
Formatting and interior design by JT Formatting
Cover design © Perfect Pear Creative
Cover Photographer: Specular
Cover Model: Adam Cowie with Boss Model Management

Tali Alexander Books Inc.
For information email Tali Alexander at:
Tali@TaliAlexander.com

Library of Congress Cataloging-in-Publication Data

First Edition: July 2016
Alexander, Tali
ISBN-13: 978-0996052986 | ISBN-10: 0996052984
1. Lost in Rewind—Fiction 2. Fiction—Romance
3. Fiction—Contemporary Romance 4. Fiction—Suspense

Adult Content Warning!
The content you are about to read includes adult language and graphic descriptions of nudity and sexual activity. This book is intended for adult readers 18 years of age and older. Reader discretion is advised.

A Note from the Author

Thank you for purchasing **Lost In Rewind** ©. This is the 3rd and final book in the Audio Fools Series featuring characters that were introduced in **LOVE IN REWIND** (Book I) and **LIES IN REWIND** (Book II). It is recommended that you read **LOVE IN REWIND** and **LIES IN REWIND** first for a richer understanding of the characters, but not necessary.

**All books in the series are interconnected,
but each may be read as a standalone.**

*He had kept all
the pain for himself*

– Victor Hugo, *The Hunchback of Notre-Dame*

Jeffery

"Daddy, are you up? Can you come give me a kiss? I had a bad dream," my daughter yells from down the hall. The acoustics in this house make it sound as if she's in the room with us.

"I'll be right there, Juliet; stop yelling or you'll wake everybody," I answer in a low tone, but I'm sure she heard me with the house being quiet and everyone still asleep.

"Jeff, who's calling? I'm up," my beautiful wife murmurs with her eyes still closed and probably mid-dream.

"Go back to sleep. I'll go give Juliet a kiss and be right back," I whisper and give Sarah a kiss, about to make my way down the hall to snuggle with my little girl while she still lets me.

Sarah suddenly sits up, her eyes wide with alert, pausing my exit. "Wait, what time is it? Did the baby not get up yet?"

"Relax, she's finally sleeping through the night. That's a good thing. Now go back to sleep; you still have a few hours." I always forget how new she is to motherhood. Juliet and Jacob have accepted her into their lives seamlessly, and the way she takes care of and loves them makes me almost not regret every single one of my life choices. It's been a long journey that I've lived without her by my side for all these years. "Sleep, I'll check up on Jolene, too. You get some rest—we have a big day today."

Her arms stretch above her head as she opens her mouth to say something through a yawn, but then she snuggles back. Right before I leave the room, I hear her mumble, "I love you, only you." I glance back, smiling at her simple statement. *She only loves me.* What else could a man ask for? What a gift it is to be someone's one and only. After all these years, we finally found each other.

I walk down the long corridor ahead of me as I think back to how I almost lost everything I ever loved two years ago.

Two Years Ago

Jeffery

"Who Wants To Live Forever" by Queen

My eyes sting as the fresh New York City air assaults my face. The change in scenery clears my head, causing the actuality of the last two days to marginally evaporate, but it won't last; I can't escape my life. I cross the street in a calm state of panic while the sound of strangers going on with their lives, even as mine continues to fall apart, hits my ears and mocks me. I move farther and farther away from my house. I walk without turning around, requiring a physical distance from the truth, as if such a thing could ever be achieved. I walk faster, I run, to get away from the place I've once called home and pretend this never happened.

Everything will be okay. Everything will be fine.

I unlock my car and shuffle in like a burglar running away from the scene of the crime. I put the car into drive. All I need to do is press my foot on the gas and I'll be gone—my troubles will be forgotten. Just move my damn foot from the brake and compress the gas pedal, but I'm frozen, motionless, and unresponsive to simple brain commands. *I'm Lost.* How did I get here? How in the world did I get here?

I close my eyes and take a deep breath as my whole life flashes before my eyes—Jacqueline, how we first met, and how we fell in love. I then see Sara, on the dance floor, in her room, and in the back of that taxi crying. I remember holding my kids for the first time, their sweet little faces—they're my whole world. *Where am I going?* I've caused a sea of pain because I loved two women. *Enough!* I need to grow up and be the man I promised Jacqueline I'd be.

I open the glove compartment and retrieve the letter my wife wrote me. The letter she handed me on the night she died in my arms. She made me promise to only open it after she was gone. It's the letter I read at least a hundred times as I held her lifeless body in my arms until I couldn't pretend she would ever open her eyes again and look at me as if nothing bad could ever happen to us.

I replay that unbearable morning, three days ago, when I came into our bedroom after speaking to her doctor for the millionth time. I'm not an ignorant fool, I knew she wasn't doing well for months, but the doctor verbalized all my greatest fears. He informed me that Jacky has been refusing treatment and that she has vowed to be finished with chemo, doctors, and hospitals for as long as she has left to live.

"Jacky, are you up? We need to talk for a bit?" I'd said while I climbed into bed next to her. She had her eyes closed and I just lay there, letting her rest while I watched the frail, weak version of my wife for a few minutes. She looked thin, small, almost child-like, not like the sexy, curvy girl I used to lust over in college.

I tried to stay strong and keep my eyes focused and clear for as long as I could to delay the inevitable fear she would see in them. *"Jacky, my love, can you open your eyes?"* I whispered into her ear. She finally acknowledged my presence and turned toward me, arranging herself at my side. We always fit so well together.

"Are the kids dressed for school? Why are you not dressed for work?"

I was still in my pajama bottoms as she questioned me in a hushed tone, realizing how late in the morning it was. There was nowhere I needed to be other than right there, loving her.

"I'm not going to work this week," I declared with a fake, forced smile. *"You don't need to pretend with me. Your doctor said we have to start chemo again. Don't even think of arguing!"* I took hold of her face, wishing things were different. *"I've made arrangements, and I'll be in the hospital with you. We'll do it together like we did before. But, Jacky, you can't stay home and refuse treatment. We need you to get better, baby,"* I stated calmly as I ran my fingers down her bony cheek. I tried to mask the horror etched in my heart ever since I had that conversation with Doctor Stein the night before. We both knew she would never get better … she was dying.

"Can I ask you for something?" Her lips trembled as the words left her mouth.

"Anything, I would do anything for you. You know that, right?"

She had closed her eyes and smiled—I wished I could've made her smile more often. She slowly reached over to her nightstand and pulled out an envelope from the drawer with my full name handwritten on the front. She handed me the envelope, which I'd accepted, and then placed her fingers over my lips to silence me while she spoke.

"I want you to hold me today, all day. No talking, no crying, I just want to be in your arms for the rest of my life. Promise you'll only read this letter when I'm gone."

I'd shaken my head and tried to protest, but she pressed her weak fingers to my lips to stop me.

"Can you promise me that?"

"I promise, my love."

I'm in my fucking car, crying and having an emotional breakdown like a lunatic. I open the letter and read it again, reminding myself that she always knew exactly who I was all along.

To The Man I Owe My Life To,

Please don't be sad that I'm gone, I don't feel the pain anymore. I want you to know that I'm actually ready for what should've been my doomed fate to finally catch up to me. I will never pretend to understand why the universe allowed me to stay here with you and survive for as long as I have, but I did. I survived, and I lived. We thought we would only get a year together but we got over fourteen, and only now I feel as if the final countdown has at last begun.

I should've been smarter and not dragged you down to hell with me. I clearly recall refusing your ring at first because I didn't want you to endure this—me, cancer, hospitals, chemo, death. But you didn't care, you said you loved me and would make me happy. You promised to be by my side every day for the rest of my life, and I wasn't going to get a better offer than that. I was selfish. I married you even though I knew somewhere in the back of my delusional dying mind that you were and always will be involved with another woman, but I was desperate, defeated and dying, so I chose to pretend. We both did. Thank you for being my selfish escape.

I promise you I always knew who lived in your heart. I've watched you quietly love someone else for over seventeen years, and yet, I pretended it would go away just like my cancer. If you only allow it, your head can make you believe lies until they stop being lies and start feeling like the truth. I allowed myself to be fooled because when you were with me, she disappeared, and I pretended you only loved me. When you looked at me, it was different than the look you wore when I knew you were daydream-

ing about her. I pretended she wasn't real, just an intangible fantasy for you while I was your tangible home. But I always knew you were never really mine.

I should've stepped aside and left you alone or made you leave me and go to her. I tried to send you away; I gave you the freedom to go to her often, but I just wasn't convincing enough ... because the truth was I couldn't let you go. I thought that I would unburden you years ago and you could finally stop choosing me. I don't understand why you chose me and not her for so many years. I know you never got over her, you never moved on, or un-loved her. I think that the years you've been apart only made you love her that much more. I don't know why you stayed with me for this long, but I need for you to believe I don't feel cheated on; I understand the choices you've made and don't ever think for one second that I didn't feel loved. Thank you for never abandoning me and helping me fight every step of the way.

I may be sick, but I'm not bitter, I swear. I still feel like the luckiest girl in the world for being granted time to see those perfect little humans grow up for the past seven years. When they get older, I hope they won't hate me for being the reason their real mother and father were kept apart for all these years.

You were, and still are, the most magnificent thing I've ever known, and the only man to make me feel alive with just a smile. Nothing about you is ordinary; those distinctive dual-colored eyes staring back at me is what I'll see in my mind as I take my last breath. Most people live a whole lifetime without feeling what I've felt in my short life because of you. Don't let anyone make you feel like a bad guy, they don't know. Only I know. I understand why you had to be two different people—my Jeff and her Jeffery—in order to survive the nightmare I pulled you into. I was always relieved knowing that you had her as an escape to alleviate the hell we had to live through. It may sound silly but I know you loved us both, and no matter how far away, who she's with, or how much time goes by, you will never recover from

Sara Klein, and if I wanted to be Jacqueline Rossi, I needed to be okay with that. And I was. I never imagined I'd stand in your way of loving her openly for as many years as we've been together, because in my wildest dreams, I didn't imagine I'd survive this long. One year turned into two years and then five and ten. Maybe if I were on my own, I'd have died years ago. I ask myself every day: why am I still here? How did I get so lucky to have him love me and never leave? I sometimes suppose that the only reason I stayed alive and beat cancer for so long was because I was never alone and you were always by my side. Thank you for being my reason to live and the drug that kept me alive.

I couldn't ask for a person to love me more and care and support me through this horrific ordeal as much as you have. And as I lay here spending the last days on this earth, I can't even wish that you only loved me. Once I'm gone and I leave you, our children, my parents, and all our friends ... it gives me solace to know that you and our babies will have someone like her to pick up the broken pieces I've left behind. And that has always been the reason I never asked you to stop loving her, never gave you an ultimatum, because I knew this day would eventually come and I didn't want you to choose me and burn the shaky bridge you two have built. I know how much you love me, and that if I asked, you would end all ties with her and choose me, because you would never hurt your best friend. You would suffer and endure not being with her, like you do now. If I only said the word, I know you would do that for me. But I guess I love you too much to make you suffer more than you already have.

I remember us in law school—you and I were only supposed to be secret lovers; that was my plan. I was okay with being your best friend, your behind-the-scenes lover, and her fill-in. I came to terms with being jealous of Sara, the imaginary, unattainable schoolgirl from New York. It was a given that you two would end up together once school ended. I will never forget that mute for-

tuneteller who sat upstairs at that bar we all used to go to after our exams. You went upstairs to the bathroom and after twenty minutes, I came to see what was taking you so long. You were sitting behind the curtain talking to that old woman—the fortuneteller. You didn't know I was there, but I've always been there. I heard what that old woman told you and I saw your face. She was right, wasn't she? Her prophecy of you and Sara will finally come true once I'm gone. You've worn the key she gave you around your neck for far too long—it's time for your life to begin, Jeff.

I wish stupidly we could make love one last time. It's been years since I felt you like I did when we were young. I wish it didn't hurt to breathe knowing I may not see you again. I'm scared and I don't want to leave you and the babies, but I can't keep suffering like this. God needs to finally let me and all the people around me have some long awaited peace. Jeff, please don't feel sorry for the hand I was dealt in life, don't cry for what could've or should've been. I want you to smile and remember all the beautiful stolen years I've had with you, how I cheated death, and for a moment in time, I had a family of my own. Please tell our kids what they meant to me and that I loved them and refused to die because of them. And I want you to know that I always knew who their real mother was. I took you away from her, but I made sure to give her a part of you I could never have. I wanted our children to come from love and not just a test tube. I don't blame her for loving you. I hold no resentment toward Sara; I owe her my family. I thank both of you for allowing me to be Juliet and Jacob's mother for a blink of an eye.

This is the end of my battle and our story. You're about to inherit a new kind of freedom, and you're about to begin a new kind of struggle. You'll need to go to war and try and bring back your rightful wife, the one whose name you have carved in your heart and etched on your skin. The girl you've patiently waited for. The woman that fate withheld from you for all these years.

Godspeed, my love. Please forgive me for all the pain I brought into your world. I pray for the music in your life to finally begin.

With all my love,
Jacqueline Rossi

I fold back the letter I know by heart and retrieve a key from inside the envelope. I remove the leather cord from around my neck and add this key to the one already hanging from it. The new bright key shines with unexploited pristine. It makes the old one I've worn around my neck for fourteen years look tainted and abused. I can still feel my beautiful wife in my arms, and I let the memory of her soothe the war inside. *She always knew; she always knew everything.* I open my eyes, and my vision is blurred, but gradually, everything becomes crystal clear. I need to go after my prophecy and find the girl who is my destiny.

Jeffery

"Dancing with Myself" by Billy Idol

I'm not passed out; I'm just pretending to sleep, and with any luck, never wake up—but so far I've failed. I don't need to choose anymore. When I'm drunk, I can pretend to be two different people and that I still have them both. Pretend I'm not a worthless bastard who couldn't make a decision. Fucked in the brain—that's what I am, but I still comprehend that I'll never be with the women I love, ever again. My spectacle of a life needs to be over, and I'm ready to let the curtains close. I don't give a shit. I'm done trying to go on with this miserable existence—I've had enough.

My kids need a mother. They don't need me. They're better off without me since the only good part of me died with Jacqueline three days ago, and the other part of me was already dead the day I saw Sara in his arms. I knew he wouldn't leave her alone. I knew it in that one moment, in the way he looked at her, that if he had gotten a small taste of my lifeline, he would never let her go.

Sara, Sara, fucking Sara. Will that name ever not make my insides ache with guilt? *Why are you etched so deep in my goddamn useless soul that I can't even take a breath without breath-*

ing you in? He doesn't know her, he doesn't deserve her, he doesn't understand that she can't love him. She will always be mine; there is nothing or no one who can make her un-love me, us, or what we should've had. I've tried unloving her my entire meaningless life, and all I've managed is to love her even more. This should be our time, not theirs. That fortuneteller predicted that we would be together—not them. She should be in my arms, letting me love her for the whole world to finally see. William Knight, a fucking child, another British piece of shit she found to hurt me. He made sure to call me to send his condolences and tell me that when I see *his* fiancée, I should congratulate her on their upcoming wedding. *How could she agree to marry him?* Does the universe think I need to be punished more? Losing my wife, my best friend, isn't enough heartache, so it made sure I've lost Sara, too? We waited half our lives for this moment in time, and now, I wish I were the one being buried, and not Jacqueline.

I can't fucking be around her and see her in the same room as our kids and watch as they bury my best friend. I wasn't supposed to lose them both. Doesn't she know it wasn't my plan for us to be apart for all those years? Didn't she understand that I couldn't leave Jacqueline? How was I suppose to leave a piece of my heart, the girl I couldn't imagine living without, the girl I never dreamed could love me back and be my wife for as many years as she was? Jacqueline was supposed to leave me; me leaving her was never an option. My head knew what was right, and I'm lucky I got to have those years with her. And Sara had agreed, she understood, she'd promised to never stop loving me. I did everything I could to keep them both happy. I tried, *God* how I tried, but I couldn't be in two places at once. I love nothing and no one like I love my family—Jacqueline, Sara, Juliet, and Jacob—they're my whole fucking life. I couldn't leave Jacqueline when she was sick, and I couldn't choose Sara when she'd lost all hope.

Most men can't find one girl to love, and I somehow found

two exquisite women who were my whole goddamn world. Now I've lost them both, and this worthless existence is finished, done, over, finito. *I lost everything.* How did I manage to fuck it all up for us? *Timing,* it's all about timing. What if Sara wasn't fifteen when we'd met? What if I never came back to see her on her birthday? What if I didn't talk to that old fortuneteller that night? *What if? What if? What if?* The truth is, I wouldn't change a thing. Loving them both didn't feel wrong; it felt right. It was my purpose. *Timing!* It's all about fucking timing. If I hadn't left her alone that night in The Pierre hotel two years ago to go back home to Jacky, she and William wouldn't have met. She would be in my arms right now and we would finally get our chance at happiness, and that old gypsy woman's words would finally materialize. I would never be happy that Jacky is gone, but I know I did the best I could and loved her with all that I had until her last breath.

I picture Sara's lovely face, but then I remember the way she looked at him. Did she ever look at me that way? That night when I came back to the hotel to see her, I'd stood there like a stupid stranger, an intruder, watching them in their own world. I had no choice but to tell him about our kids, in the hopes of him leaving her alone. But the way she'd frantically called after him when he handed her back to me and left—did she ever fight for me like that? Ever since that day at The Pierre, I knew that my dreams of the promised future I'd always imagined would never come to be, and I've been dying a slow, painful death ever since.

They don't belong together. They have no right getting married. How I've dreamt to one day make her my wife for the world to see. I want a chance to make her smile like she did that night we first made love in New York. I want the whole fucking world to know how much I love her and our kids … and yet, I'd made sure to never show anybody how I felt about her—*feel* about her. I kept her tucked away like a precious jewel, afraid someone would take her away from me—someone like him. Sara doesn't even care that we have kids together. She stopped waiting and never fought for us; she just effortlessly walked right into his fucking arms. *She should be in my arms.* I thought having children together would cement our lives and be enough to keep her from ever doubting how much I love her, but she needed more. It wasn't fair to make her wait, but I couldn't do a thing. I had no fucking choice. I'm a selfish piece of shit, and in a twisted way, I loved them both. I couldn't hurt them—or me—and let either of them go. I'm lost without them—*both* of them.

I sink into the couch, clutching the bottle of tequila like a newborn baby. I look at the bed on my left; it's perfectly made and hasn't been touched in years. It mocks me and my fantasy of a life with Sara. I look around at the place I've designed for Sara, knowing these walls have seen a sea of heartache at my orchestrating. I close my eyes in pain while I hide from everyone and myself inside an imaginary world I once shared with Sara. I'm inside the apartment that Sara sold two years ago after our children's custody hearing; only I found out two days ago that it was Jacqueline who secretly bought it. My wife left me the key inside her letter and commanded me to be the man she married and go after and fight for what is rightfully mine. I was supposed to bring my family back together and set my life to music. But I lost them both and now all I hear is silence.

"Jeff, you up, buddy? Can you hear me?" Eddie's voice filters in as he shakes me. *Fuck.* I hope we don't have an exam today. *Wait, crap, I didn't study for any tests!*

I frantically jump out of bed as my old, worthless brain tries to clear through the alcoholic haze I've been drowning in for days. My mind slowly begins to comprehend that I'm not a poor, twenty-three-year-old law student oversleeping for some exam after a night of partying, but I'm a thirty-nine-year-old attorney who's just lost everything and hiding out in what was once his secret portal.

I'm almost one hundred percent sure that I'm not hallucinating, and that the person fixed before me is not a mirage but Eddie Klein, my former best friend. *How did he find me? How did he get in?* This man standing next to me, I would trust with my life, even knowing that he hates me for loving and ruining his little sister's life. I hate me, too, so I can't blame him for trying to protect the people he loves. I would protect Sara for the rest of my life if she'd let me. I never should've kept my feelings for his beautiful sister away from him. I should've told him from the start how I couldn't stop thinking about her, that I cared and respected her, how I wouldn't touch her until she was legal. I should've told him that at eighteen, she made the conscious decision to love me back. If he'd known about us, maybe he would do a better job at keeping her away from me? Maybe he would explain to Sara that I loved Jacqueline from the beginning of time and that she should find a good guy, someone who will only love her? *Maybe, maybe, maybe, enough*!

I shake the worthless thoughts out of my mind. I loved Jacqueline, and it was my responsibility to make whatever life she had left good and happy. It wasn't supposed to be this way. I didn't intend to love them both and lead Sara on for all those years. I had no right promising his sister anything. My heart always belonged to Jacky first; she was my best friend. What we had to live through … I couldn't let my best friend go through that alone. I never abandoned either of them; they were just different parts of me. And I became dependent on both of them to function. I just wish I hadn't hurt everybody the way I did.

Sometimes I wish I was never born; they'd all be better off without me.

I just stare at Eddie as the memories of my youth flood my

veins like fire torching what's left of me. What I wouldn't give to go back in time, and yet I'm almost certain nothing would change.

"Hello again, Jeffery Rossi."

My stomach churns the second I hear that wretched British accent as I turn to meet his glare. The bastard who stole a piece of my heart; the boy who gave her everything I never could. *Why is he fucking here? Is this one of my nightmares?* As I take a shaky step toward the British fucker who ruined my life, I instinctively want to punch him and erase that victorious smile off his happy face. Mentally, I pound his face in, yet in reality, I try and swing my fist with all my strength, but I'm too weak to even lift my arm in the first place. My head weighs a ton and keeps bobbing back and forth. *This is an illusion; it's not real life.* I look up as I feel myself being carried by some big guy, and as he callously drops my naked body down on the couch, I realize it's the one and only Louis Bruel.

"Eddie, he's fucked. Let's get him some OJ and coffee—he needs food. I don't know what kind of shit he's on, but we need to get him cleaned up." Louis barks orders at Eddie. *Bossy motherfucker, always telling everybody what to do.*

"E, don't listen to him. I don't need food. Get me some vodka with ice and a lemon," I mumble as the three of them gawk back at me in silence. "What do you jerks want from me, anyway? Eddie, E, my boy, my brother, my best friend in the whole wide world, we haven't seen each other since that fucking custody hearing. And you, Louis, last time I saw you, it was at your stupid penthouse inside The Pierre hotel where you fucking talked me into going back home and leaving my Sara to calm down and run into this fucker's arms again. You guys are no good for me. Thank you for coming; now leave. I'll get my own vodka."

If my body wasn't so limp, and if I had the strength, I'd throw them all out. I can think but I can't move. Her pretty-boy keeps looking at me. He won't stop staring me down like he wants to tell me something. He wants to rub my face in him having won—by stealing what was rightfully mine.

"You see something you like, asshole? In America, it's not polite to stare at someone's dick. If you have something to say to me, fucking say it and get the fuck out. I can't stand looking at you with that dirty smirk. I-I-I should've killed you for trespassing on private property that night in that hotel." Just another rich bastard who gets to have whatever he wants, even if it's not his. Our children could've had both their parents together if it wasn't for him. How could she be with him?

"Do you have no shame?" he finally says with that holier-than-thou tone of voice.

"Shame? Did you just question my shame, motherfucker? I didn't take another man's woman like you. I'm not breaking up a family, like you. She is my life, and you just took her as if she didn't belong to me." He doesn't give a shit about what he did to us, to our family.

"Sara doesn't belong to anybody but herself, and especially not you." He shakes his head and smiles like I said something funny.

"Don't fucking say her name. You dirty piece of shit," I yell back. I try to get up and finally have it out with him like we should've done two years ago in that hotel. If Sara hadn't fainted that day, if he wasn't holding her in his arms, I would've annihilated this scum.

"You have a family, mate, and you're breaking your family up right now. Wake up! Your kids need you. They don't know where you are. They just lost the only mum they've ever known, and their father is on the other side of town getting wasted. I despise you, Jeffery. You are a coward, and I can't stand the sight of you. But I love Sara more than I hate you, and for some reason, she wants you to come back to your kids and be their father. Be a bloody man. Go help them with the loss of their mum. Stop feeling sorry for yourself," he preaches to me.

"Those kids don't need me. They need Sara, but you stole her from us. I'm nothing without her. Don't lecture me on what and whom they need. I won't go back unless I go back to her."

He smirks at my words. He thinks I have no chance with her. He clearly doesn't understand what we share and what fate has waiting for us. But one day, he will, and then I'll be the one visiting him while he's hiding somewhere drunk and confused.

"Who's stopping you? Go and get yourself and Sara sorted. She's been bloody waiting for you to show your mug for over two days now. Did you know your wife's funeral is today? If you stay here a bit longer, you may even miss the hearing where Sara is granted full custody of Juliet and Jacob, and then I'll be their father. Is that what you want, Rossi?" His words are like acid—they burn all the open, oozing wounds inside me. I want my kids and I want my fair chance with Sara. *Sara, Sara, she's my Sara!* I waited so long for this moment, and never have I imagined it would end and hurt like this.

"I'll go back and figure everything out with my kids … if you leave New York. Let me talk to her without you. I have things I need to say that have nothing to do with you, but everything to do with our kids. Respect what we share and let her deal with me without you."

William's eyes enlarge as he instinctively glances over at Louis, who simply shakes his head, and then to Eddie who makes a "don't look at me" gesture before his worried eyes meet mine again.

"All right, go talk to Sara and I'll be waiting in St. Lucia for her. We have a wedding to get to. I'm not the reason she's not with you—you're the reason," he proclaims with that cocky smile again. "She came back to New York to see you and her children, but you made the wrong decision, like you always seem to do. Your choices are to blame, not me, mate," he finishes, turns his back on me, and walks toward the door.

As soon as Louis leaves after him, I drop back on the couch. I have no strength nor will to go on. Eddie comes and sits on the blue velvet couch his sister once picked out, not looking at me but captivated by the dozens of black and white photographs of Juliet and Jacob—his niece and nephew—covering the walls.

"Jeff, I've known you for way too long, dude. I've never seen you like this. Are you high? Those kids … they're your kids, man; they depend on you. Jacky, poor Jacky died knowing that you would take care of them in every way possible, but they physically need you right now. Stop obsessing over my sister; it's over. It's been over. Get your life together, brother. Look at everything you have. You own one of the largest, most prominent law-firms in New York. There's a plethora of people depending on you. Sara is finally happy. Please, leave her alone. She doesn't have that sad look in her eyes anymore. My sister is not keeping you or the kids inside like a dirty secret." He finally looks at me. "He's a good guy, and he loves her. He makes her happy and they're getting married. I blame myself every day for bringing you into her life, but I love you despite everything you've done to her. I love you because you're the father of my niece and nephew, even though they know nothing about me. I know you're not a bad guy. You're fucked in the membrane, but you're not a bad guy. Please, don't prove me wrong. Come home and deal with your life like the man I once thought you were."

I know he's right. I just need to convince my heart to keep beating and be strong enough to go back home, even if nothing ever feels like home anymore.

"I'm sorry for all I've done. Eddie, I love her so much—you have to know that. I'm sorry I couldn't make her happy. She deserved to be happy. I tried to make them both happy and not break either of their hearts, but I fucked up. I would never have asked her to wait for me or promised her a future if I'd known Jacky and I would be together for all those years. I fucking hurt her so much. I would do anything for her." I fail to hold back the sob.

"If you love her, get up, clean up, and be present for your kids. They need you. That's what Sara and Jacky want. I'll be waiting outside to bring you home."

He gets up and pats my back, not like a friend, but more like a stranger looking down on you with a mixture of revulsion and pity. I don't blame him one bit.

I'm left on my own to chew over all the words they left floating around me in this cold, soulless space that no longer feels like home. This was once our sanctuary. When we walked through those doors, life made sense, but nothing makes sense right now. Isn't this who everybody—including Sara—thinks I am? A bastard who cheats on his sick wife with a girl he brain-washed into loving him, asking her to wait for nothing? They all think I'm a dirty lawyer who fucks anything that moves or looks my way. Would they believe me if I told them I haven't made love to another woman since Sara, in that hotel room, over two years ago? Probably not, and the only woman who knew the truth is now dead, anyway. Will Sara ever stop hating me? How do I get through to her? How can I win her love back if I'm here, hiding? They're all right. I need to stand up and start fighting for her and our family like a man or I may as well be dead.

Jeffery

"Never Gonna Give You Up" by Rick Astley

A good person, a good man, a good father wouldn't leave his children a few days after their mother died to go hide in a secret love-shack he once kept with their biological mother. Juliet and Jacob deserve a good parent, and not a shit mess like me. I'm a worthless, empty excuse for a man without my wife, I'm nothing without Sara, and they can't see me like this. If they look into my eyes, they'll know I'm dead, too.

My secretary has left no less than two voicemails every fucking hour on the hour—my father-in-law, too. The whole world wants to tell me how sorry they are for me. I only check my phone to make sure it's not my babies trying to reach me. My parents and my whole family are at my house with them, and all I can think about is how alone we are. My mind won't let me forget about Sara—the girl I once met in a New York club on a dirty dance floor, the girl that offered to blow me as a joke, only the joke was on me. Just one kiss and she fucked me up for life, but I'd do it all over again because I owe her everything. *What the fuck is wrong with me*? It's as if my heart is finally allowed to explode and all the feelings and thoughts I've trained my mind to keep under control are blasting out, and I can't do anything but let it consume me. The prophecy I've held onto for fourteen years has waited long enough, and it begs to finally play out.

While Jacky was alive, at least I had her there to remind me every day why I kept my feelings for Sara inside. I couldn't add to her pain, I couldn't abandon her and go to the girl I left indefinitely waiting. She knew—she always knew—even if we didn't talk about it, she still knew. I can't even recall the last time Jacqueline and I made love—it's been years. Why did I walk away from Sara that night at The Pierre? Why did I let Louis Bruel talk me into surrendering? When the dust cleared and I tried to fight back and finally give her more, it was too late. William found her, he got a taste of her, and our paused, twisted love story wasn't a good choice for her anymore. She wanted a new story, an untainted story.

I stand in front of the same door I walked out of two years ago and I can't imagine not being able to touch her and lose myself inside her like I did that night before we became strangers. It doesn't matter how much time passes, I can still taste the saltiness of the tears running down her cheeks on her eighteenth birthday when I kissed her in the back of that cab, the weekend fate brought us back together.

Ring the bell, you coward. What do I say to her? Don't marry him! How do I make her give me and us a real chance? *I love you, I miss you, I can't live without you.* I need to tell her there would be no more lying, hiding, and waking up in separate beds. I survived her last fake, loveless marriage, but I had Jacky and the kids to keep my mind from thinking about her every second of every day. I don't think I'll survive this one. It's different this time. I saw it that night with the way he looked at her and she at him. It tasted like love, I felt it.

I lift my left arm to ring the bell when I spot my wedding band on my finger. I remove the gold ring to reveal her name under it. She was always there with me—in my dreams, in my heart, and etched into my every fiber. I got her name tattooed on the inside of my finger the night before Jacqueline and I got married. Sara and I made a promise that I never forgot, nor do I intend to. I kiss my wedding band and place it in my jeans' pocket. *I love you, Jacky. I will never love another person the way I loved you, and I wish everything was different. I made mistakes that hurt everybody, but you still loved me and I am forever blessed for knowing you.* Before I ring the bell, I say a silent prayer and prepare myself for whatever it is I've got to do to make Sara remember our promise. I'm here to return my heart to its owner and let her do with it whatever she sees fit.

The bell rings over and over. I know she's here since the manager personally escorted me to the elevator as soon as I uttered my name. Her new man arranged smooth passage. The elevator attendant knew exactly where I was headed as well, and silently whisked us off to the penthouse. *Of course he bought her the penthouse at The Pierre hotel where it all started for them.* I vividly recall reading in the paper about a year ago of this monumental real estate transaction between Louis Bruel and William Knight.

It takes an eternity for her to open this damn door. My heart beats in my throat and I can hear my blood rushing through my ears. I've missed her, all of her. The last time we saw one another was in a room full of lawyers as she was declared a legal guardian to our kids—without any opposition from Jacky or me. I remember how broken I felt to have her sit only a few feet away from me and not be able to hold her, to calm her, and tell her how sorry I was for putting us in such a fucked-up mess. How sorry I was that we needed a bunch of clowns to negotiate the parenting terms of our incredible kids. I held on to Jacqueline instead as she told me over and over that this was a good thing. She was happy and proud that Sara finally stood up for our kids, and she felt that Sara had at last grown up after all these years. I never spoke to my wife about the girl that was a fixed, silent part of our life, my heart, and my every thought. I was afraid she'd know how much I loved Sara, too. But she knew everything. The only person I lied to was myself. She knew who the egg donor was for our twins, and she obviously approved. Looking back now, how could she not have known? She was the one who suggested we use a donor that we know, someone who would be a part of our baby's life when her time was up. Jacky always wanted a family, but at the same time, she wasn't ignorant; she knew her ticking cancer wouldn't allow her such a luxury. Three days ago, hours before she closed her eyes for the last time, she told me that her borrowed time had ended. She whispered she loved me, that she was sorry, and that was it—she was gone, and I've been lost without my best friend ever since.

Tears pool in my eyes as I realize I've traveled millions of miles away and Sara has at last opened the door and is standing there, observing me. My heart is lodged in my throat as our eyes lock on each other, completely paralyzing me. Time stands still while everything between us evaporates into memory dust. My tears spill over as my wretched heart attempts to say the words my brain continuously denies. *Please don't leave me. We promised. Don't marry him. Give us a chance. Don't do this to me again. I don't want to live without you. I love you.* My mind is bombarded all at once, and yet I'm a fucking mute—a speechless, soundless, wordless fool.

"Sara," I manage to lament on the verge of more tears.

"Jeffery," she replies, closing her eyes to break the spell she cast.

I watch her mere inches away from me, and just like a memory of some long forgotten dream, I know what will happen next. It's as if no time has passed, it's as if we didn't break each other our whole life, and it's as if nothing else matters but her and me.

I was going to wait, I was going to be respectful, I was going to let her invite me into her space to finally talk, like adults, like parents, but I can't wait any longer. I walk in uninvited and invade her space as I take all the air in the room with me. Can she see the pain leak out of my eyes and the resolve in my stare? She stumbles backward and gasps in shock at my forwardness. She knows I won't be held at bay any longer—I've waited for almost fifteen years to un-pause our story, and now that my heart is in full control it turned my brain off, because I don't care what's right or wrong. I'm here to take back what fate promised me all along.

I feel her before I even touch her. My hands and body come at her all at once. I pull her flush against me, and turn us both to the left—as if part of some well rehearsed dance—and usher us into the open powder room. Once we're in the dark, windowless room, I shut the door with a bang, quickly locking it. My heart explodes in its cage, my limbs tremble as I hold her near, and everything turns to red. I can't think as I try to breathe and not pass out with her clutched against my heart. *Is this really happening?*

She attempts unsuccessfully to say something, but it's no use, both of our brains negate to function. My body hasn't come to terms with reality, and her touch and scent are overwhelming … but she still feels like home.

"Don't tell me to stop, don't push me away, you don't have to say anything, and please, for the love of our children, just listen to me," I beg nervously with my eyes and words while the automatic lights slowly come on, illuminating her petrified stare.

She vehemently shakes her head and looks away from me. I feel like the wolf luring in a lamb, but I'm the one who's been lost in her spell.

"I love you. Look at me. I love you so much, Sara. I'm sorry for everything I made you live through. I'm sorry I can't stop loving you. You don't need to talk, baby, just look at me and listen to what I have to say, please," I continue while I loosen the hold I have around her tiny waist and lower her to rest on the marble vanity, positioning myself as close as possible between her legs.

I'm suddenly aware she's wearing nothing but a man's white T-shirt around her overheated, trembling body, and as I look down, I feel the flush of her skin rise and spread under my touch. I slide my hands up her bare legs, sending feelings to places I know I have no right to try and communicate with anymore. I haven't seen her or touched her like this in over two years, and being this close to her, breathing the same air as her inside this little powder room, only makes me want us back a million times more.

I look down at my hands placed on her thighs; I'm trembling, too. I tear my gaze back to her eyes as she breathlessly watches me in shock, waiting for me to make the next move. *I want to kiss you, taste you. I'm starved for you.*

"I don't deserve anything from you, but I beg of you to forgive me for everything you had to endure by knowing me. I want you to believe me when I tell you that you are, were, and always will be a part of everything that I am. I'm nothing without you, Sara. You are my life, my family, and a part of my heart. Please tell me you understand what you are to me?"

She still hasn't said a single word and I can tell my words are making her angry by the way she holds her tongue and won't talk to me. But her emotions toward me are loud enough that sound isn't necessary. We stare each other down, willing our eyes to say that which our words fail to express. Without warning, she slaps my face with one hard blow that makes my head jerk to the side. I let go of her thigh to touch the spot she just hit and I smile. *Finally, we're getting somewhere.*

"Do it again, but harder. Come on, you need to beat the shit out of me. Do whatever you want to me and tell me everything you need to say to me, and let's get this over with. I deserve and will accept every form of punishment from you, but I won't accept you leaving me. I owe it to our children to fight for you," I explain, no longer smiling.

She closes her soulful, haunted eyes and swallows whatever air is still left in the room before she finally allows her own tears to emerge. She's hysterical. I can taste her frustration with every sob at how our lives seem to always get twisted and bent until somebody snaps and breaks.

I lower myself closer, cupping her face to rest my forehead to hers. Her proximity makes my head spin. "I don't know why I can't let you be. I don't know why I can't breathe without you. I just know that you've been etched in my future from the moment I kissed you in your room. Sara, I need you to give our family a fair chance. Please don't leave us; we need you. You can't marry him. We made a promise."

She pushes me away from her and opens her eyes, looking at me as if for the first time. We're having a stare off again and I know that this, right here, is a conversation fifteen years in the making.

She finally finds her elusive voice that I've been dying to hear and begins to speak.

"I fell in love with you that night in the club and in my room seventeen years ago. I dreamt about nothing and no one but you ever since I can remember. Every night I slept in your T-shirt to have a small piece of you touch me. I lied to myself and everybody I ever loved for you. You were my first kiss, my first dance, my first everything, and I would've agreed to do anything you asked of me. I gave you everything that was mine to give, and you took it all. You left me with nothing! You don't know what it was like being me—just waiting, watching you have everything without me. I know you didn't want to hurt me, but you did and I let you. You didn't love me enough back then to not be with Jacqueline when you couldn't sleep with me, and you sure as hell don't love me now. You made your bed, Jeffery Rossi, and it's time for you to go lie in it, without me. If you think you love me, like you keep saying, then leave me alone.

"I will always love you as my biggest lesson of all, and as

the father of my children, but I don't want your love anymore. I'm not the Sara you kept indefinitely waiting with all those beautifully empty promises for years. I'm not that girl you once knew. I finally understand what being loved feels like, and you didn't love me. He loves me. I love William Spencer Knight, and I love our baby that's growing inside me. You can't take that from me."

As her words leave her mouth and escape into the universe, it's as if I've been shot in the heart. I let go of her and begin to stumble back, colliding with the wall behind me. I shake my head vigorously and almost inaudibly yell *no, no, no, no,* over and over.

She gets herself off the counter I placed her on and takes a few steps toward me. I want her to hit me, wake me up from this nightmare. But instead, she engulfs my waist in a hug and begs me to do her one last favor. "Please come back to our kids. Please don't abandon them now. They don't know me. I can't meet them now when they lost their mother, and I can't have them lose you, too. I've watched you and them from afar every day. I would sit at the corner café by your house and watch you be a perfect father, just like in my dreams, and it was the only thing that kept me alive." We both have tears rolling down our faces, holding on to one another as our sad reality comes into focus. Juliet and Jacob, our beautiful children, need to be our main concern. Nothing else matters—not the promises, not the broken dreams, just our babies.

I wail, not recognizing my own desperate sounds as her words continue to cripple me. Both our legs seem to give out at the same time as we slide to the floor. I've always hated seeing men cry, and hearing myself cry out seems even more painful and unnatural. I'm aching inside as my world slowly continues to shatter, crumbling piece by piece. Every last hope I've held onto for years of us finally being a real family slowly dissipates.

She's been sitting between my legs on the floor, resting her head on my chest like she's done thousands of times, only I've made no attempt to touch her back. She's not mine anymore, never was, never will be. We've been motionless for what seems like hours, and I have yet to stop crying. How can two people wreak this much havoc in one another's lives? Will it ever not hurt being around her? Will I ever stop loving her?

I look down, only to be confronted with eyes that almost feel like they're my own. The same eyes I thought I'd look into for eternity. They're my kids' eyes, they're my youth, these eyes were supposed to be my future, but they aren't my destiny. My whole life has been a mistake. "I will never stop loving you, no matter who you love or choose, my love for you will always be there. I don't care if you don't believe me, but I never thought I needed to choose you. You were always etched in my heart as a constant future."

My former lover, my so-called "affair," looks shattered. We break each other; that's what we've done from day one. I broke her by first being a delusion and then morphing into a promised illusion.

"I was always the beggar, the hungry shadow waiting for a promise to materialize, clinging on to any morsel of hope you granted me. I never asked you to choose me, but why didn't you? Wasn't I worth your choice?" Her honest words make my tears fall even more. "Jeffery, please, stop crying," she says as she puts her head back on my chest, listening to the heart that now beats for no one. "When did you fall in love with your wife?" she asks, reminding me that there is more carnage to come.

I'm quiet, not sure how to answer her question. She starts to get up when I finally tighten my hold. She looks up at me, and I at her, and I see how much she still cares for me. I feel her body react to me as if I still own it, and only God knows how much I wish I still did.

There is no use trying to hold on to her, she's not mine. If something should be yours, no one can take it away from you.

Before I let her go, I look into her troubled eyes. The same familiar eyes that all I've ever done is promise fairy tales I had no tools for building. She should be loved the way I promised I'd always love her. She should be cherished and spoiled with undivided attention. I robbed her of that with my self-righteousness covering up my selfishness. I never thought I was hurting her thanks to the strong façade she fabricated, but she's right—I took everything and gave nothing back.

Is this love? Does love need to hurt this much? Or is this a forced kind of love that slaughters all involved?

She's finally in my arms where I've wished her to be millions of times, but I'm still lost and alone. *Guilt.* I feel guilty for everything I've put her through. Was I punishing her for lying to me that first night we met when she was only fifteen? I never asked her for her age and she never offered it. It wasn't her fault I fell for a fifteen-year-old. I've never stopped thinking about that night. Have I been punishing myself, too, by holding on to her as a self-indulgent fantasy and forcing us to live in pause because years later some crazy old gypsy read my palm and told me she would be my future? I still moved on with Jacky, but I didn't release her.

I don't know how long we've been huddled on the floor, and I'm not sure where to go from here. Sara and William are having a baby—that's a reality I need to accept. She will never be my wife. She can't take Jacqueline's place and raise our kids; that's not her life. She loves him and she wants and will have children with him. She chose him, and I can't pretend that she hadn't chosen me, because I wasn't a choice. She chose me for years, and I took it for granted, accepted her love as if it was a constant unyielding entitlement. She never once asked me to leave Jacky. She never once told me how much it hurt or that she wanted a family. Was it convenient? Was it easy until it became painful? All the years between us, how could it be a mistake? Juliet and Jacob, our kids … perhaps they're the only reason our lives collided and intertwined. Did I hold on to her, waiting for her to love me the way I always thought she did? She never once stood up for us. She, too, kept us a secret like some dirty affair. Was that easier than telling the truth and moving on?

The thought that they made a baby together and that they're getting married devastates me. This is what she felt at eighteen when I married Jacqueline. Only she was a baby when I did this to her. *It was over for us before it even started.*

I wrap my arms around her as I pull her tighter into me. If I could go back in time, I would let her go. I would allow her the happiness that I promised but could never give. I would not hold on to what some fortuneteller at a bar read on my palm as if it was the word of God. "I'm sorry, Sara. I'm sorry for everything." I kiss the top of her head as I allow her familiar scent to calm me one last time. She will always be a part of me, and I owe her so much. "I want you happy. I swear, for the rest of your life, I want to make sure you never cry again." I've caused this poor, innocent girl enough heartache to warrant her murdering me out of self-defense.

"When did you fall in love with Jacqueline?" she questions for the second time.

I don't want to tell her. I can't tell her, it will kill her. "It wasn't like that. I didn't do it on purpose, Sara. It wasn't what I wanted." The thought of hurting her even more now starts to cripple me. I don't want to say another word.

She turns in my lap to face me with those brilliant, knowing eyes piercing through my ugly soul. "I know, but you fell in love with her before we even met, didn't you? You married her because you loved her. It was different than what you felt for me, right?" Her question is laced in pain.

I nod my head. "I always loved you, too," I offer as the guilt of my actions weighs me down. "We were friends. I didn't think we had a future. The things Jacky and I lived through made it impossible for me to not love her. I did try to pretend and not care—I tried to only think of you and us. I tried to not get attached to her, because I knew she would be taken away from me. I'm sorry. I was scared that I'd lose her and you, and I just held on to both of you." My wretched tears haven't ceased rolling from my eyes ever since I walked in.

"When you made love to her, did you imagine it was me?"

We've never spoken about this. We always pretended I didn't have a wife and a whole life that had nothing to do with us. I came to see her almost every evening and she was my refuge.

"No," I say honestly. "I haven't made love to Jacky since the kids were born."

Sara looks puzzled as she continues to question me. "Why?"

"How much sex do you think I can have? We saw each other every day. I never tried to force her. She was sick and the meds had all these hormonal side effects. Our relationship started out based on sex, but it wasn't what kept us together. I never wanted to be a cheater, and anyway, she didn't want us to be sexual, especially after she had the hysterectomy."

"I didn't know she had that surgery. You never told me," she accuses me as if any of this makes a difference now.

"Your brother and Louis beat the shit out of me. You left for London and married Gavin, the asshole. There was nothing for me to tell you. I couldn't even reach you," I practically bark back at her, not sure why we're having this conversation now. All this was years ago.

"Did you fantasize about her when you were fucking me?" Her harsh condemnatory tone makes me angry.

"Why are we having this conversation? Does it matter when all is said and done? Jacky is dead, isn't that what you wanted?"

She gasps loudly in shock before pointing her finger at me. "I never wanted your wife dead. Don't you ever fucking say that! I just wanted you because I somehow believed in my infantile mind that we were destined like you kept promising." She lowers her finger and continues. "I should hate you so much, Jeffery, but I don't. You know why? Because if it weren't for you, I wouldn't have Juliet and Jacob in my life, and I wouldn't have found William. When I let my guard down and allowed someone other than you in, I realized that what I felt for you wasn't the great love I'd always thought it to be. It was just my first love. I care for you so much, but it's different than my love for him—it can't compete or compare. Only now I can fully understand what you felt for Jacqueline, because I feel that for Liam. I could never abandon him, or choose not to be with him. I love him—*only* him." She genuinely smiles when she mentions William, and it's hard for me not to be happy seeing her eyes light up with hope.

She cups my face gently and brings her lips to mine for a kiss. Not the first kiss between lovers who haven't seen each other in years, but a final goodbye kiss between friends. I close my eyes as I allow our lips to touch one last time. She rains sweet, familiar kisses on my lips as the bathroom door flies open with a bang and scares the shit out of us both.

I look to the side to see the security guard, who earlier escorted me with the manager in the elevator, fill the small doorway. His eyes enlarge as he spots us nestled on the floor. I look at Sara, who's straddling me with her T-shirt riding up around her waist, practically naked, only in her underwear in my lap. The sound of the door banging against the wall behind it when the guard first stormed in caused me to pull her flush against my body while her hands still cupped my cheeks, where only a minute ago, she was kissing me goodbye.

"No, Ronny, this isn't what it looks like." She sounds panicked, flustered, and breathless. I see her embarrassment rise on her cheeks as she frantically tries to explain our predicament to the shocked guard. "Please, don't say anything to him. He won't understand. Let me tell him. It's not what you think," she pleads, trying unsuccessfully to remove herself from my hips.

He nods his head over and over, looking anywhere but us, clearly uncomfortable. Without saying another word, he leaves, closing the door behind him.

Once we're alone again, she gets up, and without looking at me, she starts to shake her head slowly and smile. It's a defeated, manic grin, and from experience, I know it'll end with more tears. She's afraid he'll think we're back together. My ego is happy, but my heart aches as I see Sara turn to me, white as a ghost and visibly in pain. She covers her mouth and begins to sob. She falls to her knees and grabs her stomach once the realization of what the guard just witnessed becomes clear to her.

"I won't let you ruin this. You can't ruin real love," she yells through tears as the color drains from her face. I know I should just leave her, go away for good. She should be with the love of her life, and I need to get lost before I ruin not just her past, but her future, too.

Jeffery

"True Colors" by Cyndi Lauper

"Please breathe, baby. Please open your eyes."

The ambulance is hardly moving. My bloody hands are clasped together as I try to make them stop shaking. They attempt to revive her, but all I see is dark blood everywhere. I replay everything from the moment she opened the door to let me in on constant loop in my mind. I try to figure out what happened. *What did I do?* Nothing bad can happen to Sara. This can't be happening. Did I do this to her, too? Did I somehow cause this? When she dropped to her knees, I caught her before she fell. But it was too late.

"I won't let you ruin this. You can't ruin real love."

"I won't let you ruin this. You can't ruin real love."

"I won't let you ruin this. You can't ruin real love."

I swear I would never hurt her. Why is she bleeding like this? I've told the medics everything I know and that she may be pregnant. I know her blood type and Rh factor and everything else a husband would know about his wife, even though she was never my wife and I will never be allowed to be her husband.

I need to call her family. How am I going to tell Eddie? I have no idea what's happening to her, but he needs to know what's going on. I need to find William. Where did that stupid guard disappear to after he barged in like a savage? Why wasn't anybody there to help me get her to a hospital? It took me too long, too fucking long to get help. *Oh God. Oh God.* I can't think that something bad will happen to my girl.

Please wake up, baby. Open your eyes. Don't do this to me. You can't go.

I look around and I don't even know which hospital we're in, all I know is that I'm on a stretcher giving blood. I've spoken to five different doctors, told them everything I know and everything I think I know. She was bleeding, her body went into shock, and they've taken her into surgery. *Oh God.* I think I may have told them she's my wife, or maybe I just wanted to tell them that. My mind keeps shutting down. They're contacting her family members, I think—I hope.

Please, God, take me before her.

I feel lightheaded, but I'm certain I see Louis and Emily approaching in the distance. Her best friend has her head down. When she finally looks up, she seems hysterical. Louis is holding onto Emily and appears to be livid.

I am the bad guy. I'm always to blame.

"What did you do to her?" Emily questions me in a whisper once our eyes lock.

"Nothing. I did nothing," I manage to expel.

"What happened? I saw her this morning and she was fine. Why is she here? You did this!" She raises her voice, pointing an accusatory finger at me.

I agree. I also think I somehow did this. I'm just not sure how, so how can I argue?

"Why are you giving blood? She doesn't need you or your fucking blood." Her disgusted tone and word combination pierce me. Doesn't she know that if I could, I'd gladly give Sara all my vital organs? Doesn't she know I'd give her every last drop of my blood? She continues to stab me with her words. "After you've cheated your whole life with God knows who, you want to give her your dirty blood?" Her assumptious remark wakes my incoherent head and clears through all the pain I've allowed to take permanent residence in my shattered soul.

"You know nothing about me, Emily. Don't you dare say that. Don't make what I feel for her dirty. She was the only person I was ever with besides Jacky. You and everybody else know nothing about us," I answer with the last bit of strength I have left in me. "She lost lots of blood. She needs everybody to give blood. I think she lost the ba—" I look up at Emily as she covers her mouth and starts to cry. Maybe she doesn't know about the baby? My eyes close, because I can't have this conversation with her. Sara and the baby are not mine to discuss.

I pry my eyes open minutes—or hours—later. I'm alone in a cold, sterile room. My tongue is glued to the roof of my mouth as I swallow the taste of my own bile. My gaze follows the tube running from the clear bag of liquids hanging above my head to the vein in my hand. I don't know anything for certain. I don't know what's left of my life except that I need to get to my children. In the end, nothing and no one else should matter but them. Jacky is gone, Sara is somewhere fighting for her life, and I have to stay alive to take care of my kids. That's the only thing I know for certain, and that's my only purpose left in this terrible, cruel world.

I hear movement as I see a nurse coming to adjust my IV line.

"Hey, can you tell me if Sara Klein is okay?" I ask the tiny lady wearing purple.

"Your wife is out of surgery. Her doctor should stop by and

see you in a bit once I finish taking your vitals." *My wife ... not in this lifetime.* Why do they need to take my vitals? I just want to go see if she's all right.

"Could you please unhook me from this IV and these machines? I'd like to go to the bathroom." I'm lucid. I feel fine. Time to go.

"Lie back, Mr. Rossi. You have a catheter, you don't need to go to the bathroom." She pushes me down with force while maintaining a sweet smile and proceeds to change the urine collection bag attached to the side of my bed. "You donated lots of blood to your wife. You've been out cold for the last twelve hours. We just need to make sure you're well before we can disconnect your IV. You're being treated for your excessive dehydration."

I don't care about me at all. I just want to know what's going on with Sara. "Can you please contact my family? I'll give you their number. I need them to know I'm okay," I beg the little stranger at my side.

"Your family is here. I'll let them know you're up. I'm sure they'll be right in to see you."

She's out the door before I can ask or say another word. I wonder if my parents, or perhaps Jacky's parents, were called in, or maybe she means Sara's folks. The door opens once again a minute later as Emily saunters in. *Here we go.*

She looks tired but calm. Not as hysterical as our earlier encounter. I don't give her a chance to say anything before I begin questioning her about Sara. "Is she okay? Tell me what happened? What did the doctors say? Did you call her parents? Does William know she's here? Is Eddie here?" I know I have zero rights to her wellbeing, but I need to know she's okay or I'll go crazy. I need to ensure I didn't harm her any more than I have up to this point. I promise that if she's okay, I'll leave her alone. *Forever, for good, for life.* I will run far away and exterminate myself from her life; I owe her that. But first, she needs to be okay. This nightmare needs to end for her.

"Her parents and Eddie are all here. Your parents are here, too. Will is back from St. Lucia. She's out of surgery; still unconscious but stable," she expels with relief.

I close my eyes and take a full breath once I hear that Sara is alive. *Thank God. Thank you, God, for this.*

"She lost a lot of blood and the baby," she whispers the last part. "But it could've been much worse for all of us."

My heart contracts at her last statement—Sara and William lost their baby.

"Why did you tell the doctors she was your wife?" Emily asks in a small, sad voice.

I look up to meet her questioning stare. "I've been to the hospital a few too many times in my life with Jacqueline. I know a spouse has different rights than a mistake like me. She was bleeding, and if she needed blood, I had to make sure they knew that our blood types match. We went through all this when we had the twins." I smile as the memory of us sitting at the fertility clinic instantly bombards my mind.

"You're sure about this?" I question her about a choice that would change everything.

"I'm sure. I only want your sperm hanging out with my eggs if I have a say," Sara answers with her usual sarcasm. "If this works, we'll be parents. Can you imagine a baby with your eyes or my nose? Promise me I can give the baby a name," she begs with hope and excitement dripping from her voice.

"Sara, of course you can name our child. It will be our family," I respond honestly, mimicking her optimism.

Instead of one baby, we got two—Juliet and Jacob. Sara was my gift in life; she made everything better, while I made everything worse. What kind of life would I have had without knowing her? She was and is a part of everything I am today. Jacqueline and I had a real family, thanks to Sara. It's funny how we assumed our kids would provide our shaky past a stable future. But that's not what fate had intended for us. That stupid fortuneteller got it all wrong.

Emily talks to me while I reluctantly come back from a memory of when I had it all. I'm back to reality, back to my doomed fate that doesn't include Jacqueline or Sara.

"You saved her life, you know? She could've died if she was alone. Thank you for saving my best friend," she mumbles with tears running down her pale cheeks.

"Emily, I can never repay her for everything she's been in my life. I have hurt her for so long that I will be saving her life for the rest of mine." I've cried more in the last week than in my entire existence combined. Just allowing my head to imagine a world without Sara stops me from taking another breath. My kids and I lost Jacky; we can't lose Sara, too. That's not an option. Whether she's part of our life or not, she needs to be a part of this world. I need to know that she's somewhere, existing, healthy, happy, and being loved.

"Jeff, I know you love her, but I hope once she gets better you'll allow her to experience happiness without you." Emily's words come out in a plea. "I didn't know how deep your relationship was, and I wasn't a good friend to her. I didn't give her good advice, but now that I know the truth, I beg of you to let her be. She loves him and he loves her and I just want her to have what she's always dreamed about."

"I know we'll never be together again, but tell me, how am I suppose to go on? I don't know anything but her. She was supposed to be my future. How can I raise our kids on my own? She loves them so much. What if I can't be a good father?" The questions I should be asking Sara shoot out of my mouth without any thought or filter. Emily doesn't have the answers. No one can help me but me.

"The doctor will be in to talk to you since they think you're her husband."

I nod, close my eyes, and promise that I'll be whoever I

need to be for her.

The edge of my bed dips as Emily takes a seat. I open my eyes as I feel her take my right hand in hers and turn it to expose my open palm. She traces the lines inside my palm before lifting her gaze to mine.

"My nana once told me that our life is mapped out and etched in history before we come out of the womb. That no matter what road we take and regardless of the mistakes we make along the way, our destiny will always find us. In the end, all our choices bring us to our providence. I believe that fate brought you and my best friend together. Nothing and no one could've changed that. Your children are a testimony of that. But souls heal one another, not break each other. One day, you'll find all the pieces of your heart that perhaps you haven't earned yet, and when you do, you'll understand all the choices that brought you to your bashert." She looks back down at my open, outstretched hand before I make a fist and close it.

Emily stands up without another word and leaves me alone to remember a mocking memory that for years I've tried but failed to forget.

"Sit, boy. I will give you a reading," the older woman at the top of the stairs had whispered with certainty. I was never the same after I'd spoken and looked into the old fortuneteller's eyes. I can't explain what had compelled me to accept her invitation. I can't decide if I was intoxicated or perhaps hoping she'd actually know my future, since my reality at the time took an unforeseeable turn. I believe she was the reason I went back to New York to see Sara again to try and explain. Try to break up with her and let us both move on. I had every intention to never see her again. Sara had her whole life ahead of her. She was a baby who just graduated high school, and I was a new attorney who had a career to build. Even if for only a short time, Jacqueline was my future, not Sara. But seeing the girl I couldn't stop thinking about, coupled with the old woman's taunting words,

was my ruin. She planted the seed, and I watered it with empty promises and willed it to life.

But everything seems trivial and too late to try and make sense of now.

Twenty-twenty-twenty-four hours to go I wanna be sedated. The lyrics circle around in my head instead of a litany I can't bring myself to compose. But the Ramones can't help me now … only a higher being can lend a hand now. There is nothing left of my insides that my guilt hasn't eaten away at already.

My door opens as William Knight enters, shoulders hunched, hands in his pockets, utterly defeated. I recognize the guilt on his face all too well. I can only imagine the immense remorse he's dealing with at having not been there to help Sara. He walks over to a window and starts talking to me without glancing my way once.

"The universe never gets it wrong. Even if you fib, con, and steal a small morsel of hope that isn't yours, the universe will find a way to autocorrect and seize it back from you. I assumed I was coming back to castigate her for allowing you to touch her. I was then gonna apologize for leaving her on her own and fight for my future wife and child. Eight hours ago, my only fear was that I'd lost her to you. I couldn't comprehend you two on the floor in our home wrapped in each other's arms. Now, mother universe, once more, demonstrates that it's not about my egotistical idealizations, but someone's life. And if I'm honest, it's the only life I care about anymore—more so than my own. The last time I saw her, she was alive, gorgeous, perfect, and had my life growing inside her, and now, I bloody hope that she stops hemorrhaging and continues to exist. I just want her okay and out of this wretched hospital and this horrible city, and as far away from everybody but me as possible. But it matters not what I want; I have no control over anything," he declares, which takes me a few minutes to digest.

"William." I say his name to try and explain what his guard

thinks he saw. But he won't let me speak. I doubt he can even hear me.

"They have her in the recovery unit and the medics should come see you soon. Being that you're her husband." He snorts out a sarcastic laugh.

I inhale his words and look over as Sara's brother, Eddie, and his best friend, Louis, walk into my room. They, too, hardly look my way and proceed to sit on a few of the scattered chairs by the wall. Both have a hollow stare in their eyes that echoes my own. I glace back as the door opens once more; Emily returns and nods her head at me.

An older, plump gentleman in green scrubs with squeaky black rubber shoes enters the room moments after Emily. He speaks first to Eddie, who then beckons William to come join the conversation. They all look my way simultaneously and begin to approach. I can hear the doctor speak, but I can't make out his words. I'm fairly certain I'm brain-dead. He suddenly turns his full attention and initiates to speak directly at me, as if he knows that his patient means everything to me.

"We were able to stop the internal bleeding, which was the main cause of the septic shock her body experienced. The ectopic mass was the cause of the catastrophic tubal rupture that led to the massive hemoperitoneum."

I continue to stare at him with a dazed, empty glance. I haven't a fucking clue as to what anything he said actually meant.

He senses my confusion and switches over to English and continues. "The blood caused by the ectopic mass rupturing accumulated in the space between the inner lining of her abdominal wall and the internal abdominal organs. That was the presenting cause for the emergency surgery, and the fluid and blood replacement. We were able to stop her bleeding and stabilize her, for now."

Now I slightly begin to grasp what he attempts to explain, but I'm still confused and lost.

"She's going to be okay, but she lost the baby?" I ask like a two-year-old idiot. I already know she did by everything he and Emily already said, but my brain is in refutation.

"I'm afraid so, Mr. Rossi. If you hadn't brought her in when you did, and if the first response team hadn't begun their resuscitative efforts when they had, we'd have lost her, too." His last words ricochet out of his mouth right dead center into the open wound I once called my heart. "We don't know exactly how far along she was since you weren't lucid enough to tell us, or how long she's been bleeding, but the pregnancy was ectopic, which means the fertilized egg implanted in the wrong place and began to grow outside the uterus. In this case, the blastocyst implanted in the fallopian tube, which ruptured and caused the internal bleeding. She's very lucky to be alive."

I nod frantically, not allowing myself to lose it and think any further than the information the doctor just gave us.

He looks around at William and Emily and then adds, "I know since you're all close relatives that you're all aware as to how rare Sara's blood type is. I can't stress enough how lucky she was that her husband was with her. He knew exactly what her blood type and Rh factor were. He also practically forced us to start drawing his own blood, which he knew was a perfect match for the transfusion. That saved us precious time as well." He keeps using the word "husband" and turning to me, which I can only imagine makes William want me dead even more. But *no,* unfortunately I'm not her husband—never was, never will be.

"Thank you, doctor. When can we see her?" Eddie jumps in and asks.

I need to get as far away from these people as I can. I won't go back on my promise. I made a silent pact with God and I will leave her alone. He kept her alive and I will leave her alone. I just want to make sure she's all right. I'll just steal a quick glance at my angelic Sara, who was once mine, and then I'll get lost.

“Sit tight. We’ll let you all know as soon as she’s out of the ICU.”

Jeffery

"King of Pain" by The Police

I've stood in this spot before and watched my wife, my once radiant wilting best friend, my Jacqueline, lying on the other side of a hospital door far too many times. But I've never been in this position with Sara. She was my rock, my salvation. I ran to Sara to escape the hell that my life was wedged in. Never once did I imagine I'd watch her helpless body connected to machines. It almost feels staged, like we're on a movie set and the director is about to yell *cut*. But the more I watch, I know that this is real, too real. This is my Sara fighting for her existence and I can't do shit about it. She's so pale, so small, but still incredibly beautiful, almost tragically beautiful, like a broken china doll.

Emily and William stand on either side of her while holding each of her hands, and I think they're singing or something, because Emily is making exaggerated hand gestures while swaying and William looks like he's yelling at the top of his lungs. I spot Louis sitting on the far right, drumming his hands on his chair, and it would all be funny and entertaining if Sara weren't lying frozen in the center of the scene. I know what they're doing … they're trying to wake her up. They're trying to make her come home from the hell she's apparently lost in.

I close my eyes and wish I could figure out a way to switch places with her. I've begged and pleaded to be able to switch places with Jacky thousands of times, but I'm still here. I pull apart my tear-filled eyes to see them all motionless on the other side of the door. Emily is crying and suddenly falls to her knees. William hangs his head down, and Louis sprints to his wife's side. *Show is over.* I move away from the door as I see Louis approaching with Emily hysterical in his arms. They leave Sara's room without noticing me standing, like an unwanted intruder, on the side. I can hear the anguish in Emily's sobs long after they disappear, and I somehow feel like I'm to blame. I feel personally responsible for Sara. I always have.

I look back into the room again. It's just her and William as he sits on a chair by her side. He's still clutching her hand and kisses it repeatedly. He lets go of her hand to touch her hair. The door is slightly ajar and I can hear him speak to the woman he obviously loves and deserves more than I ever have.

"This is my favorite strand of hair, the one that usually fancies falling into your eyes. It's the strand that drives me bananas whenever I spy it anywhere near your eyes, the one I must adjust at all costs."

I feel like a ghost witnessing a moment not meant for me. She hasn't moved and the strand he speaks of is static, suspended, devoid of life. That strand is me.

"I won't bloody live without you, Sara. You hear me? You're my life, you're my perfect ballerina. Open your eyes and say something smart, for the love of God," he yells at the top of his lungs at a motionless, helpless girl. "Do you know that today was supposed to be our wedding day? Today oughta be the happiest day of our lives, yet I feel like the last person left on Earth."

I swallow his words as if they are my own.

I want her to get up, open those bewitching eyes, and breathe on her own. I want her and him to have a life together—a good life, the kind she deserves, the kind I couldn't give her.

I'm transfixed; I can't stop watching them, and almost as if he can sense me, he turns his head and stares right back. You can clearly see every possible emotion pass on his features. He hates me. He wants to hurt me. He wants me to be lying on that hospital bed fighting for my life instead of Sara, and I want that, too.

I open the door, attempting to go against the grain and be less of a coward and more of a man. William instinctively gets up without letting go of Sara's hand to face me. He seems frantic and agitated, as if bracing himself for a fight, but I'm not here to fight; there's no competition. He wins. I don't even know what to say to him.

I'm thankful that he begins speaking first.

"When I was flying back to New York, I finally had a moment of clarity. You see if A is meant to be with B, it doesn't matter what C does. In the end, A will end up with B. C can stay and watch A and B come together, but C can't have what was meant for A and B in the first place. I'm quite sure that I'm C in this debauched equation." He lets go of her hand reluctantly, making a fist with his barren hand and continues looking me straight on. "I knew when I was returning back to New York, again, the city that hates me and my family, that I was on my way to witness the destruction I've choreographed firsthand. That I was headed back to see A and B have their happily ever after, surrounded by dead bodies and broken hearts. Because, you see, everything I love is cursed, and slowly but surely, gets taken away from me—first my brother, then my sister, now my baby, and eventually, my ballerina. And, Jeffery, I just want her to get through this. I promise, if she pulls out of this, I'll leave you pair alone. I'll go as far away from her as humanly possible and allow her to be happy. I will never ask for anything again if she makes it out of this alive." He half weeps, finding her hand and clasping it once again.

I stand and listen to him in total bewilderment. He thinks Sara chose me? Does he really have no idea how much this woman loves him?

"Thank you," I hear come out of his mouth, which catches me even more off guard.

I'm not sure if he's being sarcastic or I'm imagining things. I've had such a long, tumultuous week that I don't fucking know what planet we're on.

"I'm rather glad you were present for Sara," he adds as his voices cracks at uttering her name.

I look at him and nod, still in shock. "I'm sorry," I manage to expel and look at my peaceful Sara, who seems miles away. "I'm sorry this happened to you guys, and I'm sorry if this was my fault. I tried to get help. When she fell to the floor and I could see the blood coming out … I wasn't fast enough. I panicked. I tried to find the security guard and I wasted too much time. I should've gotten her to an ambulance faster. She seemed fine, I mean, we were talking and arguing and…"

I try and find the right words to tell him that we were saying goodbye. That we were finally letting one another go … when he adds, "Kissing?"

I look back at him, shocked, and my former self would be gloating and taking full ownership of that innocent kiss, but I love this woman. I can't do this to her. I owe the person she loves the truth since she's unable to provide it.

"It wasn't that kind of kiss! Don't be angry with her; it was all me. It was a goodbye kiss. It was an I'm-finally-happy kiss. It was an I-never loved-you-the-way-I-love-him kiss. It was a we-have-children-together kind of kiss. She already told me about you guys expecting a child together. She was so happy when she said it. It was the first time in years I saw her eyes smile and shine with hope. I never made her smile like that. I only caused pain and tears. You … you make her happy. She was never mine the way she's yours. I was just lucky to be a small part of her world, and I'm infinitely a better human for knowing her. I owe her everything."

The tears that I've held for years are out in full force. William hasn't looked away from me while holding Sara's hand tight. He looks like a different person than the arrogant enemy who stood over me in our old apartment a few days ago. He seems deflated, defeated, scared and lost, just like me. Helplessly watching the best part of you struggle to live is the worst pain in the world; I know, because that was my life for over fifteen years.

"Thank you for fetching her help. Thank you for not abandoning her. Thank you for doing the square thing. I lost one of my babies, but I beg the universe and anything that is holy I don't lose them both."

I nod my head, praying that the pretty girl I once met on a dance floor, the girl I've always carried with me in my heart, gets to dance again, even if it's not with me.

"She will make it and everything will work out for you guys. I'm going home to see my kids, now. I've been a shitty, selfish father, like you said, since my wife died. But, if it's okay, I'll be back to see how she's doing?" I reach out my arm as William still clutches Sara's delicate hand. He reaches out his left hand and gives my hand a weak shake that I wouldn't have anticipated from him. I look into his exhausted eyes; the overly dilated pupils now hide the blue that I clearly recall. I think to myself that you can take any man, no matter the size or status, and completely incapacitate him by wounding the thing he loves most. He loves her to the point of insecurity, weakness, helplessness and hopelessness; he loves her to death.

The nice thing about New York City is that all roads lead home. Each step is a memory of the last fifteen years I've lived here. I have enough happy and sad stories to last me a lifetime. I miss my children with every breath and every step. They are my only gift I pray is never taken from me.

For years, every morning I woke up with a purpose: to give Jacqueline a good life, a fucking fairy tale, to build a life that didn't seem temporary within the agony and hell she was forced to live. But as the sun would set each day on our harsh reality, all my hopes and dreams would be depleted. I would run to Sara to reignite and refuel my soul to be a man again tomorrow. *That's not a life.*

Every notion delivers me a step closer to my home, which is no longer a physical place. Home is inside my heart where Juliet and Jacob dwell. I will now wake up every day and make sure I give those two perfect humans an ideal life with enough love to never have them feel devoid of a parent.

The image of Sara bleeding in my arms and losing her pregnancy assaults my mind unexpectedly. I swallow around my guilt and pick up the pace, running to my children. They are the only things that can refill my soul now; they are my reason to live.

I round the corner out of breath as my townhouse comes into focus. I look to my left and she's there, sitting, waiting at Joanna's restaurant with her chocolate croissant and tea, watching over us like she has every morning for years. Not knowing that I've financially kept this restaurant in business for years to ensure she had a dependable place to watch her children from every morning. Only she's not there today. She's still unconscious and unaware that her happiness has been suspended once again.

I run up the stairs and fumble with the lock, unable to shuffle in fast enough. The second I enter, my little monkeys attack me. It's as if they stood by the door awaiting my return, which perhaps they have.

"Daddy, you're home. Did you find our angel?" Juliet repeatedly kisses the side of my face.

I'm too overwhelmed with the flood of gratitude I feel at holding them both in my arms that I can't even understand what my daughter is asking of me.

"Daddy, Mommy promised you'd find our guardian angel. Did you find her? Does she have wings? Does she look pretty, like Mommy?" Jacob takes my face with both his hands to direct my attention to him in an attempt to support his sister's query.

My mother must see the horror manifesting on my face as she removes first Jacob and then Juliet from my arms and explains. "It takes time to find a guardian angel. Daddy still needs time to find her. One day you'll meet your guardian angel, I promise." She smiles sadly and winks at me.

"Mommy said her name is Sara. Daddy, look for an angel named Sara."

I stand motionless, unable to breathe or speak.

"Juliet, let's go start your bath time. Daddy will come read you both a story, maybe two if you behave."

My mother offers me another sad look. I thank her with my eyes and kiss the disappointed looks on my children's faces. I pray that one day Sara finds her own happiness and comes back to meet the miracles she helped create. We'll be here waiting.

Jeffery

"Send Me An Angel" by Real Life

It's been almost six months since Jacqueline passed away. It's the first week I've stopped alternating between sleeping in Juliet and Jacob's bed almost every night, chasing away their bad dreams with my presence. Juliet is adamant on me going to find us a guardian angel. Every time she mentions that her mommy promised a beautiful girl named Sara was going to come and live with us, my heart stops beating for a second to reset its rhythm. They're too young to even understand that their mommy isn't coming back. They still think she's somewhere in a place called heaven getting treatment, and I thank God for their innocence.

It took Eddie, Louis, and William to come and knock some sense into me in order for me to wake up and realize just how much I have to live for and how blessed I really am. I went back home to try and be a half decent father to kids who, just like me, lost the most important part of their life.

I wanted to be the man that my wife thought I was and pick up the pieces and get my family back together. I was going to beg Sara to give us a chance and hope she'd agree to play a more active role in our children's lives, now that the only mother they ever knew was gone. I did run to Sara and Will's apartment at

The Pierre but since that day my life has never been the same. After almost losing Sara, I haven't been able to find myself among all the memories. The lines have been blurred and my head sometimes can't decipher who said what; was it Jacky or Sara? I'm all mixed up, and besides my children, I have nothing to anchor me down to earth.

I haven't yet gone back to work. I don't feel I should be trusted with million-dollar deals when I can't even write an email without drifting away to live inside one of my happy memories. My father-in-law has come out of retirement to help with the law firm he entrusted to me. I can't look anyone in the eye, especially not Jacky's parents; I can't handle more pain. I don't work, I don't eat, I don't sleep, and my heart only beats for my little ones while I try to stay strong and stop myself from perishing.

I spoke to Emily almost every day while Sara was back at her parents' house recovering after her near catastrophic miscarriage. Emily is my only direct link to Sara and her wellbeing, even now since Sara and Will returned to their penthouse. I'm pleasantly surprised they haven't left New York, and somewhere in my head, I hope she comes to see her children, as they patiently wait for their guardian angel to magically fix their mother's absence. Emily has mentioned how depressed her best friend is and how slow and painful her healing has been. Sara refuses to talk to me, and I have a feeling she blames herself for losing the baby, which was clearly out of everybody's hands. I still give blood every fifty-six days, against the doctor's recommendation and without anyone having knowledge of it, but it helps me to sleep better at night.

My kids have an army of people who love them and show them every day just how important they are in their lives. Even Eddie and his wife Michelle have been over a few times to let his children spend time with their cousins. We've had many invitations over the summer to stay in the Hamptons with people Jacky and I once considered friends, but I haven't been able to leave the safety of the walls within my home. I'll be okay one day, just not right now.

The last few weeks I've been having vivid dreams about being back at Brown University. I've refused to go talk to a therapist as my parents and brother keep suggesting. I don't need to talk to anybody or be put on antidepressants, I just need to reprogram my brain to accept reality and wipe from my mind what I assumed would be my life. Eddie thinks it would be a good idea for me to go back to Rhode Island and revisit where Jacqueline and I first met. He feels that in order for me to have closure and move forward I need to go visit the place where we were once young, happy, and carefree. After chewing over everybody's two cents regarding my life and wellbeing, I've decided it may be good for my sanity to take a short trip back to Rhode Island, not just to be back at the place where it all started for Jacky and me, but also to go find that old fortuneteller and return her key; it clearly doesn't belong to me. I need closure and I also want to somehow give her the prophecy back—it serves no purpose in my life anymore. She made a mistake. She got the wrong guy. When I find her, I'll finally get to ask her why she said the things she said to me that night. And how she could've possibly known the details that she said. It may be childish and silly, but my soul demands it.

I walk into Jacob's room first, but he's already asleep with his mouth open catching flies. I tuck him in and kiss his soft, dirty-blond mane. I close the door and go find his sister who I can bet my life is still not sleeping.

I peek in and I spy my little ballerina in training still fiddling quietly with her violin.

"To sleep or not to sleep … that is the question," I whisper in jest.

"Daddy, can I sleep in your room today? I think I'm going to have a bad dream," she cries out.

"Juliet, everybody has their own bed. I promise that tonight you'll only have good dreams."

I place her violin back on its stand and sit at the side of her ornate princess bed. She gives me a sad look that almost makes me want to cancel my silly trip. I should just stay home and sleep in her room, chasing away any nightmares, but the more I think about it, the more sense it makes that I need to leave New York City for a short time both mentally and physically and try to find myself for all our sakes. I have my whole life ahead of me and I need to be able to raise my children, run my law firm, and be happy with the cards I've been dealt. I ultimately need to be Juliet and Jacob's guardian angel, even though my name isn't Sara.

"I'm going away on a short trip to find something. I need you to take care of Jacob and make sure he doesn't get into any trouble. Can I count on you?" She loves being in command.

"Where are you going? Are you going to find Sara, our guardian angel?" Her eyes enlarge with hope and anticipation.

"I'm going back to where Mommy and I went to college. I think I lost something there. And, baby, listen, Sara will always be your guardian angel, like Mommy said, but she may not be part of our lives the way you're imagining. We have Mommy in heaven watching over us, and we have each other here. That's all we need." I kiss the disappointed look on her little perfect face.

"You're wrong. Mommy said Sara would take care of us when she's gone, and Mommy is always right," Juliet protests with conviction.

I nod. "Yes, Mommy is always right," I concede to my seven-year-old believer.

Providence, Rhode Island

Kali

"Beat it" by Michael Jackson

"Do you see that lost-looking guy?" Lauren points her shaker at a man sitting in the darkest corner of the bar.

"Yeah, I see him. What did he do?" I'm always suspicious of the strangers that visit us on dark, rainy days. I could probably name every person that walks through those doors, and in most cases, I can tell you who they're sleeping with or who they *want* to sleep with. That's what I get for spending every waking hour at the closest and best-known bar to the Ivy League giant known as Brown University.

"Watch this—in exactly one minute, he will get up and go upstairs to the bathroom. He's been here for over three hours, since we opened, and every fifteen minutes, like clockwork, the idiot gets up and goes upstairs to piss or maybe do something else. Here, watch, it's almost time." The clock on Lauren's phone shows a quarter past three, and the mystery man gets up and goes upstairs.

"Heads, I kick him out, tails, he's all yours," I call out mid-toss.

"No go, Frenchy. I dealt with our favorite drunk-transy last night. This bathroom creep is all yours, sister." Lauren is already on the other side of the bar as I reluctantly follow the weirdo up the stairs.

I cringe as the top stair squeaks. This throws my whole ambush plan to shit. I go with plan B and knock on the bathroom door instead.

"Sir, are you all right?" Silence. I try again, "Sir, is everything okay?" Still nothing. I try the handle, and it's unlocked. I roll my eyes, wondering why the fuck I need to deal with this bullshit, and why does the security guard's shift only start at five? Oh yeah, because we usually have four patrons before five and their tab wouldn't even cover an hour of his pay.

I proceed inside the second floor bathroom that most first-time visitors of the bar have no knowledge of, and it's dark. No fucking lights—the creep went in without turning the damn lights on. Is this the part where the crazy psycho grabs hold of me and kills me? I'm only half kidding when I feel someone tap my shoulder from behind.

"Do you work here?" His voice startles me because of my overactive, horror-movie-filled imagination. It's the same man I came up to find and kindly escort out. He's younger looking up close. He actually looks normal, perhaps even more toward the handsome side.

"Yeah, I work here. Are you lost? The bathroom is right here." I point in the opposite direction from where he obviously just came from.

"Where is the woman that used to sit here?" he demands in a deep, raspy voice.

I wasn't expecting that question from him. His words send a frozen chill down my spine. I'm sure I've misheard him. "Excuse me? The bathroom is this way," I repeat as little specks of memory begin bombarding my mind of the woman I think he's referring to. My vision begins to blur as I feel the tears building.

I'm not a crier; I'm a fighter. I need to go. Now! Without looking back, I walk toward the stairs. *Don't cry, don't cry, don't cry,* I chant over and over. I take a step down and then, as if I'm flying backward, I feel myself being jerked back up.

He holds both my upper arms while standing behind me and continues with his questions. "I need to see that woman. If she moved or started working somewhere else, please tell me where I can find her. I need to speak to her; it's important."

I glance back and look down at where his hands hold my arms.

He must notice what I see, because he quickly lets go. "Forgive me, I didn't mean to touch you or hurt you. I just need to find her. She used to sit right here." He points to an empty corner by the oval stained glass window. When I turn around to face him, still willing my tears to stay put, he adds, "The fortuneteller. I need to find her. Maybe you can ask the owner about her."

"I am the owner," I state with conviction, lifting my eyes to his. But the air is briefly knocked out of me as the chill that his words caused is replaced with recognition. The moment our eyes connect, it's apparent that I've seen this man before. I don't recall ever meeting him face to face, but somehow, I know this is no stranger.

We're both watching one another, and I'm suddenly hyper-aware of everything: the ticking sound of the clock, the hum of the ceiling fan, even the air has a taste. The peculiar color of this man's eyes makes me feel like I've been here before. I've lived in this point already. *Déjà vu.* My heart beats so fast that I can't seem to catch my breath. Who is this person? Why is he here? How does he know about her? Why is he asking about her? Why is he making it hard to breathe? He won't stop staring at me, as if he's breaking down my face into features—eyes, nose, lips, cheeks. His gaze continues to scan me. He also appears flustered, as a fine layer of sweat covers his features. I can't pinpoint or understand what's happening, but I can tell that he senses something. It's not just me.

We both begin rambling questions at each other simultaneously, and then we both stop. He gestures for me to proceed, and I do. "How do you know about the woman that used to sit here?" He seems too young to know about her. She hasn't been here in over a decade.

"I went to school here many years ago. This was our place. She always used to sit right here." He motions to an exact spot by the door again, the same spot that overlooks the entire bar, a spot which has been empty for years. "I need to find her, if it's the last thing I do."

"Why? Does she owe you money?" I snicker.

"No, she owes me an explanation. Did she leave a contact number when she left?" His question makes me want to laugh *and* cry—I choose to laugh. "This isn't a joke, this is my life." He briefly pauses as his voice cracks into a plea. "I drove for five hours to get here. You think this is funny?"

I shake my head. "No, it's actually very sad. She died two months ago." And now my smile does nothing to hold back the tears. I look away as I wipe my wet cheeks. I hear the guy with the dual-colored eyes laughing. "Is it funny to you that she died?" *What a pénis.*

"No, it's just funny that with my luck, I'm always a dollar short and a day late … well, in this case, I'm two months late. I waited over ten years to talk to her again, and when I finally got enough balls to come back and face her, she fucking dies. Perfect!" He's still laughing maniacally, and I'd love to know what was so important that he drove five hours to come talk to some old fortuneteller?

"What did she say to you anyway? It obviously seems like a big deal." I'm literally dying to know what propelled this man to come back to find her. He keeps turning around to the place he claims Joella used to sit. I always feel her presence when I come upstairs, but today more than ever.

"I think that old woman changed the course of my future. I've been clinging to her words from the day she uttered them. But she made a mistake. Everything she said was a lie—a horrible, vicious lie." He takes another look at the empty place Joella once occupied and begins to walk away.

He's midway down the stairs when I raise my voice and say, "She never made a mistake, and her tongue was too pure for lies."

He stops, turns around, and looks up at me with a smirk. "You wouldn't understand—you're just a kid." His tone has a sound of melancholic defeat.

The fighter in me needs to have the last word. I need to make this arrogant stranger, who doesn't seem strange at all, know how great Joella was.

"I'm no kid, and trust me when I tell you that Joella Gitanos never opened her mouth unless she had a reason. She never took a dime for a reading, and as far as I know, only offered someone the future when their present depended on it." I hate talking about her to someone who has no idea how gifted she was. I hate having to defend her legacy to some ignorant man. Why would she waste her time on him? People couldn't beg her enough to grant them a reading if they weren't part of her path. Maybe this guy is confused, delusional; perhaps he imagined a reading. Back in the day, I was told she chose to spend her days sitting at the top of these stairs—she said she had the perfect view, but nobody understood of what. The one thing I am certain about is that Joella Gitanos only gave readings to a chosen few, all of whom are long gone.

I look back into this man's eyes. I've never met anybody with two different eye colors—green and brown. I'm sure it would look odd, perhaps abnormal, on anybody else, but his eyes are fascinating and reluctantly they pull me in like magnets.

I suddenly have an unexplained craving to know everything behind them. I stand and stare in awe into eyes that silently promise chaos. They are not calm seas but turbulent oceans with storms brewing at their core. And I've already learned early on in life to stay as far away from any body of water, but I need to know exactly what my grand-mère said to him.

Jeffery

"Bringin' On The Heartbreak" by Def Leppard

That old woman knew nothing. Absolutely nothing. Every word was a lie. This college girl, the one who claims to own this joint, which I suspect is a lie, too, believes that the fortuneteller never made mistakes. *Ha!* Look at me—I am living, walking proof that all her predictions were a goddamn joke. What was I thinking? Did I really leave everybody behind and come here to confront some old hack and blame her instead of me for how my life turned out? I should've used my better judgment back then … *and* now. Isn't that what I'm trained to do? What self-respecting attorney takes advice from a fucking fortuneteller? I pity this confused girl who obviously has some admiration for that dead old lady. I wonder what evidence she's holding on to for her foolish convictions?

"I have a few hours before this place becomes a mad house. If you don't have any plans, I'd like to maybe chat," she hesitantly invites me, while avoiding my gaze.

"Chat?" I mock her. "About what, the quack who ruined my life?"

I feel my face jerk back before my brain can even process that this little bitch just slapped me, *hard*. I'm on the verge of being pissed, but I can't help the smirk that takes hold of my lips. I mean come on, by the look on her face, she's more shocked by her actions than I am, which makes this whole situation amusing. This little woman looks like a vicious child who is about to cry hysterically unless I defuse this situation. She nervously watches my lips in horror, still avoiding my eyes like the plague. I'm used to people evading my gaze, I'm aware that my condition freaks some individuals out. It's not natural for someone to have one green eye and one brown, but this girl's reaction is different. It's interesting. I rub my left cheek and the tingling sensation only brings me back to Sara slapping me in the same spot six months ago. Everything can change in a heartbeat—six months ago, I lost my wife, and then I almost lost Sara. And now I'm wasting time with a confused young girl.

"She's not a quack, you idiot." Her shaking voice hisses out, dragging me back to our present encounter. "Fuck you, whoever you are. Get yourself out of my bar or I'll call security."

I hear a peculiar accent escape in her outburst, which I haven't picked up on before. She finally gathers herself and looks up to meet my eyes with her dark, angry glare. It takes a split second for a chill to cover me. Where have I seen those eyes before?

It takes me another minute to collect myself and attempt to diffuse this train wreck. "I'm sorry, I shouldn't have said that. That old lady obviously means something to you, and shame on me—I had no right to badmouth her. I can only blame myself for having taken ill counsel from a total stranger." I don't like how every time I open my mouth, this kid gets angrier with me.

"Why are you so lost, sir?" Her question drips with ridicule. I hate her calling me *sir*, makes me feel ancient, which compared to her I probably am.

"I'm lost because everything I love, I lose. I thought I knew how my life would play out … but I know nothing." I'm not sure why I feel the need to explain my worthless existence to this girl.

Perhaps I feel like a dirt-bag for coming off heartless regarding the death of that old fortuneteller who once worked here.

"You can't be mad at my grand-mère just because you can't appreciate what she knew. You have no idea how lucky you are if she actually chose to speak to you. You may be the last person who ever got a reading from her." Her eyes become misty again, and she scrunches her nose to hold back tears, I suspect. I took French in high school, and I'm quite certain this girl just called the old woman her grandma. And now I officially feel like the world's biggest douche for saying what I fucking said about this poor girl's dead grandmother.

"I'm very sorry for your loss. Please disregard everything I said before. My name is Jeff, by the way. Again, don't pay any attention to anything I've said. I'm sure she was a great woman." I feel like I'm tracking up shit creek without a paddle here. I'm usually not this callous with my words, but everything that I've had to endure in the past six months has fucked me up for life. This is not like me.

She has a hard time looking directly at me, which only makes me want her to look at me that much more. She tensely places both hands in the back pockets of her jeans, and without looking up at me, says, "You can call me Kali," in a half whisper.

"Hi, Kali. It's very nice to meet you. I'm sorry for being a dick. I really believed I'd just walk right in here and find her sitting at the top of these stairs, as if time stood still. I'm delusional. Time waits for no one." Which is the truth. I tried, I failed, time to go back home. I take another look at the place I remember that alluring gypsy fortuneteller once occupied and wish that I could make her take back all her words. What if she never unleashed her prophecy? What kind of life would I have had if those words didn't float around in the universe? I take a deep, exacerbating breath, allowing myself to finally acknowledge how tired and hungry I am. I drove all night to get here. Put a gun to my head, and I couldn't tell someone what finally made me decide to come all this way after all these years. Maybe I was possessed, or maybe just desperate. I thought, I really thought that if I came back to where it all started, to the place where I accepted a promised future from a total stranger, and in return disregarded the consequences of my present actions, then maybe my life would finally make sense.

"You hungry?" Kali's voice brings me back before I let my mind dwell in the past again. I long to go back to when it was all simple. "I'll feed you and maybe you'll be less of a dick," she declares with a smirk.

I nod, thankful for her not calling security. I drove for hours to get some answers from a dead fortuneteller, and instead, I've managed to royally offend her poor granddaughter. Dinner and conversation are more than I deserve.

"Sounds good, but I'd like to treat you for dinner. I owe you at least that," I propose, stretching my hand out for a truce.

She first looks at my hand, and then finally up at my face and nods, keeping both hands in her back pockets. Her eyes have cleared up a bit, no longer black. She's not ready to touch the asshole who called her grandmother a quack, and I can't say I blame her.

I nod back, accepting her hand snob declaration and then obediently head down the stairs behind her.

Kali

"Always Something There To Remind Me" By Naked Eyes

I haven't been this emotional about the passing of Joella since her funeral two months ago. But this man coming here and mentioning her reminds me of how quickly things get taken away from me—first my maman, and now my grand-mère. I wish I had more hours with both of them. I wish Joella hadn't abandoned me so soon after we found one another. I mean, I only found out about her after my maman's accident. I had no reason to believe that a woman named Joella Gitanos residing in Providence, Rhode Island was my grand-mère. My maman, may she rest in peace, never mentioned her roots or that she had family left in America. She told me she was an orphan, for the love of God. Who knew that I had gypsy blood running though my veins? During my maman's wake, I recall a statuesque older woman walking into our little church in Cassis. The same church my parents were married in and where I was baptized. I felt her presence before anyone actually noticed her sitting in the back row. I sensed her the moment she came in, and our eyes immediately locked in a baffling recognition. My papa turned around to see who I kept looking at, and once he spotted her sitting in the back, he stood up abruptly and left without a single word.

Maybe if Joella were still alive, she'd tell me more stories about my family and why her daughter left her and America and never came back. Maybe I could've better convinced her to enlighten me as to what my future holds and why she couldn't warn her own daughter about her accident? To this day, my papa refuses to speak about his mother-in-law, and my maman died too soon. I wish I'd known about Joella when my maman was still alive, but even if I knew about her existence, I wasn't old enough to have known to ask the right questions.

I'm an only child with more questions than answers and with no one left to ask.

Joella told me, when I originally came to live here, that she first met me in the flesh when she came to attend her daughter's funeral. I was too young and shaken up over the sudden loss of my maman to question her or anybody else as to her identity. I had no idea who she was. My papa knew, but he didn't say a word, as if helping my maman keep her a secret. I only heard back from that elusive stranger a week after I turned eighteen. She sent me a long letter, finally introducing herself as my maman's mother, and invited me to come to America to attend university. My papa refused to talk to me about her. "Never listen to that witch," he warned me before I came here, but I owed it to myself and my curiosity to meet the last living link left to my beautiful maman.

Sometimes, I believe that my coming here was pointless, but today, meeting this stranger feels predestined. I've spent the last five years trying to learn and understand my past, my family, and Joella at the helm. And I've finally grown accustomed and accepted that my quest for answers was fruitless and ended with her death eight weeks ago. But thanks to this confused stranger asking about her, this is the first time since she died that I feel a twinkle of hope. Perhaps there are still things for me to uncover. Besides Lauren, I have no one left here. My lonesomeness rears its ugly head, and without warning, I long to be anywhere but here. I wish it were five years ago and I were with Florent—the only person besides my papa from my old life in Cassis I truly miss. But before I allow myself to miss him too much, I recall how he had no problems moving on to another girl. Never once coming to visit me, never once asking me to return, so maybe it's not him I miss but the feeling of not being all alone.

I make it down the stairs as I spy Lauren flashing me a disturbed smile while holding her thumbs up with a questioning look. I nod and mouth, "I'm okay," letting her know that I've got this situation under control, which I don't. I know she's still watching me as I proceed to find a semi-isolated place to sit and talk with Jeff—our bathroom creep, who's following closely behind me.

I wouldn't have been able to make it this long without Lauren. She has managed this bar on her own for years. She's taught me everything I know. I've slowly learned the job, and as guilty and as wrong as it may be, I haven't missed the life I left back home because Joella and this place felt like home … until eight weeks ago, when she left me without warning.

I legally own everything that was once Joella's. I have all of her possessions entrusted and passed down to me, and I still haven't wrapped my brain around it. I wear her dazzling scarves at home, and I swear it feels as if someone I love is wrapping their warm arms around me. I instinctively touch the locket around my neck that she used to wear. It has a picture of my maman holding me as a baby, and an empty slot. I wanted to fill the empty space with a photo of her, but I haven't been able to find one, since I haven't looked for the key to her private apartment. I'm not ready to find that key. I'm sure her second floor apartment situated directly over this bar houses all her photographs and the journals she kept in her youth, which I recall her mentioning. However, I won't be able to bring myself to open any of them even if I find them. It still feels wrong to read them, therefore I hide my head in the sand and pretend there is no key.

"Would you like to go somewhere else to eat and talk?" Jeff's voice interjects my thoughts.

"No, I'd rather we stay here and sit in that quiet corner. I'd like to keep an eye on things, especially since the security guard isn't in yet." I show Jeff back to the corner booth I first spotted him in, and then make my way to the bar to try and explain this to my favorite curious bartender who's shooting daggers with her eyes at our table.

"You know him?" Lauren begins grilling me, while unconsciously frowning and raising her eyebrow in Jeff's direction.

"I don't think I know him, but he says that Joella once gave him a reading."

Lauren turns to look at me, letting the beer from the draft overflow and drip all over her hands. "Throw him out, now!" she bellows, not at all kidding. "He's pulling a fast one on you. Throw that liar out, now! You know what? Stay here, let me do it." She mutters obscenities under her breath, and I can see that Jeff has a good chance of getting his ass kicked unless I stop this madwoman.

"Lauren, come back. I don't think he's lying. He has no reason to lie. He just came here to talk to her. He wasn't looking for anyone but her. He didn't even know she owned this place." I look over at Jeff sitting in the corner. He hasn't stopped staring my way. He's far enough that I can't see his eyes, but I can't shake his piercing gaze from my mind.

"Frenchy, listen to me, I don't know if you know this, but Joella's last so-called reading was your mom's. Strangers who weren't somehow related to her didn't know she was a fortuneteller. There was no neon sign. She hasn't even sat up there in over a decade. This guy is a jerk for feeding you lies. She wouldn't have even spoken to him."

I grab hold of Lauren's arm before she pounces over to Jeff and explain to her why I believe him. "That's why I must talk to him. Don't you see? How could he possibly know that the woman who sat at the top of the stairs years ago was a psychic, unless she actually gave him a reading?"

She stops moving toward Jeff's direction to contemplate my words. She sighs, rolls her eyes, but she, too, understands why I won't be throwing this stranger out, just yet.

"Order me two shepherd's pies and I'll grab the beers. Let me give him a chance to explain. It's never too late to throw him out later." I smile bravely, although my insides bubble with anxiety.

Lauren kisses the side of my head before she passes me on the way to the kitchen. She's all I have left here. She's not that much older than me, but she sometimes feels like my mama-bear.

"If you need muscle, lift your eyes my way and I'll come kick his ass." She makes a fist and winks at me.

I plaster my brave, fake smile and go back to find out how Jeff, owner of the most magnificent eyes I've ever seen to date, met Joella Gitanos at the top of those stairs.

Jeffery

"I Drove All Night" by Cyndi Lauper

The more I look at this girl, Kali, the more I'm able to recall the fortuneteller from that one stupid night. Up until now, I couldn't remember what she actually looked like, but it's uncanny how they have the same dark eyes. There is no question that I've seen those eyes before—even the shape is the same. I can't stop looking at her with her black, unruly hair falling down her back. The clairvoyant, Joella, or whatever her name was, also had black hair, but I don't think it was this long. But all of this makes no difference. Joella is dead and I still need to figure out how to get my life back on track.

My gorgeous children are the only reason I'm still breathing. I swallow the thought of them waking up this morning and me being away. Since Jacky died, I've had my in-laws, my parents, and my brother alternate staying with us. I had no choice but to come here and put all this behind me for my sanity. This chapter of my life needs to end for a new one to begin.

I look away from Kali while she talks to the girl bartender I met when I first came in, and I look down to my phone. Juliet and Jacob are smiling, staring back at me from my screen saver. I stroke the screen and wish I could, one day, give them a life where they have a normal family—a mother and a father like they once had. I wish I could bring my wife back to life, and I wish I could give Sara all the years I stole from her with my empty promises. Basically, I wish I was a magician and unhurt everything that I've ever touched.

"I hope you like shepherd's pie," Kali announces, placing two bottles of beer on the table and then sitting across from me. We're back to no eye contact, and she starts to clean the table with a napkin, nervously. Shepherd's pie was our staple diet throughout law school. I think back fondly to the hundreds of nights that we've spent at BlackGod Bar binging on them. I instantly remember sitting at this very table with Jacqueline, and I swear I can hear her laugh at one of Eddie's corny dirty jokes. It seems like yesterday, yet it was a lifetime ago. "I can order you a burger, I just know that most people come here for the meat pie."

"I love shepherd's pie, and I probably haven't had one in over fifteen years, because I could bet my life they wouldn't compare to the pies we've had here."

She raises her eyes to meet mine. Finally, I didn't say something to offend her. She's a pretty girl when she's not angry with me.

"Who are you and where are you from?" Kali asks me point blank.

I want to tell her that I'm a nobody, and that I just came back from hell, but I stop myself. I don't need to unleash my despair on this poor young woman. I'm not one of her issues that she needs to deal with.

"New York—concrete jungle where dreams are made of," I half sing Alicia Keys' song sarcastically, which makes her smile again. Her grin is crooked, with her lip curling to one side. I can't help but mimic her. *When was the last time I made a girl smile?* I think about the women that make up my whole life—Jacqueline and Sara—and then I think about how I haven't even been able to make my daughter smile in months. The image of

Juliet bombards my head and immediately squeezes my heart, which wipes the stupid grin off my face. It's only been eighteen hours since I left them last night, but I miss my little babies so much.

"I've never been to New York. I must go one day," she proclaims with determination. "Now, tell me why you came all this way from New York to see Joella? It was obviously important for you to speak to her." Her eyes shine with interest. "It's a little weird because it's just not normal for her to give strangers a reading—if that's, in fact, what she did for you. Only a few people knew she had the vision, and she seldom shared it with anybody." And the melancholy look in her eyes is back again.

"I feel like an idiot for coming here. It was so many years ago, and yet I can't forget a single word she said. Sometimes, I repeat her words over and over and it helps me … you know, it makes things bearable." I rub my chest, feeling the outline of the key I wear around my neck. "When I was attending school here, my friends and I would come to this bar hundreds of times, and she was always sitting at the top of those stairs. I just accepted her presence as part of the scenery or ambiance of this place. I honestly can't remember if I've ever seen her giving someone else a reading. I never noticed. Anyway, it doesn't matter what she told me back then, I was probably drunk. It's all ancient history now, right?"

Kali stares at me. I asked her a rhetorical question, but I think she's seriously contemplating it. The blond who's been behind the bar interrupts our silent conversation to deliver the prized pies. The smell of the flaky pastry derails any thoughts I had in my head. The dark-skinned woman gives me the look of death, before her face softens as she directs her attention to Kali and then mumbles for us to enjoy our grub. My mouth waters as I begin to dig into my pie like a starved caveman. I place a spoonful of the hot beef infused with the bordelaise sauce, smothered in buttery, velvety-smooth mashed potatoes, and allow myself a moment in heaven. This is probably the only place in the world that actually uses dry, aged Bordeaux to make shepherd's pie. I almost forget where I am as I devour every last bite. I see Kali smiling at me, clearly happy with my juvenile reaction to fucking peasant food. I move the plate away, taking a few swigs of my beer and try to remember what I said to Kali right before the pie derailed me.

"This may be rude, and I understand that it's none of my business, but I would do close to anything to hear what you recall my grand-mère once telling you. I don't think I'll ever have an opportunity like this again." She reaches out her hands across the table and boldly takes hold of my wrists. I let go of the bottle to allow her a better grip, surprised by her brazen behavior. Without letting go, she continues to plead. "Jeff, I'm begging you to tell me. I promise it will be our secret, and I will never mention this to another living soul, but I have a choking need to know what she predicted and why she chose to speak to you." I hear the desperation in her voice.

I look at her small, delicate hands holding my wrists and have a kind of déjà vu moment that brings my mind back to the night I met her grandmother at the top of those stairs. I turn my wrists to expose my palms and feel the fortuneteller tracing my lines and painfully sealing my fate. I look back into Kali's hopeful expression, awaiting my verdict, and it's clear what I must do.

Fortunes are meaningless unless you know the lives they forever changed.

Kali

"Take On Me" by a-ha

I'm lured by a stranger I know nothing about. I have this intensely, foreign, stomach-churning sense in my gut to take hold of him. He needs to tell me what Joella revealed to him all those years ago. I don't know what I'll do if he denies me this information. My heart beats at an unimaginable rate as I hold on to his wrists as if he's my last hope. But hope of what? What am I hoping he tells me? He has not a thing to do with my life, or my future, except having had my grand-mère choose to speak to him. My gut and every cell in my body screams for me to keep digging and hold on to him until he speaks and puts this crazy thirst of mine to rest. I hope to God this is not my loneliness clinging to anything that once had contact with my past—my dead past.

He twists his wrists in my hands to reveal his palms, still wet from the cold beer he just held on to a moment ago. I look away from his outstretched hands and back into his eyes, but they're shut, and he suddenly seems miles away. His nostrils attempt to capture more air, but I can see when he loses the internal battle that's obviously been evoked from within. I can feel his grief and his struggle to not cry. The look on his face is painful, but in an odd way, also peaceful. I know the moment when the memory hits him, and I sense him give up and allow it to play in his mind. I wonder if it's Joella's words that triggered the turmoil I both felt and saw in his face earlier. Or maybe it was the consequences of his actions to her words that caused the chaos that still lives within him. Whatever it is—*who*ever he is—I must know what Joella Gitanos predicted. She's gone, but her words are calling to me. I need to uncover the truth, the reason for his presence here, and what was so special about him to be the only living person that I know of to have been granted a sitting with the person I wish I had more time with.

"Jeff, are you all right?" Tears run down his cheeks. "Jeff, will you talk to me?"

He abruptly pulls his hands from my grip as if I forcefully held on to him, and then opens his eyes. They are the most extraordinary and tragic things I've ever seen.

"Nothing I say will make any sense to you. It only makes sense to me. She had no way, no right to know the things she said to me. I wish I could ask her why? Why did she stop me that night? Why did she say anything to me? I didn't ask for my future. I didn't want it." He's all worked up, getting himself angry. He's right. None of this makes any sense, especially if he won't tell me what she actually said to him.

"I want to understand. Only you can make me understand. I know I'm not her, but I'm the only living link left of her, and I spent five years here trying to understand her. Maybe I can help you. Maybe you can help me. If you need to be angry with someone, then be angry with me. I don't care if you yell or talk; I just want you to tell me and make me understand why you—why would Joella Gitanos choose to talk to you?"

He gets up from his seat and my heart drops. He's about to leave. *Please don't go.* He's about to go back to whatever hole he crawled from and leave me with even more questions than I already had. He can't just come here, stir me up like this, and then leave. *He can't do this to me!*

I look up in shock at a man that I suddenly have a burning desire to know. I don't want him to go. He must see the fear in my eyes, because he stretches out his hand to me. I'm confused and my brain can't decide what's happening. Does he want to shake my hand? Is he leaving? Or is he leaving and taking me with him?

"Come." His hand is outstretched in midair, and he and I both know this isn't a question. "You and I are about to get better acquainted." His words ring with a confident finality to them, while his eyes look like a Photoshopped illusion, and I feel hypnotized by both.

I take his hand without an ounce of hesitation, and at this point, I'm quite sure I'd follow him into hell as long as he keeps looking at me.

I come out of my trance-like state and realize we're upstairs again. *Did I go up the stairs?* I question my fuzzy memory. He pulls the heavy black curtains to one side and unlocks a door using a key. He's now holding it open for us to enter into Joella's old quarters—the ones that haven't been used since I moved here five years ago, the ones I haven't yet found the key to. Joella wasn't able to go up and down these or any other stairs. Everything I know about this part of the building comes from stories I've been told by Lauren and her mother. I've only seen the outside portion that every patron who visits the facilities sees. I'd never been invited, nor had I ever been asked to go beyond that point. Jeff leads the way as if he's been in this off-limits part of the bar hundreds of times before. We're inside, standing in the middle of a round room, and I suddenly feel his strong hand holding on to me. I look around my unfamiliar surroundings and gasp at the location he's brought us to. He moves us in deeper, pulling me toward him. My mind slowly allows the rest of me to process that I'm walking through my grand-mère's private chambers, and that's when I stop pretending to be strong and everything goes black.

"Baby, it's time to get up." I hear my maman and feel her warm lips kissing my head.

"Maman, I had a bad dream." I whimper and crawl into her arms as I recall bits and pieces of my nightmare.

"We don't repeat bad dreams. We allow them to evaporate with the night." I feel my beautiful maman pull me close and gently stroke my back as I inhale her familiar vanilla scent, trying to forget the man with frightening eyes who always appears in my dreams.

"Kali, Kali, please don't do this to me." His voice is familiar. Where is my maman?

I slowly open my eyes before closing them again. The dim light burns my lids and makes my eyes tear up. His warm hand rubs my cheek and it forces me to melt into his touch. But as I attempt to open my eyes again, his touch is gone and so is his hand—another illusion. I find him sitting a few feet away from me with his arms folded over his body. He's watching me intently, waiting for an explanation.

"Who are you?" I've asked this already, but this stranger named Jeff seems to be in no hurry to answer any of my questions.

"Perhaps I should be asking you that?" he counters, and I, too, don't feel the need to say more than I already have.

How did he know to bring me here? Who gave him a key? I sit up from the bed he must've laid me on, and look at him, realizing that my gut was right about him. "How did you know about this place?" I question, somehow knowing he must've been so much more to Joella than I originally thought.

"I've never been in this room, but I've seen it in my mind before. She gave me a reading in the room we first passed through. It's where you fainted. Why did you faint on me, Kali? I'm prepared to talk, but I need to make sure you'll be okay with the things I tell you."

I can't look away from him and those eyes of his.

I notice a key dangling on a black cord around his neck. He instantly grabs hold of the key and hides it under his T-shirt. He momentarily looks away from me and rubs his chest, making sure the key is in its place. He's waiting for me to answer, and I wish I could explain to him why I blacked out. I wish I could tell him that I am prepared to hear everything. But the truth is I'm scared out of my mind and I've never felt my heart beat this hard in all of my twenty-five years on this earth.

Jeffery

"Don't Stand So Close To Me" by The Police

Lately my presence seems to make the women I encounter faint on me, and this is not a welcomed side effect. I wanted to show Kali the room where the fortuneteller, her grandmother, gave me her stupid reading, but that plan just went to shit. The second we entered that room, I felt her small hand begin to shake in mine, right before going limp, as she stopped holding on and began to fall. I was instantly reminded of Sara fainting in the bathroom six months ago, allowing the familiar terror and fear to flood through my veins again. I had Kali nestled in my arms, unresponsive to my touch. I looked around to find a flat place to lay her weak body on and tried to wake her. The living room we were in only had chairs, so I proceeded farther inside and carried her to the next room before placing her on a bed. It was dark, and a strong smell of roses hit me immediately. I'd never seen this room in my life, but it felt familiar like a childhood bedroom that you never forget.

I called out her name, trying to wake her up. I couldn't help but stroke her hair and face, and that, too, seemed natural. Who the hell is she? Where do I know her from? Why do I feel like I've been here already? It had only been a few seconds, but I thought perhaps I needed to call an ambulance. As soon as the thought entered my head, her eyelids flickered. I instinctively moved away from her. I didn't need to scare her more than all of this already has. Her color slowly came back to her cheeks and my treacherous heart began to beat again.

The fear in her eyes does crazy shit to my insides. I know she's not scared of me, but I still feel like a dick for somehow causing that look. This isn't sexual or anything, but I crave to hug her fear away. *Who the fuck are you, Kali?* Why do I care so much who the fuck she is in the first place? She sat up, and as if reading my thoughts, asked me who I am. I don't know how to answer that. I don't think I've figured that part out yet. I feel as if she knows more about me than I know about myself. And my questions seem to elicit a similar mute response from her.

I get up, unable to restrain myself and maintain an acceptable distance, and walk over to sit next to her on the bed I've placed her on. I know I can't touch her, but I need to be close to her. She looks confused, like she needs someone to be close to her, and right now, that someone is me. Her eyes enlarge with an emotion I hope to God is not fear. As soon as I sit next to her, I regret our proximity. I immediately feel more than I should for a woman I just met. When I hear her gasp, I instantly get up, because I have no business feeling anything.

There are moments in your existence that you know your life will change forever. I had that moment when I met Sara almost seventeen years ago in that club in New York City. I had a moment with that fortuneteller over a decade ago a few feet from where I stand now. I had that moment when I married Jacqueline, and when my children were born, and I just had that moment with Kali two minutes ago. You can't explain it to anybody except to the person who caused it in the first place.

I hate myself for what I think I feel. I can't bring myself to even look at her and, God forbid, see in her eyes the same feelings I have. I begin to frantically look around the room for things that can take my mind off this striking girl who keeps watching me with expectations to deliver her answers, but I don't have any … just more questions. If she only knew how lost I am. If she only knew what kind of man I really am, she'd stop looking at me with hope. Everything I touch, I ruin. It's best I touch nothing from now on.

I pretend to examine an intricate tapestry hung on the wall, distancing my thoughts away from how attractive she is. Without warning I feel her arms engulf me into a hug from behind. I glance down to find her hands lace together and wrap around my waist; her chest molds flush against my back. The air I've held inside from the second she touched me deflates, allowing her to momentarily incapacitate me.

"You look like you need a hug," she whispers innocently. I shouldn't be imagining anything but an innocent hug with this girl.

I turn to face her. Her eyes study me with such anticipation I almost wish I could give her the information she so desperately seeks. Against my common sense I hug her tight to me, not letting my feelings rule this peculiar situation we're both in. "I think we both need a hug," I answer with a chuckle, hoping to hide how nervous I am.

She looks up to give me a small smile, and I pull her close again, resting my chin on her head. Embracing her feels as natural as breathing, and yet we know nothing about each other. We stand huddled in the middle of what I suspect used to be her grandmother's bedroom, and I can't help but feel for the first time in a long time that I'm in the right place, with the right person, at the right time.

"Please don't faint again," I beg her as we begin to pull away from our hold.

"Deal." She nods with a smile. "Do you think we should stay and talk here?" She's already moving farther away from me, and I'd be lying if I said I didn't like having her close.

I look around the small room covered in old books and photographs with the dried flowers immortalized in dozens of colorful vases scattered around religious statues. I look up at the ceiling draped in a dusty white fabric coming from the center where a dim chandelier gives off almost no light. I return my gaze to the bed, with Kali standing by it. It's too much for me to stay here and pretend that I don't feel the things I know I shouldn't after being numb for so long. This room feels like a hidden lovers' tent suspended in another lifetime. In a way, this room reminds me of the place Sara and I once called home, and I know I will never again have a home.

"Would it be okay with you if we talk in that first room? I don't want you to faint again, but this room feels wrong," I confess honestly.

She nods. I motion for Kali to go back through the doors I carried her across once she fainted. She leads the way, looking down as we pass first the living room and then the room just beyond the curtains, taking a seat at the round table. There are only two seats, so I naturally sit across from her. I just now noticed that this room is completely round, and if I release the black curtains, we'd be in total darkness. Maybe I've been in total darkness ever since I stepped into this room years ago. Knowing your future is unnatural. Perhaps I allowed the darkness to live inside me, and instead of forgetting it and running as far as humanly possible toward the light, I ran right back to it.

I hear a scraping sound across the floor. Kali moves her chair, positioning it close to mine. I instantly have a need to tell her how unstable I am. She shouldn't be moving closer to me, she should be running away. I can end her curiosity in five minutes and get the fuck out of here. I'll tell her the futile prophecy bestowed upon me by her dead grandmother, and then she will leave me alone and let me live out the rest of my life sentence on this earth without the ones I love.

"What are you doing?" My voice sounds harsh. I know exactly what she's doing, but she shouldn't be nice to some stranger. She knows nothing about me. "You know what? I think it's best if I just write down what your grandmother said to me and then go. You'll have all the time in the world to read it over and over and then try to decipher what her fortunetelling actually meant. I can assure you that her prophecy never came true and I have yet to understand any of her predictions." That's my head talking.

She smiles at me—a knowing, one-sided grin revealing no teeth but plenty of disappointment. She looks away, nodding her head to herself. "Okay, Jeff from New York City. You're right—perhaps it's best you go. I don't want you wasting your time on a dead fortuneteller's granddaughter. I mean, what can I possibly say to you that would give meaning to Joella's reading if you yourself haven't a clue? After all, it must not have been that important to you if you've waited all these years to come here to make sense of her words." The chair scrapes the floor with a soul-piercing sound, the loss of eye contact and her sudden withdrawal from my space begins to cause a panic that makes zero sense.

I feel like I'm letting this girl I know nothing about down. Why is she agreeing for me to go so quickly? Only minutes ago, she had her hands wrapped around me and moving her chair to be closer and now she's prepared to walk away?

"Kali!" I call after her. "Kali, look at me!" I say her name with more ownership. She finally turns with a victorious, knowing grin on her lips.

Checkmate.

She knows I don't want to go.

Kali

"I Can't Hold Back" by Survivor

He seems too old to still be playing games, but then again, some men just play games forever. I can see how badly he wants to talk to me. I can feel how much he wants me to help him make sense of things he's probably never spoken to anybody about. He and I may have just met, but we have one thing in common—Joella. I never knew enough to be able to talk about her, and I'm pretty sure he's been pretending they never met. But he can't pretend with me that this is no big deal to him. I didn't miss the look of fear that just passed in his eyes. He needs me just as much as I think I need him.

"Are you going to stop pretending and playing games? I'm not your girlfriend—you don't have to worry about me. You have information that I want, and I may have the explanation you seek. I'm not trying to come on to you … I just want you to feel comfortable enough to talk to me. If my gut is right, I bet I'll be the only person you've ever spoken to about what Joella Gitanos enlightened you with, right?"

He nods.

"Let's start over. I get that I first need to know you a little better in order for my grand-mère's words to mean to me what they mean to you. Are you willing to be truthful and open about your life with me?"

I hold my breath as I wait for him to answer. I may have just said that I am not his girlfriend, but I feel something, and he intrigues me in more than a brotherly way. I can't deny that his eyes are doing silly things to my stomach. But he doesn't need to know that, he just needs to feel at ease to want to talk to me.

He takes two huge strides toward me, and a tingle a little south of my stomach comes to life. He holds out his hand again, as if to shake mine, and I comply. But instead of a handshake, he just holds on to me, and then turns his hand in mine, opening it to show me his open palm. He lowers himself close enough to whisper, "I'm not happy about how I feel around you. I can count the number of times in my life that I've felt this way. I promise you, I'm not playing games. I'm just trying to play it cool. I know you think that you'll be able to understand your grandmother's words, but once I tell you about myself, I'm worried you'll only inherit the burden of knowing me."

My heart stops beating as his breath warms my cheek, while my shaking hand still rests in his palm. I'm certain of my attraction to him, and I'm certainly not proud of it, either. I have no business being attracted to a man that is probably married, or at the very least, has a girlfriend waiting back in New York. I tilt my head to the side to try and move away from him, and I swear it's harder than it seems, because I feel the electromagnetic pull between us.

"Do you feel that?" I ask him.

"I do, but I don't want to do anything about it," he declares, retrieving his hand.

His response leaves me livid; I don't like feeling rejected. But once I calm the petulant only-child-complex that lives in me, I'm silently thankful for his dismissal of the things we're both feeling. I agree that we shouldn't be trying to explore some weird emotions we've stirred in one another, and start exploring the reasons why Joella chose Jeff—an unknown bar patron—to bestow one of her last known readings.

"Let's not talk today." I need to clear my head and catch my breath.

His eyes enlarge at my statement.

"I mean, let's just take it easy today. It's too much for me to take in, and I'm not sure what I'm feeling … my brain is all out of sorts, and I'm sure you're tired, too, from driving here. Let's meet up in the morning."

He sighs at my words and takes a few steps away from me to go sit back down. He watches me, and once again, I feel as if he's breaking down my features. His gaze finally lands back on my eyes. "Did I offend you, Kali?"

I shake my head, which we both know is a lie.

"You don't need someone like me to come on to you. Trust me, I'm nothing." He can keep saying that, but I know that my grand-mère wouldn't choose a "nothing." He's special, and hopefully soon, we'll both find out why.

I begin to leave when I feel him grab hold of my arm and slowly pull me toward him. "Don't go, Kali," he whispers. I turn without looking directly at him. I take a few small steps back to where he's sitting, and wait for him to make the next move. He continues addressing me in a low, desperate voice. "I can't wait until tomorrow. I want to tell you everything now."

I instinctively bring my hands to touch his face, as if I have a right to touch this man I know nothing about. But the tone of his voice gave me consent to touch him. I run my fingers around his eyes, which forces him to close them, and allows me to keep touching him. My hands eagerly graze his mouth. He opens his lips and lets out a breath, almost as if to kiss the inside of my hand. His breath against my palms sends responsiveness down my entire body. I never knew attraction could feel this way. It's tangible. I have this slow-simmering hunger, a need to climb into his arms and kiss him until we both pass out. What's happening to me? Who am I?

"You feel that?" he asks.

My eyes are closed to allow myself a moment to enjoy the feelings he speaks of. I nod my head, shouting *"yes"* on the inside. Every part of my body can feel him.

"Are we going to do something about it, or should we ignore it?"

I open my eyes at his question. I want nothing more than to do something about it, but this is not who I am. I don't just recklessly act out on my lustful desires. I'm not one to have this kind of reckless desire in the first place.

"Are you married?" Time stops as I wait for him to answer.

He looks away from me and exhales heavily, before whispering, "Yes."

His answer sobers me up. I almost slap him again, but then I realize that I am the one coming on to him.

"Shouldn't you be with your wife?" I hiss out, failing to not sound bitter and hurt.

"I should be, but I'm sure they wouldn't let me into heaven with her."

It takes me a few minutes to make sense of his words. He watches me, giving me time to process what he just made known to me.

Suddenly, it all makes sense, the reason for him being here. "Is that why you came back here? Did Joella warn you that your wife would die?"

He shakes his head. "I told you already that nothing your grandmother said would make sense unless you knew the whole story, or at least my side of the story. I don't think you'll look at me the same way once you know the things I've lived through." He stands up, forcing me to look up at him. "I feel what you feel. There's a charge between us that I won't deny, and I'd be a liar if I told you I don't find you intriguing and attractive. I've hurt enough people that I can't consciously add you to the list of casualties. I just want to be able to talk to someone who knows nothing about me. I want to share how I felt when I did what I did with a person who doesn't already hate me. I want you to listen, and I will tell you what your grandmother read on my palm or saw in my eyes that night, and how her words could never be."

This would be a good time to tell him that Joella wasn't a palm reader, but I won't tell him anything until I understand exactly who he is. "Did you kill somebody?" It's a legitimate question, to which he shakes his head with a smirk. "You don't seem to be a bad guy, and now I want to know about your life even more. What could you have possibly done to make people hate you?" Hate is such a strong term. Why would someone hate this good-looking man?

He nods and smiles, as if he can't wait to share his life story with a stranger.

"Are you not tired tonight? We can wait for tomorrow, or if you're worried I'll disappear, we can still talk tonight." I guess since it's not the weekend, Lauren and the staff can handle the bar without me. I can invite Jeff to my place and we can get comfortable and talk. I haven't spent time alone with anyone since Joella passed away, and he definitely feels like more than just *anybody*.

"I need to get back home to my kids. I actually thought I'd be back in New York before morning to take them to school tomorrow. But I can make some arrangements to stay another day or so, to explain everything."

I didn't hear a word after he mentioned having kids. I mean, what was I thinking that some perfect stranger was going to come in and everything would just click. I'm insane for attempting to get close to this guy. I wonder how long ago he lost his wife and how old his kids are? He seems to be in his mid-thirties but I clearly know nothing about him.

"I'll tell you everything about the kids, too, but I don't want to wait for tomorrow," he almost begs.

I calm the internal war his last comment caused and try to talk my juvenile sense of jealousy, which has spread inside, into calming down. "Would it be okay if we go back to my place?" I ask, feeling less sure of the shameless feelings I had before.

"You're the boss—you lead, I follow." He gives me a wink, which makes me smile. How can anyone hate him? He's very likable, almost *too* likable. "How far away is your place?"

I smile as I point to the ceiling. "I live upstairs. This is my building now." And that reality stings as it comes out of my lips.

"Nice, I had no idea this place had another level. Let's go before you change your mind."

The thought of him in my little apartment does funny things to me, and once again, I catch myself getting hopeful for no reason at all.

Jeffery

"Animal" by Def Leppard

I saw the way her face dropped: first, when I said I was married, and then when I mentioned my kids. I shouldn't be here. I should be home working on myself, and on my head. I need to figure out how to go on with my life without them and stop caring about some random girl's facial expressions. This girl, Kali—or all the other girls in the world—can't possibly hold the key to my salvation. I was given two gifts, and I somehow managed to lose them both. If only I could ask her grandmother why she told me what she did and how she knew the things that I never spoke of out loud? But she's gone and the answers are gone with her.

I follow Kali up the stairs while attempting to look anywhere but at her ass right in front of me, which literally holds the power to hypnotize me while swaying from side to side as she obliviously leads us up a back flight of stairs. With every swing of her hair, I catch a whiff of her shampoo or perfume, and it smells really fucking nice. I haven't felt like a man in years, and this girl reminds me of what it feels like to be a kid again. The nostalgia of this place brings back my carefree college years and makes me feel as if the future is mine for the taking. But that's the thing about life—our future doesn't always resemble our childhood delusions. I'm deep in thought as I walk right into her backside on the last step, crushing her with my weight into a closed door ahead.

"Shit, I'm sorry. I didn't realize you stopped walking." I'm an idiot, and now I'm completely mortified.

"It's okay, I shouldn't have just stopped like that. I mean I should probably be able to walk through doors by now, right?" She turns her head to offer me a smug smile, and I have zero control over my face as I immediately chuckle back. She's making me into a giddy fool.

Women usually don't affect me this way. I have trained my mind and my heart to only have this kind of response to two women in my life, two women I've lost forever. The image of Jacky and Sara pops into my head and my foolish smile is immediately wiped off my face. I have nothing to smile about.

I hear a squeaking sound as Kali holds the door open and motions for me to enter. I immediately have a flashback to The Pierre hotel, with Sara standing by the door watching me. I hope to God today, or any other day in my life, never ends the way that one did. A sharp pain radiates through my chest as my heart painfully constricts, tightening every muscle to the point of agony. I attempt to take a few deep breaths and not allow myself to think and agonize about Sara.

"You keep going somewhere far away," she says in the distance, catching my attention. I adjust my vision that has slowly begun to blur with unshed tears. The painful memory turns into a sharp knot as I swallow around it, reminding myself to stay strong and be a man.

"I'm right here. There's nowhere I want to be but here," I state firmly, to convince us both. I rejoin the land of the living and finally begin to inspect my surroundings. I spot one, two, three, four violins, with one prominently displayed on a stand, and piles of sheet music stacked on the floor. I pivot slightly to see an upright piano by the wall, and at least three other string instruments I don't know the names of. This must be where the band meets. I snicker to myself and idiotically ask, "You play?" The moment the question escapes my mouth I already know how stupid it sounds.

"Nah, I just like to collect various instruments and use them for firewood once it gets cold." Her smartass comment to my ridiculous question was expected.

I look toward the kitchen where she's standing, and smile at her and her sarcasm—Sara used to be sarcastic until I realized her sarcasm was a way to mask the hurt and cynicism.

"Don't ask me to play anything because I'm not a show pony. I don't perform on demand," she warns me playfully.

"I wouldn't dream of it. My neighbors and I usually skip town when my daughter practices her violin. So no request here," I assure Kali. The thought of hearing the screeching sound of that retched instrument—that I swear Jacqueline's parents bought Juliet just to punish the entire Upper East Side—is enough to make me contemplate running away.

"We wouldn't want you to skip town just yet. I promise I won't touch any of my instruments while you're here. I wouldn't want to make your ears bleed."

"You can play all these?" I question as I scan and mentally count the number of different instruments littering her tiny apartment.

"Not well." Her sly smile reappears, and I must admit, I'm starting to like it, a lot.

"Your parents must be very proud," I say only half mockingly, recalling how happy Jacqueline would get at Juliet's home recitals. How I promised her that I would make sure the kids would continue their music lessons. Then I think of how Juliet and Jacob learned to play their mother's favorite song, but their mother died before they had a chance to perform it.

I'm on the verge of crying, which I can't allow myself to do right now, so I instantly switch to think about Sara. I would send her videos of Juliet playing the violin and Jacob attempting to play the piano, but it does little to stop my tears. I can only imagine my tormented Sara watching those videos over and over and how it must've hurt to watch her little babies grow without her.

"Where do you keep disappearing to, Jeff?"

I hear her voice in the distance like an echo while I struggle to come back from the taunting past. A painful past that I would give anything to go back and relive instead of my present hell.

"Why are you crying? Did someone break your heart?"

I hear the concern in her voice. I process her question and wonder what would she think of me if she knew my story and how many hearts and lives I've broken. Would she still want to talk to me? Or would she despise me, like everybody else?

"If you had one wish, what would it be?" I have no idea why I just asked that question.

Kali's confused look says it all. She probably thinks I'm bipolar. "I'd go back thirteen years ago and try to prevent my maman's accident." Her answer knocks the air right out of me. My French is coming in handy today.

"I'm sorry about your mom." I feel terrible, why did I ask such a pointless question? You don't get to go back. You live your life forward not backward.

"I'm sorry, too. I always wonder what it would be like if I grew up having her in my life longer." She forces a smile, no doubt fighting her own tears. "How about you? What would you wish for?" She shuts off her emotion with that fake smile and turns the tables on me.

I wanted her to ask me that question, that's why I'd asked it in the first place. I knew I'd never be able to come up with an honest answer had I asked the question to myself—I'd tried before, and failed miserably each time. If I had one wish, what would it be? Would I rewind time and undo everything that has led me to where I am right now? Would I choose differently?

"I would go back fourteen years ago and unmeet your

grandmother." It's the truth, which I'm aware isn't the polite thing to say to her.

She swallows my harsh response and counters with a question. "Do you know what my grand-mère once told me about fortunes and futures?" She doesn't wait and answers her own question. "She said, 'no matter what you do, no matter how far away you run, what's written in the stars cannot be undone.'" Her smile is still very evident on her face as a renegade tear rolls down her cheek. "You see, Jeff, it doesn't matter what you or I may wish. We can't change the outcome of our futures by going back to the past and undoing something, because it's already done."

I take a few steps toward Kali. She's barely able to stand without holding onto the table in the middle of her small kitchen, her whole body trembling violently. Her gaze is set beyond me. I follow it to see her transfixed on one lonely violin displayed separate from the rest, and the haunted look in her eyes tugs at me. I can almost taste her sorrow, and it's fucking with my brain. I wonder if my sorrow can recognize hers?

I don't know what she needs, but I need to touch her. I engulf her in a tight hug without any consent. I may be out of line, but I'm starved for any kind of human touch, and I sense her approval when her stiffness vanishes in my arms as she melts into me. The lingering sweet scent of berries that's been driving me crazy physically assaults every last pore, allowing her to practically diffuse into me. Her hands move from inside my embrace and trail up my body, around my neck, as she pulls me even closer. That's all the consent I need.

I look down at her face innately resting against my chest. *She's lovely.* She draws her attention back to my face and whispers, "Kiss me." And the dormant animal inside me begins the attack.

Kali

"Can't Fight This Feeling" by REO Speedwagon

How many times in life do we pass a stranger on the street and think they're attractive, sexy … perhaps even beautiful? Most of the time, we just keep walking. We don't stop and explore our attraction. I'm aware of every part of my body, and how Jeff affects it. I have never felt such complete and utter desire toward a person I just met. The last thing I willed my lips to say was, "kiss me," and I'm quite sure nothing will ever make sense again.

His lips ram mine without any reprieve and zero regard for what is right or acceptable. His tongue swipes in and mingles with mine with such ease it's as if they've been acquainted and danced before—thousands of times. His hands are on my face, in my hair … he's everywhere all at once. He pulls and positions my head to gain even deeper access into my mouth, and this kiss feels like the most erotic act I've ever been involved in. I've never been kissed this way, nor have I ever felt anything close to this. My legs become unstable and I'm not sure if I'm standing or levitating. I'm not even sure any of this is actually happening to me. Is this what lust feels like? Is this what makes ordinary people go mad with passion?

"We shaaaa stop," he half moans, half mumbles, while still

frantically licking into me.

"Hhmmm," I moan back my agreement.

"Table or floor?" is his next proposition.

"Bed."

I need for whatever this is right now to happen. I'm starved to have every part of him immediately, and by the incoherent sounds coming from him, I know he wants me just as much. This is what every woman wants—whatever it is that Jeff is making me feel is what *everybody* wants—to be the object of someone's obsession. We've made each other go mad. I've never felt this desired by a man before, not even by Florent, my only lover. I'm so turned on that I haven't even noticed that we're moving while he has me straddling his waist. I only realize our arrangement when he pulls me down into his hardness. I'm afraid that after having zero love life for the past five years, this may kill me.

I open my eyes when I hear the sound of a door open, but this door leads into my bathroom not my room.

"Wrong door," I say into his mouth.

He captures my lips again and continues to kiss me. I try to pull away to tell him that the last door down the corridor is my bedroom, but he won't let me say a word. There's a good chance we won't make it to my room because I can already feel him lowering us to the carpet in the hallway.

Jeff finally pulls away from me, attempting to subside the unexplained urgency and madness we've elicited in one another. He kneels over me on the floor, and all I want is for him to fuck me. I don't want to try to rationalize anything. I don't even want to think about the next second—I just want him, all of him, right now inside me without any words or explanations.

He's suspended above me, not moving, just panting and catching his breath as he studies me. Fear strikes me hard in the chest at the thought of him changing his mind. I become frantic, because this could all be an illusion, a dream, but I want this to be real. The panic propels me into action, finding his pants and undoing them before everything evaporates.

I find his belt without losing eye contact, except he grabs hold of my hand in protest as I struggle to open it. The euphoric lust cloud is gone and once the smoke begins to clear, like in all good fairy tales, the princess turns into nothing more than a common farm girl while the prince goes back to being a regular frog. I brace myself for the inevitable rejection.

"How are we suppose to have a meaningful conversation if I'm about to disrespect you?" He removes my hand from his crotch, bringing it to his lips for a kiss in an effort to soften the blow.

I'm not sure how to answer that, so I ask him, "How do you expect us to try and have a meaningful conversation if we don't get this tension between us out of the way?"

He cracks a smile.

He needs to know this is not normal for me. "I haven't had this kind of reaction to anyone in my life, and this irrational behavior may be normal for you in New York, but it's not for me."

He lowers himself and shuts me up with another kiss … a slow, soft type of kiss. "Nothing about you or this is normal to me. My life has been a series of unfortunate events navigated by poor decisions and bad timing. I don't want this between us to be added to my running tally. I'm going to take you to bed and try to lose myself in you because you're driving me crazy, but once we get this itch out of the way, we're going to sit down with our clothes back on and make sense of everything." He pauses to look at me before he begins to kiss down my neck, sending goose bumps along my hyper-aroused body. "I guess it will be nice to share a bed with someone who doesn't have a past to hold me to, someone I don't need to promise anything but an orgasm or two. I can't remember the last time I fucked someone without at least knowing her last name."

His crude words are harsh, and the delicate girl in me should feel hurt and offended, but the truth is, he really is a nobody, and sometimes in life, we need a nobody to un-numb us and make us remember that we're a somebody.

His lips find my nipple and begin to suck expertly through my ribbed top. He lifts his gaze, no longer intimidating, to make sure I'm watching. "I can't wait to see you naked," he declares while inspecting the wet spot left behind by his mouth on my white shirt. He shifts over to suck my other protruding nipple, and with every lick, I fight the urge to lower my hands and rub my throbbing clit for instant relief. "I can't wait to be inside you."

That makes two of us. I haven't had actual sexual intercourse since I came to America, so this day has been long coming—literally and figuratively. Sex with someone other than my imagination should be a treat. And the thought of Jeff inside me is mind blowing and completely intoxicating.

He gets up and towers over me, giving me a chance to observe him—*all* of him. For the first time since we met earlier, I see him as if he were mine to watch and enjoy. Even unshaved with his hair disheveled and no doubt tired, he's still very attractive. It's undeniable; however, it's his inimitable eyes that make him one in a million.

"Shall we?" He offers his hands as I grab hold to let him lift me up.

"We shall." I give a crooked smile. "I've never disrespected someone as much as I want to disrespect you," I jokingly say.

"Very funny. Now, show me your bed, femme fatale, or I'll go back to disrespecting you on the floor."

He got the femme fatale part right, but I haven't felt any lack of respect from him—not yet, anyway. I like that he tries to impress me with his French speaking and understanding skills, not many people do. His appeal in my mind keeps growing, which may be very good for my soon-to-be rousing sex life, but very bad for my sleeping heart.

Jeffery

"Need You Tonight" *by INXS*

I try to stay in the moment with Kali and not think about what having sex with her will say about my character. Maybe this is what I need in order to move on and finally let the ghosts of my past go. I haven't been on the same page with a woman in a long time. It's a nice change to want and be wanted back equally. My whole life I wanted what I couldn't have, and promised what I couldn't give. Right now there are no promises … just sex.

She tastes amazing and I don't want to think about anything other than fucking her tonight. I just want to be a regular guy who picked up a stunning girl at a bar, a guy who didn't lose his wife and the love of his life six months ago, a guy who doesn't know the inside of Sloan Kettering hospital better than his own bedroom, a guy who didn't cheat and lie to his wife, a guy who hadn't ruined an innocent girl's life, the type of guy who can give his kids a happy life. I just want to be a guy who doesn't destroy everything he touches. I just want to be anybody but me tonight with this fascinating woman who seems to crave me just as much as I desire her. I know I don't deserve it, but I've already lost everything, so I have nothing left to fear losing. I just need to lose myself between her legs tonight.

I follow her blindly like a starved man as she leads me to the end of the hallway. I still have time to stop this, turn around, and go home. I can tuck her in and never look back. I may be physically ready to fuck, but emotionally, I'm a goner. She enters her room, which I can't bring myself to notice because my eyes seem to be glued on her. Once again I'm hypnotized with every sway of her hips. She sits at the edge of her bed and waits for me as I stand in the doorway. She appraises me shamelessly from under her long, black lashes, and I'm still on the fence as to who's the wolf and who's the lamb in this scene. I look at the two wet spots my tongue left behind on her shirt, and my dick grows harder the second I see the outline of her stiff nipples through the wet fabric.

Moments ago, we pretended to play it cool and back off, for each other's sakes, but who are we kidding? I'll die if I don't fuck her immediately. And by the wild, desperate look in her eyes, I suspect she suffers from the same syndrome.

"I want to see you naked, really bad, but I'm not sure it's going to happen," is the last lucid statement I'm able to make before reality ceases to exist, and in its place is pure lust that fuels my every move.

I come at her like a wild beast—a predator. The way I attack her breasts and thrust my hips into her, you'd think I haven't seen tits and a pussy in years—and in a strange, fucked-up way, I really haven't. My only goal is to have her twisted and wrapped around every inch of me. She asked for this, and who am I to deny this young woman the thing she wants most—*me*. She can have every part of me tonight. Everything her eyes and hands touch is all hers, nobody else's. I don't belong to Jacqueline, I don't belong to Sara, and I certainly don't belong to myself. Right now, I only belong to Kali.

She owns me … whoever the fuck she is.

I'm operating on autopilot as I remove the condom from my pocket. I've carried this hackneyed piece of rubber for over two years now. I only needed it for Sara, to make sure she never got pregnant while Jacky was alive, because I wouldn't know how to tell Sara that I couldn't leave my wife. But I loved Sara too much to stop dreaming about her, seeing her, making love to her, promising her a real life one day. I slip the condom on my dick before I change my mind and begin to remove her jeans. I fumble with her button as she grabs my impatient fingers to unbutton her pants herself. She slowly removes her tight jeans, leaving her underwear on and offering me another chance to stop. *I'm not stopping now.* This, us, is unstoppable.

My jeans are still around my knees as she moves to my feet in order to remove my shoes. I allow her to do whatever she wants, because I'm certain once I sink inside her, I'll come in a minute flat. I haven't been with a woman since Sara, and that was two fucking years ago, so unfortunately for Kali, this will definitely be a short, fast ride.

The sound of my shoes hitting the floor brings me back to the present, and I observe her delicate hands peel off my socks. She has her enticing ass on display for me as she proceeds to remove my jeans and Calvins in one hard pull. Her pussy is covered by a scrap of white material, and I can see it's completely drenched. *I caused that.* I grab the string of her underwear as I move it over to feel exactly how wet she is. She freezes as she senses my fingers at her opening, but then moves backward, almost forcing my fingers inside her. Hot liquid coats my finger and my dick twitches in response. I come at her from behind, unable and unwilling to pretend anymore. I push into her with one long-awaited thrust, and forget my own stupid name. Her pussy welcomes me, opening for me, swallowing me slowly, inch by inch—just like I've imagined.

A moment in heaven and a lifetime in hell, that's the story of my life.

Kali

"Dance Me To The End Of Love" by Leonard Cohen

Please, God, don't let this be a dream. Please, Dieu, make him real. I've never once asked for a boy or a man to be mine, except for right now. I've accepted every painful hurtle along the way, but I beg of you now, for this moment, for this man to be real.

He replaces his gentle fingers with his hardness and plunges into me like a bullet. Never before has a perfect stranger taken me to the emotional depths like Jeff just did. He didn't even need to penetrate me for me to feel him inside. He pumps himself into me over and over while pressing almost painfully on my clit with his whole hand. I'm all feeling—there are no words that can describe my state of arousal, only sounds and movements. We are in sync every step as we fuse our bodies as one. I feel him reluctantly slow down while he harshly begins to rub my pubic bone with manic force. He's jerking the orgasm out of me like an expert, and it only takes a few moments for me to go lax under him and moan out my release. I've never had a man provoke and incite my orgasm, and from now on, it's the only kind I want. He gradually allows me to fall back down to Earth, and only then lets go of my clit to take hold of my hips and resume his own climb. It's a frantic pursuit up until he desperately comes inside me with a loud roar.

It's over. It's done.

We satisfied every last ounce of hunger we evoked in each other and now we're both empty—nothing more to give.

I never understood how people, especially some of the college students who frequent the bar, could just meet a stranger and agree to have sex with them sans amour. I often asked myself why would someone want an empty one-night stand? But I now feel like a naïve bébé for thinking that way, because this, right now, is the closest I've ever been to a man in my whole life, and love had nothing to do with it.

I'm deep in my own thoughts, permitting my mind to catch up to my body and acknowledge what just took place in my bed, when I feel his warm touch as he grazes my flushed cheek with the backs of his fingers.

"I'm staying inside you forever," are his first words to me after he's no doubt ruined me for life.

"It will be hard for me to pee with you inside me." I try to keep this light and funny, or it will be heavy and sad if I tell him how I really feel. I sense him smiling into my back, which sends cold shivers throughout my body. He's still inside me as his shaft twitches and pulsates, ready to leave me.

"What the hell just happened?" he whispers, while playfully biting my ear.

Now that's the right question to ask!

"I think we basically just fucked each other's brains out," I answer in all honesty.

"We didn't fuck—fuck sounds dirty. We just had really good, fast, animalistic sex," he defends our manic fucking with a hint of sarcasm as we both begin to laugh. "I'm serious, that was different than what I'm used to."

I turn inside his embrace, releasing his hardness—which is no longer hard—to get a better look at his face, or more correctly, his eyes.

"It was nice, let's just leave it at that. Are we still going to talk tonight? I feel myself drifting off." Once again, I don't understand what's going on inside me. My body is restless and my mind is shooting a thousand feelings per second, but I sense myself contently floating away in his arms.

"Do you want me to stay in your bed, on the couch, or outside?"

I taste the almost subliminal longing in his question. I know he wants to stay in bed with me, and I want that, too.

"I want you to stay. I feel safe with you, for no good reason, but I'd like you to sleep with me anyway … if it's okay with you?"

He cups my cheeks and gives me a kiss. Our eyes are wide open as we gaze into one another.

"Thank you," he whispers between pecks. "By the way, I'm Jeffery Rossi. It's nice to meet you, Kali." I'm about to tell him my name too, but he continues kissing my sensitive lips, not giving me a chance to speak. "I'll see you in the morning, beautiful girl, and hopefully, life will make sense again," he mumbles into my mouth as I drift off into a peaceful slumber, cocooned in the arms of a stranger, who at this point in my life, feels like a hallucination. "Sweet dreams," I hear his deep voice echo in my head as I shut the world off.

Jeffery

"Hold On To The Night" by Richard Marx

I'm both euphoric and repulsed with myself as I watch my hand glide up and down Kali's smooth body. She's been asleep for hours, but I can't succumb to my own fatigue. My mind won't allow my body any form of elation after doing what I did with this innocent woman. She has no idea who she's peacefully sleeping next to. She doesn't know what I'm capable of. Before we had sex, I was prepared to tell her everything. I had it all worked out—I would tell her about Jacky and Sara, as it happened in history, but now, I can't. I don't want her to hate me the way I know she will. I don't want her to look at me the way the world sees me—as a lying, cheating piece of shit opportunist. She doesn't think I'm scum. She actually thinks I'm special. She's under the impression that her grandmother chose me, and I wish more than anything that I was special.

But I know I'm not.

The thought of leaving Kali and going back home enters my mind every few minutes. *Run, leave her alone, do the right thing, be a man for once in your life.* My head attempts to reason with me, but I haven't moved an inch. What does a young, pretty girl like her see in me anyway? All I see is anguish when I look at myself in the mirror; years of lying and nothing but heartache. I already recognize that everyone I touch pays the price of my sins, so why haven't I stopped touching her? And why don't I want to? Because I know exactly how this will all end, and I refuse to waste a single moment on sleep while I'm still allowed to touch her.

I haven't stopped strategizing all night on how I plan to unravel my past without alienating this beautiful stranger that has aroused a part of me I gave up on long ago. The part of me I thought would forever die with Jacqueline; the part of me I then tried to disastrously keep alive with Sara. It's the part of me I unconsciously gave to Joella that night fourteen years ago in exchange for knowing my future.

I catch myself dozing off with an image of Kali straddling me at daybreak and us having slow, sleepy, lazy sex lingers and surfaces in my mind, but I'm certain we only made love once, enough to sanction my delusions of her to materialize in dreams.

I open my eyes to a sun-flooded room, and to a far away hum haunting my mind that can only be explained as a requiem from my dream. I'm alone in a bed that seems much smaller than I remember lying down in last night. It's just me, alone, with sheets wrapped around my naked body. There's only one pillow, which is strange—didn't Kali and I sleep here together? Did we both sleep on one pillow? I don't even recall falling asleep.

"Kali," I call out. I hope she didn't leave. I spent all night practicing in my mind how I plan to tell her my backstory. I spent hours listening to my own words in my head just to make sure I don't forget any crucial details, or sound like a heartless bastard. "Kali, who I still don't know your last name, can you hear me?" I try to be funny, but I sound like a shmuck.

I spy my clothes neatly folded on a chair and I proceed to get dressed. I grab my underwear that Jacky bought me—come to think of it, she'd picked out *all* my clothes. I haven't lived on my own since college, and back then, she helped me go clothes shopping, too. I miss my wife in everything I touch; even in the small, stupid, everyday things, I feel her absence. *She left me forever.*

I notice it's almost seven in the morning as I grab my phone on the nightstand that Kali must've plugged in to charge, and then dial my house. My daughter picks up before it even rings.

"Daddy, why are you not back yet? Yesterday Grandpa said you're taking us to school today." Her voice reminds me of how big of an asshole I am. Why did I leave them?

"Grandpa didn't know my trip ran overtime and that I still need to finish talking to somebody before I come back home. Is everything okay? Is Jacob okay?" She's quiet on the other end of the line, just sad at my absence. I can picture her unsmiling little disappointed face with her lips downcast in a frown—it's Sara's frown. *I shouldn't have come here. I shouldn't have left them.*

The familiar feeling of failure spreads inside. I always let someone down.

"I miss you, Daddy," she whimpers, breaking whatever's left of my worthless heart. My sweet little babies are my world and the only thing that matters. That realization made it clear I had to return to them. Now. I'll make arrangements to meet Kali another time. Right now, I need to be there for my kids. They need to feel safe and loved after losing their mother, and I'm the only one that can give them that.

"Baby, don't be sad. Listen to me, I promise I'll be home to drive you and Jacob to school tomorrow." I need to keep that promise.

"Will we stop at Joanna's for chocolate croissants first?" Her words kill me a little more. Sara didn't raise her children, but she somehow managed to pass along all her idiosyncrasies. I wish Juliet knew how the woman whose blood she has running though her body, Sara, could practically live on chocolate croissants just like her.

I swallow down years of memories in an attempt to block

them out and compose myself. "Yes, first croissants then school, but please be good and don't give Grandpa and Grandma a hard time, okay? And don't forget to help Jacob pick an outfit for school just like Mommy used to. I promise I'll be there very soon. I love you." Juliet loves to baby her brother. He's older by a few minutes, but that doesn't stop her from pretending that she's his babysitter half the time.

I say a few words to my dad that all is well and that I should be on my way back home soon, before I hang up and go locate Kali. I need to try and explain why I have to leave and put our conversation on pause for now.

I find her in the middle of her living room. It's the first room we entered last night, the small room that was littered with at least ten different musical instruments. I also observe the lack of a couch or a TV, just a few pillows dispersed on a big rug. Kali sits on the floor at the center of a vibrant floral carpet facing the window with her long black hair up and bare legs spread open around scattered sheets of paper between them. She has her back to me, and I now understand why she couldn't hear me calling her earlier. She's wearing headphones plugged into an electric violin. She's clearly zoned out while animatedly playing a few soundless cords and then writes something down.

I watch her from afar, transfixed, not daring to interrupt her. I'm completely captivated by her. She reminds me of an untamed animal or an exotic creature that needs to be left wild and untouched. The way her fingers methodically move across the strings is spellbinding. I can't hear a single sound, but the way her body sways I can only imagine the melody being dramatically sublime. She's wearing a colorful cloth around her body tied over her breasts like a dress, and the image of her under me last night comes into perfect view. She looks like a beautifully tragic gypsy right out of a Victor Hugo novel, and I wish I could watch this passionate woman in her element all day. *But I can't.* I need to go home.

I wonder how long I could stand here without her noticing me? But, I don't have the luxury to play this game, and therefore, I come and sit on the floor beside her. She instantly removes her headphones, puts down her violin, and attempts to cover herself.

"Whoever invented the soundless violin is a fucking genius." *That was the stupidest thing I could possibly say.* It's a proven fact that this girl makes me stupid.

"I did make you and your ears a promise," she quickly counters, no doubt silently agreeing with my internal diagnosis of my stupidity.

"I don't know why I say the silliest things around you. You make me nervous." Which is the whole truth, so help me God. I either offend her, jump her bones, or say the most inappropriate comments around her. You'd think I was a kid and not a thirty-nine-year-old widowed father of two.

"Well, your eyes do silly things to my stomach, so I guess we're even."

She's already off the floor, creating distance and walking toward the kitchen. The material tied around her body is some kind of scarf, and I'm pretty sure she's completely naked under it. I adjust my dick that just sprang to life again and refocus. I have to remind myself that I need to get the fuck out, go home to my kids, and leave this poor girl alone.

"My eyes usually make people uncomfortable. They want to stare, but you know, it's not polite to stare, so they try to look away, unsuccessfully," I offer small talk when I should just tell her that I need to go.

"I've never met anyone with two different eye colors like you. I didn't even know such a thing exists." She smiles, which makes her even more attractive.

She makes us coffee and slices a loaf of bread, glancing my way every couple of minutes.

I grunt inwardly. How am I supposed to just leave when

she's making us breakfast? I promised her we'd talk. *Fuck.* Instead of telling her that I need to go, I keep talking as if everything is going as planned and I'm not about to run back home. "What I have is called complete heterochromia, it's a hereditary gene mutation where one iris is a different color from the other. I was born with it, which made for a fun childhood." I cringe recalling my tortured youth.

"It's very sexy, in a freaky-can't-explain-it kind of way," she tells me, still smiling while giggling to herself.

God, I'm fucked.

"Don't be upset with me, but I need to leave soon. I just spoke to my daughter and I promised I'd come back home before tomorrow morning."

Her carefree smile vanishes and she begins to nod her head frantically while buttering the toasted slice of bread with more force than required, pretending to agree with my decision to go. "Okay, yeah, yeah, you should definitely go back to your kids."

I wish I could split myself in two and be in multiple places simultaneously, but history already proved that is not my goddamn forte. However, thanks to my occupation and the countless clients I've encountered as an attorney, I do specialize in body language, and I can write a book on this girl—power blinking, lip chewing, loss of eye contact, murdering the toast with butter, shifting weight from leg to leg.

She's livid.

She hates me.

"Kali," I say, but she's giving the toast her undivided attention and won't look at me. I have this feeling she's about to cry, and I don't fucking need that. I have enough shit to dig through. "Kali, just look at me," I beg her and she complies. I was right, she's seconds away from crying, and my numb heart just went from existing in my chest to roaring back to life with petulant pounding against my ribs and is about to burst. I walk over to stand behind her. I probably shouldn't escalate this by touching her, but I think she's already crying by the ever so slight movement of her shoulders.

I engulf her from behind, which only causes her to cry harder. There is no way I'm leaving this girl in this kind of state after spending a night with her, but I need to go. "I need to get back home, but it doesn't mean we won't talk again. How about every day after I drive my kids to school I call you? If it's okay with you, the hour from eight to nine every morning will be Kali o'clock. I won't schedule anything, and you and I can talk a little every day. I'll tell you everything and you'll listen and tell me things about you as well. I want to know about your life. This isn't the end, it's a kind of a beginning." I hold my breath as I wait for her verdict. I don't want my actions to hurt anybody. Why can't it be simple for me? Why is it always like this?

"You don't need to worry about me. Your children should be your first and only priority. I'm sorry. I wasn't crying because you were leaving, it's because I feel guilty and horrible for keeping you away from your enfants—ta famille," she cries out.

If every time I open my mouth around her only stupid shit comes out, this woman is the complete opposite. Every word that leaves her lovely mouth is perfect. I could listen to her speak French forever.

I turn her around to face me and kiss those puffy, overchewed lips. I can't help but want to be wrapped and tangled inside her again. I hope every man that touches her knows how perfect she is. I play my thoughts back, and I hate the feeling of ownership and entitlement that blooms inside me like the plague. I can't possibly presume that this young woman, the one I just met and fucked last night, can actually be anything more than just that. And yet, the thought of another man touching her, the way I touched her last night, makes me want to scream. I'm emotionally and mentally unstable.

"Did you imagine my face when you were buttering that toast?" I question my gorgeous, angry host.

She snorts out a laugh and brings the over-buttered piece of bread to my mouth for a bite. I oblige and allow her to feed me—another intimacy that's been long forgotten. She kisses my lips clean between bites, and I wish she knew how every kiss fucks me up more and more. I wish I was fifteen years younger and that I didn't have to go and be a responsible adult and recklessly lose myself in her company.

"You're very pretty. I don't even know how old you are. I should probably ask you about your past relationships, and I'm assuming you're not seeing anyone, since we, you know—together in your bed." It's none of my business, but she's becoming my business with every kiss, and my brain demands some answers before I leave her.

"I'm twenty-five and I'm just fucking some guy I met last night, so I'm not sure how to answer that." She winks and releases herself from under my hold.

"Lucky guy." I really am lucky, maybe *too* lucky, and that could be a problem. I don't deserve the women that make up—or *used* to make up—my world.

I follow her around the house like a lost puppy and she leads us back to her bedroom. I collect my few belongings and look around before exiting.

I hand her my phone to input her contact information. She punches in her number and then takes a selfie of herself, a non-smiling, sad one.

"When will you call me?" she inquires while handing my cell back.

"I can call you tomorrow, or the day after—you call the shots." There's a flash of disappointment in her stare following my words. I'm not sure if she trusts that I'll call her at all.

I hate goodbyes. Every night I had to sneak away from one life to go join another, therefore I don't do goodbyes, I just leave.

"Thank you for the last twenty-four hours. You may have

unintentionally saved my sanity. I can't wait for Kali o'clock. I have no doubt it will become my favorite time of day."

She nods her head while forcing a fake smile, which I can already detect, and holds the door open for me to leave.

"Au Revoir." The French words roll effortlessly off her tongue.

I scan her face like a painter committing features to memory for later use. I need to go quickly before I change my mind because my heart is waging a campaign; it's demanding more time with her. *I'm a fool ... don't you dare say another word to her.* I can't be trusted to speak to this woman with my wavering feelings. I offer her instead a forced smile and against my better judgment, I lower my head to kiss her cheek. The moment I inhale her scent I take hold of her face and kiss her lips as if for the last time. As if by kissing her I could take a part of her home with me to help keep me hanging on. She doesn't protest and wraps her arms around my waist.

God, I don't want to go. This feels like goodbye forever.

Kali

"Only The Lonely" by The Motels

I've been in a depressive haze that can only be described as a kind of emotional unconsciousness, since Jeff left me yesterday. I thought of nothing but him all day and even dreamt of him at night. I have new questions that keep stacking up in my head with no one who can offer me any kind of answers. I've checked my phone six thousand times and I still haven't received as much as a text from the man who's kidnapped my sanity and made me question every single aspect of my life.

After Joella's sudden death, I was completely lost and alone. The only real family I have left is in France—thousands of miles away. Besides Lauren and the bar, I have nothing left here in Rhode Island. I even contemplated selling the bar and the rest of the buildings that Joella left me in the will and starting over, maybe even go back home to Cassis to recharge for a bit and then travel the world, meet people, and try to find myself. Perhaps I would find a place where I belong. But forty-eight hours ago, I crashed into an iceberg known as Jeffery Rossi, and now I feel myself capsized and drowning, slowly allowing the feeling of solitude to pull me under. He doesn't owe me anything, and just because we slept together I can't pretend I know him or expect for him to call me and keep his word.

He's not going to call. My brain keeps taunting my heart, proving that it's always right, while my silly heart is always wrong.

I go back to a routine I've called my life for the past five years. I go through the motions, I make conversation, I pretend to be busy though I spend most of the day hiding like a leper in the kitchen, because who am I kidding? I'm not me anymore. As the day progresses, I grow agitated and bitter, snapping at the busboys for no reason. *Why do people make promises if they have no intentions of honoring them?*

Lauren has already asked me twice today if I feel sick because I look like shit. If I look even half as bad as I feel, I must look like death. I try to recall Jeff's exact words. Did he say he would call me today or tomorrow? Maybe I typed in the wrong number into his phone by accident. Why didn't I take his number? Thank God I don't have his number or I'd be in even deeper shit. At least the choice to call or not to call is all his.

The day continues to drag on painfully and I can't wait to close the bar and go upstairs, take a long hot shower before I crash into bed—the bed that, without a doubt, still smells of him and me.

It's way past midnight when I enter my empty apartment. I look around my couch-less living room and smile the moment I notice my instruments. When life takes things away, you learn to love things that cannot be taken from you. My music is everything. It has always consistently been there for me, good or bad, and it stays with me. It's a part of me.

My maman had a thing for mushy eighties songs. She hated French music and her car was littered with cassette tapes that reminded her of her youth. She would only speak to me in English, and I was only allowed to watch American cartoons and listen to English songs, which probably explains why I speak English without an accent—it was, after all, my first language.

People are usually shocked when I tell them I'm French and not American. I remove my locket to look at my favorite tiny reminder of the person I love most in the world. She was perfect, too perfect, and the water took her from me. In a moment of weakness, my tears roll down my cheeks as I see through blurred tear-filled eyes that my phone is flashing with a text. I look at my watch and it's one thirty in the morning. I know it's him—who else would dare text me in the middle of the night.

-I thought of nothing but you for the last 24hrs. I want every hour to be Kali o'clock-

I smile as I let out a loud cry of relief. I'm still sobbing, but his words have just calmed my doubting mind, allowing hope to bloom again. My fingers shake as I attempt to type back a reply.

-I didn't think I would ever hear from you again-

It's the truth and I'm not embarrassed for him to know that I have very little faith in him.

-My son has a nasty cold. I had to take him to the doctor and spend most of the day begging him to take medication. I wanted to call you the second I drove away, but I'm also trying to give you some space and a chance to change your mind about talking to me. I still don't understand what happened between us-

I'm not a big texter, since I don't have too many people I speak to on a daily basis. I usually want to hear someone's voice, like when I miss my papa and some of my friends back in Cassis. Therefore, I'm a bit surprised at how easy it is to just communicate with him through text. I can picture his face and his smile as if he's actually saying those things to my face. I think I can probably type anything as opposed to having the nerve to say it out loud.

-Are we going to talk only through texting?-

I need to hear his voice, make sure it wasn't all a dream.

-No, I'll call you in the morning. I've been dying to hear your voice. I'd call you now but I have Jacob sleeping in my bed tonight-

I like the image of him nursing his child back to health. I actually like him a little more than I did before he texted me.

-I hope Jacob feels better. Goodnight, Jeff-

I'm about to put my phone away when I hear another message coming in. I look at the screen to see that he sent me a picture. It's a dark photo, obviously taken at night, of me, with his hand stroking my cheek while I sleep.

-This picture makes me smile. You make me smile. I haven't had anything to smile about in a very long time-

I beam as I read over his message. *I wish I could hear his voice.* I put my phone away and finally give my overworked, beaten mind a chance to shut down. Kali o'clock can't come fast enough.

I wake up with a smile that quickly morphs into a frown, once I glace over at my watch and see that it's half past nine. *He didn't call?* I find my phone under my pillow and it's completely dead. I can't believe I forgot to charge it! I jump out of bed and plug the damn thing in and wait impatiently for it to spring to life. *Fuck.* He must've called and got my message. He probably thinks I don't want to speak to him. *Fuck.* My retched phone finally illuminates back to life but shows zero missed calls, zero messages, and zero texts.

Is this really happening, again?

Jeffery

"If You Were Here" by Thompson Twins

I'm disoriented when I see a nurse hovering over me. It takes me a few minutes to realize I'm at the hospital. I blink away the grogginess and sit up, only to have the whole room spin out of control, forcing me to lie back down again.

"Stay down, Mr. Rossi."

The familiar voice of my favorite nurse helps me recall my location and the reason for my visit. I'm giving blood, like I have every fifty-six days for the last six months.

"They don't want you donating blood as often as you do. It's not good for anybody if you blackout on us."

I nod my head. I don't care what the doctors think anyway. I will give blood as long as I'm alive and I have blood to give. I close my eyes as I try to take deep, long breaths and calm the lightheadedness.

"Why do you do this to yourself?" Nurse Lily questions me.

"Because it's my duty." An ache squeezes me from inside as I open my eyes to see the elderly nurse shaking her head at me.

"You're a good man, Mr. Rossi. Take care of yourself. She doesn't need your blood." She pats my cheek while directing my face with a bit of force toward a glass of orange juice by my cot and then leaves.

I gulp down the sweet beverage and try to sit up again. This time the room stays still. I fish my wristwatch from my pants' pocket and almost pass out again when I see the time. It's fucking ten o'clock in the morning! I was supposed to call Kali at eight. The acidic drink burns my throat as it comes up, and my lightheadedness is replaced with nausea. I can't get anything right. I ruin everything I come in contact with, and without a doubt, this poor girl thinks I'm playing games with her head. I find my phone in my back pocket and call Kali at once. It rings and rings and rings and rings. I hang up and call again, still no answer. *Shit.* I type out a message reading it twenty times before I hit send. I hold my breath and wait for her response—but nothing.

I read over my text again and again.

-Kali, I'm sorry I didn't call. Something out of my control came up. Please pick up and let me explain-

I imagine how disappointed she must feel if she won't answer or text me back. I may have to go and explain to her in person that I'm an idiot. *I usually don't faint from giving blood.* I have bad thoughts coming and leaving my mind at a steady rate as I conclude that this is fate stopping me from talking to her.

My phone vibrates in my hand with her sad selfie appearing on the screen. Elation is an understatement. I exhale in relief and take in a deep breath through my nose and answer.

I say, "I'm sorry," before I even say hello and begin rambling off a defense. "I fainted this morning when I was giving blood. I slept like shit and haven't been eating well for months and I must've blacked out. That's the only reason I didn't call you. I swear." I wait and listen.

"Why were you giving blood?"

I smile and close my eyes upon hearing her familiar voice with her peculiar sweet accent, thankful as hell that she's still talking to me.

"I've been giving blood regularly every fifty-six days for the last six months. I promise to tell you all about it." I collect my things and walk out of the hospital. "Is this a good time for us to talk?" She makes a sound that I accept to mean that it's as good a time as any. Fresh air coupled with her on the other line is a gift. Across the street I sit at the first empty bench I spy and get ready to spend time talking with a woman that hasn't escaped my thoughts in days. I still feel a little woozy, but there's no way I'm hanging up with her.

"Talk, we've danced long enough. Now you need to talk to me." She sounds defensive and who can blame her? I need to win her trust and show her that us talking is important to me. She can't think this is some kind of mind-fuck. I get comfortable and begin like the lawyer that I am, painting a picture for my jury of one. I've won hundreds of cases in my career but assuring Kali doesn't despise me at the end of my life story narration somehow feels more significant.

"Okay, but before we start, I'd like to explain to you that you're about to hear the first part of my story. The part of my story that everyone thought they knew. It's the good, simple part." I close my eyes and shut off the noise of New York City around me as I begin to describe to Kali how a boy once accidently fell in love with his best friend.

"When I was twenty-one years old, I realized that what I had always perceived as a horrible genetic mutation was actually my best asset. It attracted a special girl, so I ran with it. I'd never been a ladies man, never popular, average on all accounts—until I met Jacqueline Boyd. We were accidently matched up as roommates in our junior year of the pre-law undergraduate program at Brown. When I walked into my new dorm room and found my roommate's bed made up with pink girly sheets and motivational posters covering the walls, I almost pissed myself. It turned out to be a glorious computer glitch where they accidently registered Jacqueline as Jack Boyd—who was her father and happened to be an alumnus of Brown University.

"I had transferred to Brown that year in the hopes of having a better chance at getting admitted to their law school. I'd only had one girlfriend, if you can even call her that, back home in Florida, and believe me, I wasn't getting anywhere close to the action every college kid dreams of. This girl—my new roommate—was freaking gorgeous. She was everything someone like me never stood a chance with. When you looked at her, you knew she came from a long line of pedigree. Everything about her screamed refined class and sophistication. She was beyond my league—she was in a different stratosphere. But all my initial assessments couldn't be further from the truth. Yes, she was wealthy and came from a long line of respected attorneys, but she chose to live like a regular college girl. She was down to Earth, humble on all accounts, and never once made me feel like the loser I was." I hear Kali stifle a laugh on the other end of the line. I smile to myself recalling how Jacky and I first met.

I continue telling her about one of the happiest times of my life. "Jacqueline and I laughed for hours about our predicament, and after getting to know each other, we chose to keep the current boarding arrangement for as long as possible, since it could always be worse. I could've gotten some smelly guy, and she could've been paired up with a crazy wild girl. We liked each other right away, and so that's how I met my best friend.

"We made a decision early into our roommate-hood to keep our relationship platonic. We didn't want to jeopardize our living arrangement since we actually liked each other, but honest to God, I was insanely attracted to her. After months of watching and secretly drooling over her, I finally got tired of jerking off in the communal toilet to the image of her assets every morning, and one day, I thought I'd take my ritual a step further. I locked the door to our room knowing that she had an early class and then a test later in the day. I got naked and climbed into her bed with one of her T-shirts and her floral covers spread around me. I wanted her smell on me as I wacked one off, and mid-jerk, maybe a few seconds before I was about to explode, I look up and see her standing there watching me, dick at hand." I stop my story and wait for Kali to say something. I hope I'm not being too crude with my narration. "Kali, are you still there?"

"I'm still here. I have a pretty clear picture of you in bed touching yourself. Keep going. I'm sure this is going to be an interesting story." I can hear the amusement in her voice.

I swallow hard as I think back to the two of us in bed a few days ago. The thought of her naked under me makes me smile, too. I shake Kali's naked image from my mind and continue telling her about my wife. "Jacky, sounding more hopeful than upset, asked me, *'Jeff, why are you in my bed and is that my shirt?'* I decided that it would be fruitless to lie, and since most of my blood had traveled south to my dick anyway, I just told the truth. I told her that I wanted her smell on me. I said to her, *'I'll take whatever I can get of you, Jacky.'*

"It took her less than three seconds to frantically remove all her clothes and join me before she lost her nerve and changed her mind. She finished jerking me off with her mouth and the upgraded version of our roommate-hood began. My new roommate and I had so much sex that I made up for all my missed sexual opportunities growing up. I had a built-in sex partner. I distinctly remember us, like the two stupid lawyers in the making that we were, sitting down and negotiating the terms of our fucking at one of the tables at your grandmother's bar. We naturally decided to keep sleeping together, but not complicate things by putting a label on us or being exclusive or public about our relationship. We also didn't want the dorm advisor to catch wind of our fornication. Jacky convinced him I was gay and the worst thing would be to put me in a room with another guy, so he never changed our co-ed room status." I hear Kali giggling on the phone and I love making her laugh. I wish I were telling her all this in person and seeing, not just hearing, every reaction come out of her.

"She was the first girl that loved my eyes, and she called me perfect. It was straight out of my dreams—a refined girl like her finding a mutant like me perfect. We were voracious; endlessly explored one another. She was my favorite subject, and I ran back to our dorm room every day to study her and learn how to pleasure and escape into her.

"I never imagined I'd have someone like Jacky allowing me to do anything I wanted to her, which in a way gave me the confidence to be more social, outgoing, open to things. I started looking people in the eye, willing them to not look away from me. She made me feel wanted, sexy, invincible—building my ego up like a false God. I stopped fearing rejection since she was always in my bed waiting for me. She made me reach beyond my means in everything. And like the stupid idiot that I was, I believed her when she told me I could sleep with whomever I wanted, and that she didn't care, and our relationship wasn't that serious. I told her the same, in a pubescent way to cover-up how I really felt about her. I convinced myself she wasn't one of those jealous girls—she was progressive, confident. I never wanted to imagine that she would actually sleep with someone else, it just sounded cool to say that. But in reality, I monopolized her whole life. She physically couldn't sleep with someone else; there just wasn't time. We did everything together—we were even more than best friends. We studied together, we ate together, we shopped together, and we slept together. I met her parents and she met mine. And slowly, she became my family…my love.

"You know how guys always complain about their girlfriends nagging them, being possessive or clingy? Well, I didn't have that with Jacky. We spoke about everything except what we did with other people. She never asked if I slept with anyone besides her, and I didn't, I wasn't about to volunteer any information about the random girls I'd talk to or dance with at some party or in a bar from the rare occasions we were apart. I came home to her, and she to me, and that was enough."

"You guys were friends with benefits," Kali concludes. But it was much deeper than that. I only wanted Jacky and her benefits, no one else's.

"You could say that," I offer her back. It's hard for people to grasp what I had with Jacqueline, but I need for Kali to understand. "We had our own group of friends that we collected along the way. Eddie Klein was my best friend besides Jacqueline. He was an amazing guy, and is still the kind of guy you'd want as a brother: smart, loyal, loaded, a chick magnet, funny as sin, and a heart of gold. We spent endless nights at BlackGod bar binging on those sinfully delicious shepherd's pies and local beers. Eddie was the king of corny dirty jokes—Jacky loved him. I don't think I've ever met a man or a woman that didn't fall in love with him.

"Jacqueline and I knew our bubble would eventually burst once we all got into law school. We would have to give up our sleeping arrangement or come clean to all our friends—who knew nothing about our sex-pact. And for the record, I clearly recall telling her that I wanted us to be a thing, since in my mind, we already were. It was perfect between us, and I swear, I believed we would eventually end up together. I didn't like the feelings I had when she wasn't in my arms at night. I didn't want to pretend to be interested in other girls for the sake of our pretenses. She was always on my mind, and the possibility of her finding and loving someone else crippled me. She was mine, but she somehow always kept me at bay and slowly pulled away. I knew she cared and loved me as a friend, but she kept a certain distance between us when it came to publicly displaying our feelings. I guess you could say it was part of my own hang-up of not being good enough for her. So in my head, her rejection and decision to keep our relationship private was because I wasn't refined enough for her family, or smart enough for her. My parents were simple folks, I didn't have a trust fund … maybe even because of my weird eyes, I thought she was ashamed of me.

"The summer before we all started law school, I spent a few weeks with my friends in New York—one of those friends was Eddie. We partied like college students should: visiting every club in New York City getting drunk and reckless. I want you to understand that I'd felt rejected by Jacky for a long time. It appeared to me that the girl I was in love with was embarrassed to hold my hand in public and be my girlfriend in the daylight. All I wanted was to validate my appeal and show her that other women in a similar socioeconomic class as her found me desirable—even if she didn't think I was good enough for her. I wasn't born into wealth and privilege. I had to work for everything. I was just a regular guy from Florida with creepy eyes."

"Your eyes are out of this world, Jeff. I haven't been able to think of anything but your eyes for days," Kali confesses, which only makes me long to be close to her.

"Thank you." I acknowledge her kind words and wish I could tell her just how much every part of me misses her, but I can't get distracted. I simply continue narrating my tale of doom. "While I was visiting New York that summer, which by the way was Jacky's hometown as well, she didn't once call me, find me, or want anything to do with me. She was too busy for me in the real world outside of our bubble. I needed to prove to myself that Jacky wasn't the only fish in the sea. The sea was actually overflowing with fish." I get angry as I relive that summer. Back then I was pissed at Jacqueline, but now, thinking back, it's me I despise.

"When we all got back to Rhode Island and back to Brown, she felt the change in our relationship. I wanted to make her feel the distance the way I felt it from her. I forced myself to go out any chance I would get. I would flirt shamelessly and hit on every girl that looked my way. If she was around me, I'd be Jeff the social butterfly to the tenth power, but she didn't seem to care. She didn't mind, which meant she didn't really love me the way I loved her. We would only succumb to our old habits when we both got obliterated, usually after a big exam, and only when nobody was around. After not being able to hold her in my arms, being allowed to touch her was a gift, but at the same time, it made me get even angrier with her for not allowing us to be together.

"I was just dumb and didn't realize she was hiding something from me. I should've made her talk to me. All I wanted was someone to be as obsessed with me as I was with them, so I looked for love elsewhere.

"I explored and allowed my heart to venture out and imagine a life with other girls, because I'd already given up the dream of ever being her real boyfriend. We continued with this charade for years until I found out from her best friend, Michelle—who was Eddie's girlfriend—that something was very wrong with Jacky. And suddenly, everything started to make sense. I found Michelle crying in the room Eddie and I shared, and after an hour of intense interrogation, she finally told me the truth. She made me promise not to say a word, but finally broke down and told me that Jacqueline, *my* Jacqueline, had battled cervical cancer since she was twenty-three. Her being sick put my whole life into perspective, and she became my priority. I couldn't question her about it because I promised Michelle, but I was dedicated to being around her at all times.

"At this point, we hadn't slept together in over a year, but were slowly becoming friends again. I began to reconsider her attitude, her behavior, and stopped letting my ego and my pride overrule my heart."

I pause and look at my watch, realizing that we've been talking for over an hour. Time seems to melt around Kali. I can listen to her breathing on the other end of the line all day, but I still have to get to the office and get back to running a law firm. We'll have to pick this up tomorrow. I will make sure that nothing and no one keeps me from calling her at eight AM sharp!

"I'm really sorry about your girlfriend having cancer. When people you love suffer, it changes your life, I know," she adds and I assume she is referring to her own mother's accident. I don't know anything about this girl's life, and the more I talk to her, the more I realize I need to—I want to.

I hate to end our call on such a depressing note, but I have to go. "What are your plans today?" I ask in an effort to make this conversation sound marginally normal.

She answers my question almost immediately. "You, listening to your story was the only thing I had planned today." She then adds, "Could you text me a picture of yourself?"

I chuckle. "What kind of picture?" I haven't dated, which is not what we're doing now, but I haven't felt like a regular guy in quite a while. I don't know what kind of picture I'm suppose to send.

"Send me a picture of your face. I keep forgetting which eye is green and which is brown. I want to be able to look at you whenever I forget," she clarifies.

Her reply silences me. It can't be a good thing if I miss her this much already.

Kali

"Lost In Your Eyes" by Debbie Gibson

I hang up and say goodbye to Jeffery, no longer confident if and when our next conversation will take place. He didn't tell me why he gives blood every fifty-six days—*more questions.* My emotions are yo-yoing, and as usual, nothing makes sense. A few days ago when I met him, he was nothing more than a creepy stranger at the bar, but now, he is the furthest thing from a stranger. We may have just met, but it's as if he's always been a part of my life in some mysterious way. I want to know him—all of him—and his story more than anything. For the first time in my life, I actually got just what I wished for. I got to experience every part of him physically, and now he's slowly giving me a taste of his past.

I sit on the floor and I replay our phone call as I realize I may not be ready for his story, and all I really want is to give it back and pretend that he doesn't have one—a life and a history with a woman he obviously adored and loved.

I'm not even sure I should know the things he's already told me. I've buried my head in a pillow in an attempt to shake off how every word he says affects me. I need to figure out a way to somehow disassociate my feelings and not make this about us.

Just because he's been inside me shouldn't constitute a bias listener. His story has nothing to do with me. So why am I making a big deal of this part of him, anyway? This is merely a background into Jeff's history for me to be able to appreciate Joella's words—nothing more, nothing less. All I am is just the granddaughter of the fortuneteller he once met years ago. The only part of his story I ought to take to heart is the part where he meets and speaks to Joella Gitanos.

I wonder if this girl, Jacqueline, is the girl he married, whom he loved and then she tragically died? Naturally, he came back to the place he once met his wife and where it all started for them—the good old days. This man mourns her loss, and he came back to find my grand-mère to try and get closure. I can live with that kind of story. He's not a bad guy—he's just human. I also arrived here in search of closure, seeking to find pieces of my maman by getting to know her mère who is my grand-mère.

I've always been a good judge of character, and everything I've heard so far matches up to the Jeff Rossi I was attracted to a few nights ago. Even the fact that he went back to his kids makes me like him a little bit more. I just don't understand the guilt I hear in his words. Does he regret us having sex? Is he upset we went too far? Or does his guilt have nothing to do with me and I'm just imagining things? This needs to stop being about me in my head and go back to Joella's last known reading.

I call the bar downstairs and tell Lauren that I'm, in fact, feeling sick and need a day to myself. I fetch an empty book that I haven't filled with notes or song lyrics yet and begin to write down the things Jeff has told me thus far. I write them down in my own words as I remember them. The inside of my head has become a messy minefield and writing his story down will hopefully help sort my scattered thoughts and feelings. Once he gives me all the facts and finally utters the actual foretelling, hopefully his life choices will become clearer to me and I will be able to help him decipher Joella's prophecy, and perhaps, find his significance in her life.

I lose track of time writing and sluggishly rolling in bed all day as I imagine Jeff sitting in my bed and telling me about his past in person. My phone pings with a text, startling me and my daydream of him. I glance at my screen as the most intense, haunting eyes I've ever witnessed stare back at me. It's as if we're looking right at each other and I can't look away. I don't want to look away. I bet his wife loved his eyes. I can't imagine any woman not being utterly spellbound by his gaze. A moment later he sends a written message.

-Can you talk?-

It's almost ten o'clock at night and all I've wanted to do since we hung up earlier is to talk to him. I've thought of him all day and yet I'm still starved for more of him.

I type out a simple, *-Yes-* and start to giggle as the phone rings in my hand with a call a second later.

"It's not Kali o'clock, are you sure we can talk?" I say playfully.

"I'm fucked, you know that, right? I can't even wait for morning to hear your voice again." His voice sounds relaxed, he's probably in bed already.

"I will not hold that information against you, Mr. Rossi." I can hear him chuckle softly at my attempt to make a light comment, but his words vindicate my obsessive thoughts of him as well.

"How was your day?" This is us doing small talk, I think to myself and smile.

"It was fine. How about you? How are you feeling? How's your son feeling?" I hear him take a deep breath and then silence.

"It was a hard day today for all of us, me included. Talking to you was the only thing that helped me get through it. But I didn't call to tell you about my day. I need to hear a little about your life. I know it wasn't part of our agreement, but I hope you can give me something about you, something I can hold on to. I don't even know your full name, and all I can think about all day is what I'm going to say to you when I call you." He stops talking and it's quiet again, just the steady sound of him breathing.

"What do you want to know?" Maybe he only wants to hear about my favorite food or the kind of music I like to listen to.

"Tell me about your mom. Her accident."

I close my eyes and smile, which is my anti-cry mechanism, but it's been failing me miserably lately. When I asked him to tell me his story, I pictured this conversation being one sided, but he wants to know about me, and he deserves my truthfulness. After all, he seems to be honest and forthcoming with me. He started divulging parts of his past like I asked of him, in the hopes of giving me another piece of the enigma known as Joella Gitanos. I must stop fixating and overthinking our sexual encounter and be thankful for the things he's made me feel: safe and wanted—two emotions I haven't felt in a very long time.

"I'm sorry, I shouldn't have asked that. That was stupid and insensitive of me; of course you don't want to talk about this, especially over the phone." He sounds flustered and nervous.

"No, it's not that. I want to tell you, I just haven't spoken out loud about her in years." I feel my throat closing in.

I hate talking about ma famille. I would never just tell someone about the most painful moment of my life. But at the same time, I'm not one of those girls who pretends everything is perfect when it's not. I don't dance around topics, I say things as they are, and so before I overthink his question, I get right to the point. I tell him about the moment I go back to in my mind at least once a day, and how it always ends the same way. I carry the guilt of my maman's death every hour of every day like a badge of pain. She was too young, too beautiful, too talented, and too good to die suddenly and leave me alone without her love.

My plea is always the same. I wish I was with her when she died. I wish we were both in heaven together and I wasn't left on this earth alone to wonder how I could've possibly saved her. I feel the flood of tears coming. I feel the wall of regret building up as I try to smile through the painful memory. If we weren't talking on the phone, I would pick up her violin and submerge the pain in one of her favorite melodies. I would pretend I'm seven years old and her hands are guiding me across the strings of her cherished instrument, which is one of the only tangible things I have left of her.

With my eyes still closed, I cringe and dread the pity he will feel for me once I tell him. But sometimes, you don't have a choice, and the only acceptable thing to do is to smile and expel the pain that lives and blooms inside you.

"My maman died when I was almost ten. It was her thirtieth birthday. I was waiting for her to pick me up from school, I made her a card out of flowers and my papa and I had a surprise waiting for her at home, but she never came." I take a few deep breaths and smile as hard as I can to make the silly redundant tears go away. I go on recalling the nightmare. "The local fisherman found her car capsized two days later at the bottom of the sea. Her body was still inside. They found her on my tenth birthday." *I hate my birthday and the sea equally*. I hate the water that took my maman away, and I despise the day that will forever commemorate it.

"I'm so sorry. I'm so fucking sorry," he chants repeatedly, sounding more alert and even closer. His words are wasted on me. I'm numb to those words, because I've heard them millions of times before and no one could be more sorry than I am.

I feel horrible for telling him—I hate making people feel sad for me.

"A child having a mother is the most important thing in the

world. I think about my kids growing up without their mother, the only mother they've ever known, and I wish I was dead instead of my wife every day." I hear the genuine pain and anguish in each of his words.

I'm all choked up as I try to tell him that kids need both their parents equally and nobody deserves to die. That this is how life works, shit happens, we need to go on and do the best we can. But his words begin to resonate in my mind, and I realize that I've heard them somewhere before, not a million times, but just once coming from Joella. She mentioned to me years ago when I first came to live with her that she wished it was her covered in water and not her daughter, but the universe wouldn't listen. She said the universe doesn't negotiate.

I pinch the bridge of my nose to calm myself—as I feel the panic begin to pour and radiate through my skin. I'm not a time traveler, nor can I rework the hands of fate. I can't change the past, but I do want to forget sometimes what causes my pain. I put him on speaker as I look at the picture he sent me. I long to get lost in his eyes and try to forget. When we kissed a few days ago, the past disappeared, time stopped running, and the future became irrelevant. I'm ready for his eyes to suspend reality once again.

"I wish I could hold you and kiss you, right now," he whispers, reading my mind with his eyes staring at me through the screen while he lets out an aggravated breath.

I want nothing more than to kiss him and mute the memories that hurt me. But the reality is that we're worlds and miles apart. I must remind myself that my grand-mère's words to him needs to be my only priority. I fail to hold back my feelings for him and admit, "I want to kiss you all day, but we don't have that option. You need to tell me more, and I want to listen. You have a busy life and every wasted minute you're talking to me is a minute that you should be spending with your enfants." I mean every word I say, I'm not delusional when it comes to my role in his world.

"Talking to you is not a waste, Kali. Us meeting wasn't an accident—it was predestined." He sounds annoyed or perhaps upset.

I keep staring at his eyes on my phone's screen, which helps recharge and ignite both my body and my soul. The more I look at him, I begin to feel myself disappear. Maybe that's his purpose—making me forget reality. He doesn't know it, but he's sparing me the grief I keep bottled inside one glance at a time. When he calls and texts me, even if it will only last for a few minutes, I stop feeling like the only person left in the world. It's comforting to feel needed by someone other than myself. He's currently my only form of escape, a kind of window, but I'm not sure if it's his past or future that I long for.

"Tell me more," I request against my better judgment, steering the conversation away from my sordid childhood. I like him so much, and the stupid reality is that I don't like hearing about a woman he loved, even if she's gone, but I push him for more anyway. Isn't it funny that even when we know something is going to cause us pain, we still ask for it, still want that ache? Perhaps it's our way of punishing ourselves, or seeing just how much somebody else can hurt us if we let them.

Jeffery

"Livin' on a Prayer" by Bon Jovi

I don't like hearing the sadness in her voice, and I wish I could kiss her pain away, but whether I like it or not, that's my curse—being unable to make the people I treasure happy. Is this how my daughter will one day remember her mother leaving her? I don't care how late it is, I have no intentions of hanging up with her. If it were up to me, we'd talk all day and all night. I continue telling Kali my one-sided truth. The side that makes me seem like a decent guy. And as trivial as it may be, it's become important that she doesn't hate me. I want her to understand what I did and not think of me as a monster. I didn't want to ruin everybody's life. I continue narrating my manipulated truth in the hopes of a beautiful stranger's acceptance.

"It didn't take me long to know that Jacqueline was, in fact, very ill. She went to New York City alone every weekend for treatment, and I followed her—she just didn't know it. I used a portion of my school loan and rented myself a tiny place in the village by NYU hospital. I'd stay there through the weekend, making sure she was okay while going in for her weekly treatment on her own, and I felt good knowing I was close in case she needed me. But she never called me, never needed my help, not once.

"Michelle, her best friend, was the only person I could talk to about this. She was in the know about our hush-hush relationship and she constantly tried to prepare me. She knew it was an inescapable fact that Jacky's illness could take a turn for the worst. I was also, in my own way, trying to condition my head and my heart to not build an imaginary life with her, realizing that I may lose her—not to another guy, but to fucking cancer.

"This went on for a year. Maybe about a month before graduation, Jacqueline's father, Jack, invited me out for dinner to a swanky steakhouse. I was nervous and a bit excited, hoping that maybe he'd offer me a job once I passed the bar. I expected that Jacky might have put in a good word for me. Her dad's law practice was no joke; it was fucking legendary, spanning many generations and covering high-profile cases. We actually studied many of their cases in class.

"I definitely didn't expect the horror I heard from him that night. Jack Boyd had been waiting for me at the table with red-rimmed eyes, and when I saw him hunched over a scotch and his pale expression, I knew that nothing he would say to me could possibly be good. I was right. He told me how his only daughter, Jacqueline, the joy of his life, the center of his universe, the most beautiful girl in the world, had been diagnosed with cervical cancer—which I already knew. But then he continued to tell me that the doctors had given Jacky less than a year to live, with the advanced stage of her malignant cell proliferation.

"I sat at that restaurant numb, dead, and unresponsive. In the back of my mind, buried under a pile of shit and lies that I'd told myself in order to sleep better at night, I knew this day would come. I had tried to distance myself emotionally from her, but I wasn't ready to lose my best friend—the girl that had turned my whole world upside down, the woman that I was in love with. I couldn't imagine a life devoid of her existing in it somewhere.

"He approached me with sort of a favor, if you will. He asked me how I felt about his daughter. I spoke honestly and told him that I loved her with all my heart, and that I wasn't sure how I'd be able to live without her. We both sat in the middle of a steakhouse crying like two little boys. He expressed to me that he and his wife, Sofia, would like Jacky and I to get married as soon as possible. They wanted us to try and pack a lifetime of happiness into whatever time she had left. Mr. Boyd informed me that I wouldn't have to worry about money or work, that my life would be made, and that my only concern should be his daughter. It all made perfect sense. I adored her, I worshiped her, I loved her, and she was dying. How could I not marry her? How could I not try to give her the world? And that's exactly what I did.

"I had no funds to buy an engagement ring, or pay for another apartment, but her parents weren't concerned about money. They more than took care of everything. They had the money, but they couldn't use it to buy their only daughter time and health. I honestly thought I had my whole life figured out. I'd ask Jacky to marry me and move to New York City with her after we graduated. Her parents had already purchased a place that was waiting for us. She would get the best treatment money could buy, be close to her friends and family, we would finally play house for all to see, and I would start working in her father's law firm. Simple, right?"

"So what happened next? When did you and Joella meet? Did you get married?"

I hear Kali sigh with impatience as I try to imagine her. I'm about to tell her the part where I met her grandmother, but I can't tell her everything yet, it still won't make sense.

"I had the ring in my pocket the night I met your grandmother. I had just gone upstairs to use the bathroom and this old, graceful woman that had been a permanent fixture at the Black-God bar spoke to me. I wasn't sure at first if she was actually talking to me, but she got up and beckoned for me to follow her to the other side of the drapes. I immediately protested and told her I didn't want or need a reading, and that I didn't believe in fortunetellers, but she knew my name and her words compelled me to oblige.

"She took my hands, and the minute I looked into her eyes, my whole life changed. She spoke about things she couldn't have possibly known. She opened wounds that I've kept closed and hidden from everyone, including myself. I had no choice but to accept and believe every word she gave me. If it wasn't for the things she assured me that night, I swear on everything holy I would've gone on with things the way I had planned. But her prophecy changed the course of my life. She planted a seed, and my actions made that seed grow and unravel, and ultimately, ruin lives. I promise, I will tell you her prophecy word for word once you hear all sides of my story, but not yet. It will make more sense after you know all the choices that I made along the road to hell."

"Jeff, I want to hear everything the way you want me to hear it. You don't need to explain or apologize. This is your story, your life."

This girl will make me fall in love with her if she's not careful. I imagine my sexy juror curled up in bed while I whisper in her ear stories I wish were someone else's.

"Don't stop, tell me more," she incites me.

"I proposed to Jacqueline the same night I met your grandmother, which was a few weeks before we graduated. After finally having semi-drunk sex for the first time in over a year, I said, 'Jacqueline Catherine Boyd, will you marry me?' I'd been kissing her shoulder from behind—a much thinner and bonier shoulder than the last time I had her naked inside my arms—she wasn't well. I fetched the ring from under the pillow and held it out for her to inspect and realize that this wasn't a joke. I knew what I was doing. I was dead serious.

"She immediately said no. Her voice was strong, not an ounce of hesitation. She actually said, '*No way, Jeff.*' I knew she would say that. She didn't even want us to date, and there I was asking her to get married. At that point, I was aware that most of her reserve concerning our relationship stemmed from her deteriorating health. I wasn't going to tell her that I knew about her disease. I wasn't going to sell Michelle or her father out. I wanted her to be the one to tell me about the cancer herself. I couldn't have her think it was somehow a pity proposal, which it wasn't. I didn't want her to think it was a make-a-wish kind of offer. I mean, obviously, if she wasn't sick and dying, I probably would've waited and dated her properly for all to see and try to get our lives on track before tying the knot, but we didn't have time. She had a ticking time bomb living inside her, and I had all the time in the world. This was the right thing to do. I wanted to give her everything, but the reality was that I could only give her love and memories for whatever time she had left on this earth.

"We didn't sleep all night and negotiated the terms for our marriage like the juvenile lawyers that we were. That night, through lots of tears and pain, she told me everything. I finally fully understood that she was never pushing me away or rejecting me for all those years, like my ego had once chosen to believe. She loved me and had honestly thought she was safeguarding me in her own fucked-up way.

"Jacqueline said that she was the one with cancer and it was her burden to deal with it alone. She didn't want it to be everybody's problem. '*I didn't want to be the sick girl who's dying,*' she explained. She was sick and she just wanted to feel like a regular college girl who recklessly got to be promiscuous with a boy, and not the girl who was battling to live. She pretended from the first day we met that she was healthy, normal, just another student, even though she was dying inside. She wasn't just lying to me—she even kept the cancer from her freaking parents for all those years. The only person who knew the truth all along was her friend, Michelle. I think Jacky was going crazy trying to cope on her own for all those years and finally needed someone else to share the burden she was forced to live with and help her be strong. She even made Michelle sign a confidentiality agreement."

"Wow, I can't believe she was dealing with something as serious as cancer on her own. She sounds like a tough woman." Kali correctly appraises Jacky.

"She tried to be strong and optimistic; however, everything changed and became critical when she got her last results. Her type of cancer hadn't responded to the treatment she was undergoing, and with the horrible prognosis that accompanied her last visit to the oncologist, I think it ultimately hit her that her time was running out. And that's when she finally allowed her family and me to help her and be by her side for the rest of her battle.

"Jacqueline swore that she always loved me and wanted me to be hers in every possible way, but she thought it was unfair to inconvenience me with her disease. That night, she described in great detail what it was like to have a terminal disease and what kind of life we'd have before reluctantly accepting my ring. She warned me about the chemo, the radiation, the surgeries, the hospitals, and eventually her death. She presented every disclaimer and warning you could think of, but I didn't care. I made a vow that I would make whatever was left of her life the best for her.

"Eddie, Michelle, and all our other friends were happy and sad for us, knowing what kind of shitty hand Jacky and I were dealt. Knowing that our happiness had an expiration date. Nevertheless, we promised to try and have a normal life and enjoy every day together, however long that would be, and fight the cancer together as husband and wife."

Kali listens to every word of mine, swallowing whatever information I choose to feed her in whatever order I choose to present it. I'm thankful to be the one telling her my fucked-up story.

I know if someone else narrated my life, she probably wouldn't be on the phone with me, looking at my picture and thinking that I'm a good guy. *Tick-tock, tick-tock* … she'll know the whole truth soon enough.

Kali

"All Through the Night" by Cyndi Lauper

My heart slowly breaks as I hold my breath and listen to every word that comes out of Jeff's mouth. It's one thing to lose a person you love in an accident, but to know that they're dying and agree to watch them fade away is a whole level of love and devotion that I've never experienced. He keeps dropping hints that he did something wrong by the way he tries to defend his life choices, but his actions seem noble and pure. Perhaps I'm missing something in his story telling?

The way he described Jacqueline, I can't help but like her. His wife sounded like an amazing woman. She kept the pain to herself for all those years in an attempt to unburden her family and the man she loved. I'm not sure I'd be that strong if something as horrible as cancer were to plague me. From everything he's told me, she sounded like a selfless saint. I bet that when people looked at her, they assumed she had it made—attractive, smart, rich, with a gorgeous husband … yet the truth was that she was dying.

My grand-mère evidently played an important role in his life, yet my imagination does nothing to help me predict what she could've possibly said to him to have the negative impact he keeps implying. Obviously, he lost his wife, but I still don't know exactly when or how anything that Joella once said to him could've had such a harmful bearing on his life?

"What are you thinking about?" His sexy, tired voice comes in softly. We've been on the phone for over an hour and I could easily get addicted to his voice.

I have no desire to pretend with him. I want honesty, and that's what I give him. "I'm getting impatient. I want to know everything the second the questions pop into my head." I draw imaginary question marks on my covers, knowing it won't help ease the plethora of questions that keep adding up with every piece of information he provides me. However, I can't help but wonder.

He sounds sleepy as he assures me that more answers are coming. "Believe me, I want you to know everything there is to know about me, but I can't lie and tell you that I don't care what you'll think of me once you know. It's different now. You're not just a pretty girl I met at some bar. You're you, and I've had a taste of you. I care what you think and I don't just want for you to know my past—I want to make you understand it. Only then you can judge me, after allowing me to present all the facts on the table."

"I won't judge you. Why would I judge you?" I don't like the assumptions he keeps making about my opinion of him.

"You will judge me; it's inevitable. Trust me … I may be described by some as an asshole, but I'm not ignorant. I just want you to know all the circumstances that my actions were based on before you come to a verdict." He lowers his voice, sounding closer. "You may not let me call you and talk to you after all is said and done, so I better get my fill of you now," he whispers, probably on the verge of sleep.

Another foolish assumption on his part—I can't imagine not wanting to talk to him. I want to do more than talk to him, I want to touch him and be touched by him. His presence has been a godsend, and talking to him is the only thing I look forward to.

"You have no idea how thankful I am for you. I don't deserve your company but I can't get enough of you. I think that's what I'll hate losing the most, knowing that once upon a time I was able to call and reach you on the other line. You know something? If I stop my story here, right now, I'll always be able to recall how this stunning girl looked at me without contempt. I don't want to tarnish this memory of us. If I keep talking, my words will only strip you of your good opinion of me, and you'll hate me. I think it may be better if you don't know the whole truth and what your grandmother once said. I promise you, her words will mean nothing to you. They are only meaningful to me. She's human, she made a mistake, and that should be the end of it. People make mistakes. I need to grow up and come to terms with her words and accept that her prophecy will never be, and that, ultimately, my choices were entirely my fault. I shouldn't have listened; no one forced me—it was all in my head."

When he finishes his cryptic speech, I'm ready to drive over to New York, find him, and make him tell me everything. If he thinks I'm going to let him stop his story without me knowing it all, he clearly underestimates my curiosity. I don't do well with rejection; the words "no," "can't," "impossible," or knowing that something as simple as the truth is being withheld from me is not acceptable in my world.

"Do you want to hear a story?" I know it's incredibly late, but I have no doubt that he will. The more we talk, it becomes clear to me that this should be a give and take kind of exchange. I can't expect to just take information without giving him something in return, and in this case, I need to tell him more about Joella Gitanos. He should appreciate and value their interaction as much as I do, and I suspect that once he hears who she really was, he may want to share her prophecy with me in spite of his unease regarding my opinion. My opinion about him should be irrelevant. I am nothing in his life; we're miles away from each other, but I am hoping that our exchange of information will bring him—and maybe me—answers to questions and some much-needed closure.

"Go on." This seems to pique his curiosity. I can imagine his gorgeous eyes twinkling with excitement at my new shiny offer. "I'm going to pretend I'm with you in bed and you're spread naked on top of me while telling me a bedtime story." His voice is causing a familiar rousing reaction.

"That sounds amazing." I wonder if he could hear the arousal in my voice? "I also wish you were here and I could look at the real you and not at your picture as I tell things not too many know."

"I miss you very much, Kali. Now tell me a story before I go crazy and come after you." I smile as I think that I would like nothing more than to have Jeffery Rossi go crazy and come back to me. But business is business, it's now my turn to tell stories.

"When I came to America five years ago, I didn't know what to expect. I knew very little about the mother of my mother, la mère de ma mère. I had no idea she was a descendent from the Romani people, or that she was a fortuneteller, which is not how she would ever describe herself. I had no knowledge that she owned this bar or that my maman grew up here. I never even knew my parents met downstairs at BlackGod while my maman worked at this bar. Imagine finding a whole life—la vie—that you knew nothing about, yet that life is part of your roots, your history." I take a deep breath to recall exactly how it all began to unravel and make sense to me back then.

"Joella couldn't look at me at first. She said it was like looking at the ghost of her daughter. I do look a lot like my maman, which used to affect my papa quite a bit, too. He never said anything, but you could tell that whenever he looked at me, he thought about his wife—growing old without her, missing her silently. That was one of the reasons I left Cassis. I wanted him to move on with his life, he was still young when she died, maybe if I left he would stop feeling guilty because as long as I was there, I was a constant reminder of the woman he once loved and lost. I rationalized that coming here would give me a new start, my own identity, but when I got here, everybody who once knew my maman in her youth thought I was her, too. I can't tell you how many times Joella called me by her name." I hear a rustling sound as I picture him getting comfortable under the covers. I can't deny that I wish I really were in bed and in his warm arms like he described right this minute.

"It must be hard to always be reminded of something so painful. Every time I look into my children's eyes, I see my sins, and it makes me want to love them even harder in the hopes to exonerate myself."

I unconsciously cling on to my pillow for dear life, only to realize that my arms are clenched around a pillow rather than him when the pillow doesn't reciprocate.

"Go on, I didn't mean to interrupt you," he offers.

"Every day after my classes and before I would begin my shift at the bar, Joella would tell me a little story. If she were too ill, she would make me read a passage out loud from one of her many diaries. I got to hear her life of hardships as a single mère. How much she loved her only daughter and attempted to safeguard her from all foreseeable evil. She was never married. She said her heart only belonged to one man, which fate had denied her. The love of her life couldn't marry a poor gypsy runaway without any family, and instead, was forced to marry his equal: a nice Irish girl who came with a respectable last name and money."

I hear Jeff snicker. "I know a thing or two about how it feels to love someone in a different league than your own. I'm sure it must've been awful for her being on her own, falling in love with someone way out of her reach."

I stop my story to consider his comment. Maybe Joella, Jeff, and I were all alike; I, too, am alone and have almost no family left. Maybe that's part of my attraction to this man, his loneliness. I don't dwell on my thoughts and continue recalling the little I know about my family. "I asked her once if the man she loved, the one she bore a child from, if he knew about his daughter? But she admitted to me that he never knew. Joella didn't understand or recognize that she possessed the vision until she accidentally thought she saw a picture in her mind of what looked like his future. The only thing she could clearly see was that he had a child with her eyes and his smile. Upon realizing she was in his future, when he came to her to say goodbye, she professed her unconditional love, promised him to never love another man, and gave him her body. She said he already owned her soul, so her body was only meant to ensure and lay the foundation to the future she already knew from her vision they would have.

"At that point, she explained her foresight to me and that she couldn't see herself or her own involvement in the future, but could only see the lives of those souls that matter around her; the ones that held pieces of her heart in their hands. She was very young and misunderstood her gift. It took her years to recognize that she couldn't create a future with someone if there was no future in the first place.

"When Joella made love to Kenny—the young man she described as the blood running through her veins—he was a month away from marrying the girl he hardly knew, or loved—a girl his family had chosen for him. But a few weeks later, he was drafted to the Vietnam War and was never heard from again. Joella had a baby girl eight months later, but the love of her life was taken away. When my maman was three years old, Joella finally introduced her to the boy's parents; the same parents who wouldn't allow their son to be seen with a poor uneducated gypsy. They didn't believe Joella at first, but my maman had a sharp resemblance to her handsome father. She also had the same odd-shaped birthmark on her leg that was almost identical to his.

"Joella explained that in times of war, even the very proud become humble. They stopped feeling superior once they lost their only son, and accepted that a piece of him lived on in his daughter. Although they wouldn't have selected Joella to be the mother of their grandchild, they were still thankful she chose to keep the baby, not have an abortion, and raise her without any help, and that she had the heart to bring and share the child with them. I asked Joella if she knew she was going to get pregnant? And she explained that when he came to say goodbye to her, he told her that he couldn't make his parents understand and accept her, and that while they both held onto each other crying, that's when she had the vision of the child they created together, which she assumed was their joint future. She couldn't clearly see his future, but when she touched him, she saw his descendant. She desperately wanted a life with him and she believed that her way of guaranteeing a life with the man she loved was to have his baby. But the reason she didn't see his future was because he didn't have one. She assured me that the universe wanted his soul to live on through his little girl and she was just a messenger. She didn't see him have a future, but she saw the future that was paved by his existence."

I smile and imagine Jeff as he listens to my tale. "I know what you're thinking," I say. "Why would this old fortuneteller give me a reading? Right?" I don't need to be with him or be a psychic to read his thoughts. He makes an 'a-ha' sound. *Good.* Maybe now he can begin to appreciate why I need to know everything my grand-mère said to him on the night he claims their paths crossed.

"So your grandmother had a relationship with his parents?" he questions, mumbling the last word through a yawn.

He must be exhausted, but I'm glad he's still talking to me, listening. I was worried he'd fall asleep on me.

I nod a silent yes. "The boy's family owned a very big distillery and almost every bar in Rhode Island. They were a well-known Irish family with deep roots spanning over three generations in New England, and thanks to prohibition years ago, they were extremely wealthy. Not many people know this, but Rhode Island was the only American state that didn't consent to the 18th Amendment of Prohibition. This building I'm in and all their other buildings in Rhode Island were eventually assigned to a trust to their only beneficiary—their son's daughter, their only granddaughter, my maman."

I assume by the sounds coming from the other end of the line, this information has caused Jeff to wake up and perk up a bit. "Go on, I'm intrigued," he expels, sounding less tired, confirming my assessment.

I continue, "They gave Joella a free, warm, clean place to raise their granddaughter. She never asked for a penny, but she couldn't afford quality food and a place to live while working as a waitress in some small bar. And she refused to work as a fortuneteller. She said her sight was only limited to family, and she wasn't a fraud, a charlatan, or a performer who just took people's money. With their help, she opened her own bar downstairs and called it BlackGod. She claimed that all the profits were set-aside for her daughter. She was a simple woman, she didn't need much, and she never married or loved anyone else." I mentally count down until he starts his line of questioning, as only an attorney would.

He clears his throat and begins. "So what you're telling me is that your mom basically owns half of Rhode Island?" It's a statement more so than a question, and I can see I've just impressed him a little bit with my story.

"Yes, she once did," I reply with a melancholy smile. I have no desire to offer him any more information tonight. It's late, we both need to rest, and it's now his turn to talk. After all, this is a game of give and take. "Goodnight, Jeffery."

Jeffery

"Talking in Your Sleep" by The Romantics

This girl is smart—a sexy kind of smart that you don't see coming. She reminds me of Sara more than I care to admit. It's crazy to think that I didn't even know she existed a few days ago, and now she's all I think about. Her essence, her voice, her thought process, even the lingering memory of her scent has slowly oozed into me and has now become familiar. Her grandmother is a baffling mystery that has piqued my curiosity to impossible heights. With every word from Kali, she becomes an even bigger conundrum. Why the fuck would she talk to me that night? Why did she hand me a freaking key to her goddamn home, a talisman, she called it? It makes zero sense. If I was confused about her words before, I'm at an even bigger loss right now.

While I ponder the reasoning for being given a reading by elusive Joella Gitanos, I finally close my heavy lids and shut off my brain and pray for sleep.

I feel Kali slide from under my arm and move her body to straddle my stomach. *Fuck yeah.* She's completely naked, which is screwing with my current thought process and I can't recall what the hell I was thinking about or the last thing either of us said. I'm not sure about anything, except that this is not where our relationship needs to go right now. I need her to allow me to keep all my blood in my brain and not lose it to my dick. I need to think and make sense of everything.

I put both my arms behind my head. *I swear I won't touch her.* "Just do me a favor and don't make any sudden movements or come in contact with my dick," I say the last coherent thought in my head before I become a stuttering, inarticulate fool. "I have zero self control or condoms left. Understood?" I manage to expel, but I'm already hard, so I doubt my noble speech will have any lasting affect.

She nods and immediately un-straddles me without uttering a single word. *I'm such a stupid fuck.* It's just that she makes me forget everything. I can't think straight around her; I wouldn't even recognize myself. I think I've hurt her feelings, again, with my idiotic, self-righteous outbursts. When a young, gorgeous girl that you've had the pleasure to previously fuck sits on you with her bare pussy, you shut the fuck up and let her do whatever she wants, for the love of God.

"I'm sorry, Kali, it's not that I don't want you sitting on me, or riding me, or doing whatever the fuck you want to me, it's just that you're making it hard to function. I haven't been with a woman like this in over two years, and before that, it wasn't like this. It was with someone I had a long, painful history with."

She continues to nod, clearly pissed, clearly not understanding that I like her way too much, way too soon. She looks away from me, turning her body toward the window.

"You're right, let's try and keep this nonsexual. We don't want the dorm advisor finding out about us. We still have lots to talk about and time is running out."

A minute later, she practically jumps out of bed and walks over to my mirrored armoire in the corner of the room. She has her enticing ass out for me to drool over as she finds one of Jacky's dresses to cover her naked body with. She turns around with her outstretched arms for me to inspect and approve her chosen garment, but I'm no longer lying down. I stand by the bed, watching her with a smile that only the devil should be allowed to wear. I knew this would happen. I can't keep my hands off her, especially when she shows me how much she wants me to touch her.

I come at her with such speed that could only be explained as manic and superhuman. A beat later, I have her pinned against the armoire. She's breathless, trying to suck up whatever air is left in the room. I ingest the sounds she makes. I'm the world's biggest hypocrite. I'm the same man who just asked her to cool it, and now I have her pinned to the mirrored door, rocking my erect dick into her.

"You want to kill me, don't you?" I mumble, frantically inhaling the thin fabric around her chest. I squeeze her nipples through the tight dress around her tits, breathing her in as if I'm drowning and she is my last gulp of air before I go under. I am once again lost in a sea of lust that starts and ends with her. "I think you're a fucking witch—a perfect, beautiful, sexy witch that wants to kill me."

I continue to kiss and bite down her stomach. I fall to my knees while my hands can't help but find her smooth legs from under the dress. She knows where my hands will end up. She closes her eyes and lets her head roll back against the mirror, moaning in anticipation.

"My mouth wants to do some fucking, is that all right?" I ask the question that my mouth is obviously not going to wait for the answer to. My head is already under her dress as my mouth waters the second I smell her arousal. I haven't done this to anyone in over a decade, but all I want is to kiss, lick, and suck every inch of her.

I start my attack soft and tender, but the second my fingers plunge and feel her wetness, I let my mouth do exactly what it wants—*fuck her pussy.* It's not gentle, it's anything but tender, it's hard and rough and it's the most erotic thing I've ever felt in my life to eat her out like a savage.

I lift her leg and place it over my shoulder to get my tongue farther into her, if that's even possible. Every time I gently bite her clit, she makes this sound that literally reaches my dick, making it pulse. She takes hold of my hair for balance as I grab her ass with both hands and pump her into my mouth. I feel her trembling in my hands and shaking around my tongue, which means I need to make my beautiful enchantress a bit more comfortable to help her come. *Who fucking knew that oral sex could feel this incredible?*

I slide my hand up her back, and without stopping my X-rated wet feast, I get up from the floor, lifting her up with me in the air as if she's weightless and I'm some kind of Hercules. I bring us back to the bed and lay her down. I feel young, carefree, and euphoric; I'm strung up and high on Kali. I can't believe I'm on the receiving end of her stare. She's looking at me with everything I've ever wanted a girl to look at me with. I don't see pain. There are no broken promises, no regrets, no time limit, no guilt, and no disappointment in her gaze. All I see in her expressive eyes is something between need and love.

I drop back on my knees as I continue to shower her with hungry laps of my tongue and lips. I can't get enough of her. I spread her legs as far as they will go and move back to look at her sprawled out before me. *Fucking perfect.* As I take a moment to catch my breath and look down at her, I realize it's Sara I'm with, and not Kali.

I'm a monster.

How did I get here? I didn't want to hurt her. I didn't ask for this.

"You see what you do to me, Sara? I become a fucking animal around you. I don't even know who I am right now," I say with something resembling revulsion in my voice. I'm embarrassed by my lack of self-control as I wipe her wetness from my mouth and chin.

I see the tears running down her cheeks, and then notice the blood running down her legs and covering my hands. She won't take her eyes off me when she speaks.

"I won't let you ruin this. You can't ruin real love."

"I won't let you ruin this. You can't ruin real love."

Why would she let me touch her after everything I've done to her?

I jump up as if free falling and wake up drenched in sweat, crying like a baby. It takes me a few minutes to calm my racing heartbeat and erase my horrific dream from my mind. I practically run into my bathroom, remove my wet T-shirt and boxers, and discard them. I'm still hard as I turn the shower on and let the cold water wash away the taste of Kali, the blood of Sara, the memory of Jacqueline, and the endless guilt I live with every day.

Kali

"Total Eclipse of the Heart" by Bonnie Tyler

I wake up with him on my mind and quickly find my phone and swipe to his picture to see his eyes again. He's technically not married; his wife passed away. He was here with me in my bed, and yet I still feel like I shouldn't want him, like I'm doing something wrong. Three days ago, I was being consumed by him, and now the eyes that glare back at me through the screen have a kind of warning etched in them.

This feeling, these emotions are why I stay away from boys, men, or anybody who tries to flirt with me. The young ones are just looking for a good time, and the older ones don't know what the hell they want. Jeff Rossi doesn't fit any one of my categories, and those eyes of his are still telling me to run. Maybe he's right—I'm better off not knowing his sordid tale.

I feel my phone vibrate in my hands as I read my screen with a smile.

-I wish we never met and that you just kicked me out of your bar-

His text interrupts my thoughts. I can't look away from his words—I stare in disbelief with tears running down my face. I try to close my eyes and move as far away from the phone and him as possible, but I can't. It's like I'm glued to him through our only form of communication. My grand-mère made a terrible mistake; he's just another guy, a stupid, insensitive nothing!

And then a moment later, he sends, *-I'm sorry- No, you're not.* I chime in my head as I finally will my eyes to close. My pride wins, it can't look at his words anymore. I've failed in my attempt to read between the lines and his mixed signals. It's clear what he thinks of me, and he's right—I should've kicked him out. I pry open my tightly shut lids, and manage to type out,

-I figured you out, Jeff. You blame everybody around you and make them feel bad for your actions. It's who you are. I was hoping you were special, but you're not. I don't care about the stories inside your head anymore. I have my own problems, and you're only making things worse. Goodbye-

I scream the last word out on the inside, on the verge of a massive panic attack. My body stiffens as chills spread like wildfire covering every exposed inch; every pore within me knows it's over. My head is beyond confused. I'm mortified with my feelings, disappointed with his behavior, but more than that, I'm heartbroken that it finished before it even began.

The reality of him going silent on me and taking with him all hope of ever finding out the reason Joella spoke to him strangles me. The fact that Jeff Rossi will soon cease to exist in my lonely world forces me to sprint off the cold bed and symbolically pretend to leave him first.

My attempt to escape the room and him first fails when the sound of my phone ringing halts my exit. I stand by the door and listen to it ring, over and over.

I won't answer.

He's not for me. He will just cause more pain. The phone stops ringing as the sound of a new text begins to ping.

I won't look.

His words are meaningless. My internal battle stops when my phone becomes silent. No more calls, no more texts. I walk back toward my unkempt bed and circle my cell phone as if it's a wild dangerous animal, and in many ways that's exactly what it is. It has the power to rip me apart.

His last text is prominently displayed on my locked screen.

-I'm a fuck up. I can't seem to get anything right. Please let me explain. It's not what it sounds like. I don't even know why I said that. I can't stop thinking about you. I'm crazy for you. I need you. Please let me explain what I meant-

I hear the plea and the turmoil sheath every word that stares back out at me. I know if I listen to the voice message he's left I'll hear the remorse in his tone. Yet despite my heart's recognition of the danger, I still pick up my phone to look at his words closer, because my self-preservation mode has been turned off from the moment our lips touched.

I look at his photo again, like a silly schoolgirl admiring her latest crush. Eyes, his eyes tell stories of dozens of love affairs, and foolishly, I pray to be one of them. Stupidly, I hope to be lost in those eyes for as long as fate will allow me. I'm not thoughtless, I understand that the kind of maddening desire I feel for this man I just met won't end well, and the potential of him leaving scars inside me is absolute. But walking away and ignoring him doesn't seem like an option.

I haven't made up my mind if I'll ever talk to him again, but my heart knows; it recognizes his and won't allow us to separate, not yet. Another text from Jeff pops on my screen.

-If you only knew how confounded I am by the things I feel for you ... I have no right to feel anything, but I feel so much. Please, don't throw me out. Let me talk to you. There's an urgency inside me that needs to tell you everything-

I'm lost in his words, in his story, and in his world, which I feel I belong in. Lost and found, I guess you could say.

Wordlessly, I wrap my arms around my waist and give my poor body a hug. There is no room for my ego or my pride today. My heart is running this spectacle. I let out a long, defeated breath. Look at me—a confused, curious fool who can't let go of hope. How far will I go to satisfy the curiosity he ignited?

-Kali, please let me hear your voice-

His texts sound as if he may be suffering just as much as I am. I decide to type back a reply. He obviously knows I'm reading his messages, and I'm not about to start playing games.

My fingers seamlessly type out candid words that my common sense tries but fails to block. *-I don't know what to say to you. Every part of my body is at conflict. I want you and I don't, I like you and I don't, I want you to leave me alone ... but I don't. I have no idea what this is-*

I wish he were here for me to see his reaction and talk this out.

-I'm sorry for making you feel that way. You're a smart, incredible woman who only deserves respect. Please forgive me. I'll make sure I'm clearer next time on what I mean. I had a horrible nightmare. It's not an excuse for being a total piece of shit, but that's the truth. I didn't mean what I said. I only meant you have me so twisted up inside ... I can't think straight ever since I met you. I only wanted you to know how lost I am without you-

I fight back the smile his words give me, hesitantly accepting his apology. He hadn't meant to belittle or offend me, but his words betrayed him and did so anyway, no matter how he'd meant them to come out. I ponder if his bad dream had to do with his past demons or me?

I walk out of my bedroom and head to the kitchen to make some coffee and try and put this morning train wreck behind me.

-How do you like your coffee?- I inquire in an attempt to get us away to a safer, superficial type of conversation.

-I like it dark, sweet, with a slice of lemon-

My face twists in disgust.

Almost as if being able to see my facial expression he adds:
-Don't knock it until you try it-

I smile at his ability to read me through texts.

-Let's make a deal, don't ever make me try your coffee and I'll never make you listen to my music-

I laugh to myself. We don't need to make any promises, I'm one hundred percent sure we'll never see each other again. This has been too complicated, and I'm not even sure it's healthy.

-I didn't mean what I said to you before about not liking to listen to the sound of a violin. Any music is beautiful, especially if it means something to the person you love-

It's clear in my mind that his words are not intended for my sake, but more so for his. I'm certain there's a story behind his text, and maybe I will one day hear it. I look at my phone and press the call back button, because deep inside, my heart already decided that Jeff Rossi and I are not finished, and I'm convinced that the heart is always right.

Jeffery

"She's Like The Wind" by Patrick Swayze

I can't run away from this or her, and I won't let myself make a mess of things like I always do. She deserves the truth. Whether her reaction will have a shit effect on me or not, she earned the right to hear about her grandmother's words, like I've promised. She has put up with my mixed signals since the day we met, and there is no way I can just leave her alone and pretend we never met. I can't stop thinking and dreaming about her for the love of God. I fear I've become obsessed with her.

I walk to the kitchen to make myself coffee. I look down at my phone, clutched tight in my hand; this is my subconscious attempt to hold onto her. I wait for a reply as if I wait for my sentence to be read by the judge. I busy myself with my coffee while I sit at the kitchen counter and continue to wait. I look around the grand opulent space I call home and realize it has become increasingly cold without my wife. I think about Kali's cozy little apartment and recall how warm and familiar it felt. I've done this already. I've carved out an imaginary world with a girl to escape my harsh reality, and here I am once again. Until Kali knows everything about Sara Klein and me, she won't know anything.

I see a text come through asking me how I take my coffee. I look at my dark coffee and can't help but smile at her line of questioning. I playfully type back my response, tempted to send her a picture of the slice of lemon floating in my black coffee as I long to hear her voice and kiss the sadness my callous words have caused.

My phone begins to ring and her perfect face fills the screen as if God heard my plea. If her just calling can have this kind of effect, I can only imagine what her voice will have the power to do to me.

"Thank you, thank you for giving me another chance," is the first thing I say as I clutch the phone to my ear, beyond thankful for the opportunity to still speak to her. She's silent—all I hear is the sound of my own heartbeat.

She clears her throat and softly adds, "No worries, Jeff. This shouldn't be personal." Her voice cracks—along with my heart—when she says my name. "I want to hear more about you and Jacky. I still can't understand why you said there were two sides to your story. Did you remarry someone else?" Kali fires off questions, which I can't yet answer. I ought to calm her concerns, but I need to tell this tale my way. I halfheartedly continue with the story of my life.

"No, I was only married once. Jacky and I moved to the city right after we got married. It was a small ceremony for our closest friends and family. We couldn't even go on a real honeymoon due to all her scheduled treatments, but I didn't care. I just wanted to give her the fairy tale like a stupid delusional kid. Her parents moved us into a multi million-dollar townhouse on the Upper East Side," I say as I look around my home. "I had it made. I was surrounded by everything I loved. I was even within walking distance to my best friend—Eddie—and his family. I began working for my father-in-law's firm. If I closed my eyes, it almost felt perfect, like everything would be okay.

"Her parents did everything to make our lives more bearable—they hired a chef to cook special foods to keep her strong, and every other imaginable luxury money could buy. Our days revolved around Jacky's chemotherapy and attempting to get her as comfortable as possible. It was awful. I wouldn't wish cancer on my worst fucking enemy. I chose this life with her, and I had to be strong, keep the morale high, be positive, be her rock and continue fighting and believing, or I would lose her even sooner.

"If I were the one diagnosed with cancer, I'd lock myself in a room and fall into a deep depression, or possibly just jump off a building. Not Jacky, though. She was amazing. She never complained, never demanded a thing. She was usually more concerned about everybody going out of their way for her than her own wellbeing. I constantly felt like the asshole who was mad at the world on her behalf. I wanted to blame someone and hold them accountable for her suffering. Why her? She was a fucking saint; she didn't deserve it. I hated feeling sorry for myself when *she* was the one getting punched and beaten by life—not me. I couldn't watch her die. I know I promised to be by her side physically, but emotionally, I was shattered and I had to cling onto some kind of hope or I would go insane.

"Jacky was always upset about me spending too much time in the hospital or at home with her. She wanted me to go out and try to pretend I had a normal life, make friends at work and other places. She was stubborn, forcing me to socialize and live for the both of us. She wasn't just my wife, she was my best friend, and she could read me better than anyone else could. She knew what watching her suffer did to me, and she tried to keep me busy. The times that she would be too tired or too sick to leave the house, she would somehow find errands for me to do all over town, or literally arrange meet-ups with some of my buddies. I was a weak, spineless fool who had plenty of escapism when I should've had more realism. I wasn't a good friend or husband to her. I was always selfish."

"How were you selfish?" Kali's voice is defensive on my

account. I can sense her growing irritated with my negative self-assessment, but she just experienced my egotism firsthand, so how is she asking me this?

"Remember I told you that I will be presenting two stories in order for your grandmother's words to mean anything?" She immediately "a-has" me. "Ask me that same question after you hear the second part of my story, deal?" She agrees with an "a-ha" once again.

I know once she finds out about Sara, she'll understand exactly what kind of selfish person I really am.

"Do you believe in miracles?" I question, already knowing her answer.

"No, there are no miracles. My life has proven that whatever is meant to be will be, and nothing a person does can change their destiny."

I smile, even though I don't agree.

"What if a person that had a year to live was granted fourteen instead?" She's silent, probably doing math in her head.

"Jacqueline, your wife, survived cancer and lived for fourteen years?" Her voice is alert and shocked.

"She was never cancer free, or worry free, but she was in remission, and we had fourteen years together. If that's not a miracle I don't know what is. I prayed for my best friend to get better and stay with me for as long as possible, and my prayers were answered—to a certain degree. I can't tell you how much she suffered, the fear I felt every time we sat down to talk to one of her physicians, or how many surgeries we lived through, but she was always the happy one, convincing me how blessed she felt, even though I felt cursed. Instead of trying to cram a lifetime's worth of happiness into a year, we got almost fourteen. We've never spent a day away from each other and I always woke up to Jacqueline in my arms." Every word I tell Kali is true, it's just that in my case, I have two truths.

"Tell me about your enfants. I'd love to hear about them …

if that's okay," she questions cautiously.

Her voice sounds different—hopeful—and it makes me want to smile, but before I answer, I look down and unclench my left hand. I touch my colorless tattoo that lived silently for years under the place my wedding band once occupied, and I no longer want to smile.

One life, two women, two truths, two lies—infinite pain.

"My wife was the most nurturing, caring, loving person I've ever met. Us having kids was never something she allowed herself to dream about. But after her surgery, and after living cancer free for over two years, she started to bring up the subject of us having babies. At the time, the doctors told us it was possible since she didn't have a hysterectomy, but nature wouldn't allow it. We couldn't have kids and I'm glad we didn't; her body didn't need more exertion. I think part of Jacky's problem was that she never permitted herself to stop and feel sick and fully acknowledge her condition. In her mind, she was just another girl trying to get pregnant. We all deal with things in different ways. I guess that's how she protected her sanity and dealt with our fucked-up reality."

"But you guys did have kids. Did you adopt?"

I clench my fist again and try to swallow the memories. But some memories aren't meant to go down smoothly; they're meant to choke you until you suffocate.

I graze over one truth and choose to tell her another … the one that will be easier for her to comprehend, at this point. It's the same truth I've used to lie to myself every day. I hold on to this truth with both hands every minute of my life, because the second I let my mind recall the other, my life becomes unbearable.

"Jacqueline wanted our children to be biologically mine. She was extremely pragmatic when it came to our future. Her exact words were, '*We don't have time, we just have a moment in time.*' She longed to raise her own family like everybody else around us. I could see how much she wanted a child every time she would hold one of her friend's babies, and the sad look that would take over her face when spotting random strangers with strollers walking down the street. She wanted to be someone's mother, even if it was for one day. She stupidly felt that she somehow robbed me of a normal life, and she was adamant about our children being biologically mine. She told me, '*I'm just a visitor that got held up, but once I'm gone, I want you to be able to look at your kids and always see yourself in them the way I get to see you.*'

"We used a surrogate. At first we were going to choose an egg donor that we both knew. It was Jacky's idea to have the egg donor not be a stranger. She preferred someone that would care and have a relationship with the baby if and when she wouldn't be around. But we ended up using a donor she didn't know." I swallow the tears I feel in the back of my throat at the memory of my kids being born. "We didn't get one baby; we had twins—Juliet and Jacob." My voice cracks as I expel their names. I smile past the pain as their faces appear before me in my mind's eye. Another name floats around at the tip of my tongue, and my grin disappears, her name is not ready to come out yet.

"How old are your children?" Kali quickly pulls me out of the dark haze with her melodic voice.

"They're almost eight. Next question." I help Kali along, knowing what question should logically come next.

"When did their mother die?"

I want to tell her that their biological mom isn't dead, but she won't understand yet.

"Six months ago. My wife lost her battle to cancer, six months ago. She didn't want to go into a hospital. She refused further treatment and died in our bed, in my arms." I say all that in one breath without permitting myself to hear my own words, or I may die, too.

Kali doesn't need to say a word. I've started to recognize

every emotion just by listening to the rhythm of her breathing. She can't hide how she feels from me.

"Go on, say it," I goad her. "What kind of asshole sleeps with another woman six months after his wife dies? Isn't that what you're thinking?" I question with a fake smile plastered on the surface to hide the excruciating pain inside. "I told you … I'm a monster. I warned you not to touch me or you'd get dirty."

I straighten my posture as my body instinctively braces itself for an attack. In an attempt to calm the rage I've just ignited, I hear her slowly inhale as I'm sure she deliberates on the tainted words I left between us. No doubt she wants to un-know me. I want to un-know me, too.

"I'm not here to judge you, Jeff. You seem to have that under control," she says my name with unearned familiarity. "I'm just some girl you fucked six months after your wife died, to get your mind off your real life." We both know that's a lie, but it still stings to hear her say it. "I'm just here to listen and figure out why my grand-mère wasted her time and waited at the top of those stairs for you for all those years." I can hear the defiant smile in her voice, which is in direct contrast to her comment. I'm not the only one telling stories out of order. Kali clearly knows more about her grandmother and her life-ruining prophesies than she's let on.

"You're not some girl." She needs to know I wasn't looking to get laid.

"No? You mean you don't go around fucking random girls you meet in bars?"

My body reacts to her statement before my brain catches up. In a blink of an eye, I slap my hand against the stone counter. But the sharp ache I feel is in the empty space my heart once occupied. "I'm sorry. I wasn't using you. This isn't about the sex, it was about the warmth—the sex was just unavoidable. I didn't intend to drag you into my hell. I'm sorry," I repeat, hoping she believes me.

She doesn't say a word. I'm not some kind of misogynist. I care deeply about every woman I've ever had the honor to touch. I didn't love them the same, but I did love them, and it was never just about the sex. I lived over two years without having sex. It's about being with someone who makes you want to live.

After a long awkward silence, she asks, "You said you haven't been with a woman in two years, I assumed your wife passed away two years ago. I wouldn't have come on to you if I knew how recent it all happened. I wouldn't have behaved like I did. I feel like a dirty prostitué."

I'm to blame, not her.

There is so much she needs to know, but am I ready to tell her about the last woman I've been with before her? The woman that I've slowly ruined because I was a gluttonous pig waiting for a prophecy that never came true? I'm not ready to tell her, yet I also know our time is running out.

Kali

"Don't Stop Believin'" by Journey

When someone tells you a story, especially their life story, with each revelation you should feel closer to that person. However, every new piece of information I collect from this enigma of a human sends me down another bottomless spiral of questions. His wife died freaking six months ago! That's twenty-four weeks, one hundred and sixty-eight days, four thousand and thirty-two hours ago. *Fuck.* The guilt of my actions makes it hard for me to stay objective. He has enfants and he was here, fucking a stupid French girl that literally attacked him and begged him to kiss her. *Merde!*

I recall how I fell asleep in his arms as he stroked my hair melodically as if to music, and with all the guilt and taboo surrounding what we've done, a small, tiny part of me still can't help but believe that he was here for a reason. That he was singled out for a purpose, which I pray to God isn't some kind of cruel joke at my expense.

I pace my room, philosophizing our interaction, while withdrawn to the point of forgetting that I have a phone pressed to my ear and Jeff is still on the line.

"How do you know that Joella was waiting at the top of the

stairs for me? Did she tell you about it?" His question drags me back to our present predicament.

"No, not exactly, but a short time after I got to know her, I asked her why she hasn't sold this bar. I mean, I think you get the picture of how wealthy she was. She didn't need this place and the headache of running some bistro. I thought she would tell me about the sentimental value of BlackGod because of my maman growing up here. But that wasn't her answer. She told me she couldn't sell this place because she was waiting for someone, and I naively thought she was waiting for me to come back, but perhaps it was you she was waiting for?"

I think about the key he had hanging around his neck. She must've given him that key. I shake my head to stop the silly thoughts running loose in my mind. Joella was old and mostly spoke to me about my maman, because I suspect she thought I was her half the time, like everybody else.

"Journal, diary, you mentioned something about reading from her book. Is there a way for you to read it and maybe see if she mentioned talking to me and giving me a reading fourteen years ago?"

I hope I don't find anything about him in the book he's referring to. I'm not even sure exactly how to explain her journal to him. He'll want to see it, and that's not an option. He's not going to like what I'm about to say.

"She kept a ledger, an account, a book about all the people in her life that were once important. It doesn't have names marked prominently before each entry; it's not really clear. I only found the prophecy about my maman's future amongst others I didn't recognize because I knew how she died. Joella wrote down her premonitions in a kind of long sentence without any commas or periods. It's almost as if it had no beginning or end. Once I read her words, I understood why my maman left America and pretended to be an orphan." I close my eyes as I reread that passage in my mind.

If I could see his face, I'm sure he'd look frantic with his mind racing. Without a doubt, he's already mentally on his way back here reading Joella's journal, trying to find his fortune among her scribbles. He thinks I'll just hand him that book. He thinks it's as simple as coming here and finding an old gypsy waiting for him at the top of the staircase fourteen years later. But that's not going to happen. That book is titled "The Dead, le mort," and unless he's dying on me, I won't let him read it. The living does not need to know about their end of days, because that's when they stop living and start dying.

"You won't be reading that book, Jeff." I close my eyes. I don't need to see him to witness his disappointment at my statement. I can imagine it vividly. I'm sure I've just crushed his hopes of getting an explanation of his so-called fortune. "You need to trust me and accept that you are not permitted to see if and what has been written about you."

"I trust you," he offers instantly without any hesitation.

His voice travels and warms my body.

"I don't know what I want, or need anymore, and I don't think it matters what that book says. I just want to set things right, but I can't … it's too late. I can't undo the years of damage I've caused, and I will be reminded of my sins for the rest of my life. That book can't help me now."

It hurts listening to him, and I don't believe for one minute that he's this horrible person he deems himself to be, even if he slept with me six months after his wife died. What kind of monster can make you feel safe and loved without being anywhere near you? The kind that isn't really a monster at all, I suppose. I almost want to make him believe that he's not a monster. And a small voice inside me whispers for me to go find my grand-mère's book and look for anything that has similarities to his attributes amongst the many inscribed, because her written words might possibly be his salvation.

I hear the sound of another phone ringing coming from his

end of the line.

"Kali, could you excuse me for a minute? That's the house phone. Let me see who's calling."

"Yes, sure, answer, I'll wait."

I hear him pick up the phone, silencing the ringing. I can't pretend to not be curious. I want naively to be a part of every aspect of his life, whether I admit it to myself or not. I sit quietly and listen to every word I can make out from his one-sided conversation.

"Hello … Hi … Emily, what's wrong?"

Emily, Emily, Emily … I search my mind. He never mentioned anyone named Emily. *Who's Emily?* With each word, he sounds as if he's walking away from me—one step, two steps, more steps. I listen intently as I hear him, a-ha-ing and yea-ing, whomever he's talking to, but he sounds far.

"Thank you for calling me. I was away on a … business trip." His voice begins to diminish and he sounds even farther away now. The last thing I hear before his conversation disappears is "…I'll bring the kids with me when I come." I can't hear him anymore. He must've walked into another room, and then it hits me—I may have kissed him, slept with him, I may have even listened to him recap a huge portion of his early life, but I still know close to nothing about him, and sadly, what upsets me most, is that I don't know if I'll ever get to know more of him.

I walk back to my bedroom. I need to get dressed and get back to my own life. I have a bar downstairs waiting for me. I think I have enough strength to finally go and check if Joella's old apartment was left unlocked. I could always call a locksmith and break the lock. It's time for me to look through her belongings and decide what to keep and what to part with. In the past five years she's sold, with my consent, almost all the properties that once belonged to my maman, except, of course, this building. But perhaps, it's time to separate with all my past and forge a new beginning for myself.

I sit on my messy bed and inhale the imaginary faint scent of him still lingering on the sheets. Jeff feels like a mistake right now, but I needed to have that bond with someone. I got a chance to discuss my family with a man who cared enough to listen. I should be thankful for our time together and just move on.

I hear movement on the line.

"Kali, can you hear me? You still there?" *Where else would I be?* I chuckle to myself. "I have an hour before I need to go, but you deserve to hear the whole story."

A loud thump, as if a door closing, sounds in my ear. I get in my bed and cover myself as a stranger holds my heart strings on the other side of the line and continues to tell me a story I'm not sure I want to hear anymore.

Jeffery

"Obsession" by Animation

Emily Bruel calling to invite me over with the kids, while Kali waits on the other line has me reliving my nightmare all over again. I slide down with a bang as my body hits the hardwood floor of my bedroom, and I'm grateful that I won't have to see Kali's face when I tell her about the other life I've lived in secret. I won't need to recall the look of disgust on this pretty girl's face when she learns who I really am. I'm made up of two lives that were both rightfully taken away from me.

I clear my throat and begin regurgitating the real past. "Do you remember when I told you I spent some time in New York City with Eddie Klein? It was right before we started law school, and right after I was convinced that Jacqueline didn't want anything to do with me. She was also in New York staying with her folks that summer, and never once had she called to talk to me or answered any of my calls. I got her message loud and clear—I wasn't good enough for her and her New York high society.

"My reaction to her rejection was to party it up with my friends, go to the best nightclubs, and dance and flirt with countless girls. On one of the last nights before we were headed back to school, Eddie brought along his younger sister and her best friend to the club. He had to pay the bouncer to let them in, since they were both underage. Our job was to make sure that nobody touched or even looked at these two girls.

"Eddie and his girlfriend, Michelle, wanted to step outside for a few minutes and I was left in charge of guarding the youth. I saw a few assholes trying to dance too close to Eddie's little sister and her friend, and very gallantly, I proceeded to step in and make it clear those two were spoken for. Until that moment, until I came face to face with her, I'd never actually paid any attention to his sister, or properly been introduced to her. I'd been too busy trying to find a girl for the night to get Jacky off my mind, but for whatever reason, she made me take notice. His sister, this teen, did something to me … I don't know, I guess she rattled a part of me that hadn't been engaged in a while. She was just different than Jacky—taller, lighter hair, she had this smile that was angelic and mischievous at the same time. I liked how she looked at me. She was confident but still made me think I was in control. I didn't feel inferior standing next to her. I felt like a man.

"I didn't like what my best friend's little sister evoked in me, the curiosity, the desire to touch her and see her reaction to me. I couldn't keep my eyes off her, but I knew it was wrong to feel anything. Even though I could sense she was all for it, she was still off limits. I'd imagined she was dancing just for me, taunting me, knowing I couldn't have her for a list of reasons. I also had enough tequila that night to last me my whole life, and by the time I went back to crash at Eddie's house, I'd become completely obsessed with her. In my intoxicated mind, I was convinced she was perfect for me. I couldn't get her out of my head that night. It was impossible to sleep in the same house with her and not go talk to her at least.

"Like a stupid, horny fucker, I barged into her bedroom in the middle of the night. I startled her, and when she looked at me like a deer in headlights, scared in bed, I realized I'd made a terrible mistake. I was just mad at Jacqueline; this young girl had nothing to do with it. I apologized and was about to leave, but we somehow ended up kissing. I can't recall who instigated it, or how it happened. I don't remember what I said or what she said, but I remember that kiss. She tasted different, new. I wanted to continue to kiss her all night, but then I realized that I was drunk and in bed with my best friend's little sister. She wasn't even eighteen, and she just offered to suck me off in an attempt to impress me. That whole night was ridiculous and I ended up running away before sunrise. I didn't even wait until everybody woke up to say goodbye. I got my shit and left the Klein residence before I did more damage. It was a moment of stupidity and weakness, and I wish I could go back an undo it, but I can't."

I stop and adjust my ear against the phone. Kali hasn't said a word. I hope I haven't put her to sleep with my trip down memory lane.

"I'm still here. What happened next?" I hear her soft voice filter in. Her voice makes me smile, but her question reminds me of all the mistakes I've made and the lives I've damaged.

"Once law school began, Eddie and I became roommates. Jacqueline and I went back to our normal arrangement as if nothing happened, as if my world hadn't been turned upside down by some girl I had no right kissing. I couldn't look at Eddie without thinking about his beautiful little sister. I tried to pretend that kiss meant nothing. I tried to pretend she didn't have permanent residence in my dreams. I tried to pretend I wasn't using her to feel wanted, and I tried to pretend I wasn't dying to see her again—I became the great pretender. If I had been smart, I would've asked Eddie questions, but I felt guilty for kissing and touching her that night, and I couldn't trust myself to say her name without my body betraying me and giving my intentions away. So I kept her buried inside.

"Jacky and I were back to our usual friends with partial

benefits status. I got to lose myself inside her on the nights we got buzzed, and she got to wake up the next morning and pretend we were just friends. She seemed content with our arrangement, and who was I to complain? Eddie was happy I was getting laid while spending a few nights a month somewhere else, so he and Michelle could have some privacy, and I was happy that Jacky still let me be with her. I had two girls—one imaginary and one fictional.

"I tried to conceal my ridiculous feelings for my roommate's sister. I had zero contact with her after that night we kissed in her room. It wasn't until about a year later, Eddie was heading to New York to attend a big party his family was having. He mentioned it was his sister's birthday party. I thought about her so much that in a way I felt close to her, like I knew her. He asked if I wanted to drive back home with him to keep him company since Michelle couldn't make it, and I jumped on it. I was going to New York to a swanky party to wish the girl I'd been having X-rated fantasies about a happy eighteenth birthday. She was finally legal, and maybe I'd let her do what she'd offered to do to me the year before in her room that night after the club. It was a great plan, but there was just one problem: his sister wasn't eighteen, or even seventeen … she was *sixteen*! I came to her fucking sweet sixteen bash like some kind of a molester. She didn't look fifteen that night at the club, nor did she sound fifteen in her bedroom. Could you imagine I'd been jerking off to the image of a fucking fifteen-year-old girl?"

Kali gasps, "Jeff, that doesn't sound good? But at least you didn't actually do anything but kiss her. Could you imagine if you'd slept with her?" She's one hundred percent right and that was exactly what enraged me.

"I was livid. I had a need to yell and scream at her. I don't know why I blamed her. She never told me her age and I never even asked—I just assumed. We never spoke to each other about that night, or that kiss, or her blowjob offer, or how in the morning we were supposed to talk about possibly hooking-up. We didn't speak at all. It was all make believe. I was a good boy and waited for her to grow up, but when I came back to see her, I got a good dose of reality.

"Thinking back, I had no right to take her to the side and yell at her that night, considering this was my doing—she didn't owe me anything. I shouldn't have allowed myself to speak to her or freaking kiss her again that night. I shouldn't have asked her to grow up and wait for me, so I could make all our fantasies come to life, because all I did was ruin us both." I open my eyes with the memory of Sara lingering in front of me. I've spent more time with Sara in my head than in the real world.

"Why did you kiss her again, after you found out she was only sixteen?"

Her question is filled with anger and confusion. She's angry because I kissed an under-aged girl. Wait until she hears the rest of my story.

"I was mad at her … and myself. I felt humiliated for how I had allowed her to make me feel, and I acted childish, wanting to punish her. But when I looked into her eyes, as much as I wanted to make her feel what I felt, I couldn't. I felt sorry for her. The guilt of my actions sobered me up, and I realized that all I wanted to do was protect her. I didn't want anybody else to touch her or hurt her. I wanted her to just be mine. She was the most angelic, untainted thing I'd ever seen. She looked innocent, but the things she said sounded like she was a grown woman, like she was experienced, but she wasn't.

"I couldn't hide my feelings; she knew how much I wanted her, and she was angry, too. She began to infuriate me, mock me, by speaking about being with other men. We were set on driving each other crazy from day one. When I stopped listening to her vulgar words and just looked into her eyes, I realized that she was just a pretty little pretender, like me. I asked her point blank how many men she'd been with. She responded with, 'Too many to count.' That's when I knew—there were no other men. I was her only man. Her words meant nothing, because her eyes told me everything—I had been her first kiss, and at that moment, I wanted to be her first everything."

I stop talking to give Kali a chance to ask me questions. But we're both silent, allowing my words to settle. I glance down at my watch. We don't have the luxury of silence; our time is running out. I have meetings, I need to be at court today, and I promised Emily I'd come with Juliet and Jacob to her house for dinner.

"Can I go on with my story?" I inquire to make sure my judge is still paying attention.

"Yes, of course, go on."

There is no anger or warmth in her voice, but then again, why should there be? She's bracing herself for the storm that's about to descend her ears.

"I went back to school and back to Jacqueline's bed as if nothing had happened. She didn't notice a change in me, and truth was, nothing really happened. My job was to study and become an attorney. I didn't waste my time chasing pussy like the rest of my friends. I was content. I got to make love to my best friend, a girl that was perfect in every way—just too good for me. So what if she was embarrassed to tell the world I was her boyfriend? I didn't need a title or a sign. I didn't care, because when it mattered, she always ended up in my arms. I was never a pig; I was always respectful of our relationship. From the first day Jacky and I started having sex, I may have flirted or joked with other girls, but I never slept with anybody but her, until … well, until I did.

"I spent years working my ass off with my nose pressed inside books to ensure a future once school was over. I didn't have a rich daddy to make sure I had a career when I graduated. I was conditioned and focused, spending half my life in the library studying. I only allowed myself a few distractions. After exams, once a month, I'd get drunk and call Eddie's little sister to hear her voice and make sure she knew I was thinking about her, and then I got to go and sleep with the girl I loved.

"Maybe if I hadn't kept calling his sister she would have forgotten about me, maybe she would've found a nice guy to love, but I couldn't help myself. I had this scenario all worked out that I'd go back to see her on her eighteenth birthday and fuck the fantasy out of both of us. Finally give her what she'd asked for on that night in her room. I'd dreamt about being the first man to touch her, take her virginity, and teach her what pleasure was about. I loved pretending that she was obsessed with me and waiting for me. Being denied or held back from having something can create an artificial demand that maybe isn't really there. It was all premeditated in my mind, but then something happened.

"About a month before all my dirty dreams with my best friend's little sister were to come true, my worst nightmare came to be. Like I told you before, I found out from Michelle that Jacqueline, *my* Jacky, was suffering and battling cervical cancer on her own. I was angry. I couldn't understand why she would withhold something as serious as cancer from me—*me*, of all people? Did she think so little of our friendship that I wasn't even worth the truth?

"Her weekly trips to the city to see her parents started making more sense. At one point, I honestly thought she had a real boyfriend in New York, someone her parents had approved of, not some guy she fucked in school in secret. I spent a whole month following her into the city every weekend to see for myself that this wasn't some kind of horrible joke. She would go by herself into the hospital for treatment for two whole days every week. I remember waiting for over thirty hours on a park bench across the street from the hospital for her to come out, just to make sure I didn't miss her. I couldn't let her do this on her own. The cheap, decrepit, five hundred-square-foot studio I'd rented was by the hospital where I could keep an eye on her from my window. All it had in it was a clean mattress and a pillow. It had no fridge or a kitchen, just a hot plate for boiling water for coffee. That's when I stopped putting milk in my coffee. Sugar and lemons don't spoil as fast as unrefrigerated milk."

I hear Kali take a deep breath, which reminds me of our distance. I need to stop. I'm already late to my first meeting.

"Why are you so far away from me? I have things I need to tell you and real life keeps catching up. If I hang up to go be an attorney for a few hours, will you promise to pick up the phone when I call you back? I won't take lunch today, I'll call you as soon as my meeting finishes and I'm on my way to court." I hold my breath for her reply.

"You don't have to apologize or ask permission to speak with me. I need to know what Joella said to you more than what I can offer you back by hearing it. We both should get back to our lives and talk later."

"Kali—," I'm about to tell her that she's becoming a huge, important part of my life, but then I stop myself. Maybe it's not wise to engage her with intimate words until she fully understands who I am and what I've done. "I'll talk to you soon."

I agonize over Kali's reaction to my affair with Sara by milking the revelation, but it's inevitable. If I crave any sort of a normal relationship with this woman she ultimately must accept me, including all my mistakes. My involvement with Sara wasn't a mistake, since our union produced the most beautiful children in the world, but the way I kept Sara waiting indefinitely with the hopes of us having a real life, was.

The meeting I'm in slowly drags on for hours with back and

forth behind-the-scenes negotiations between our clients. I'm thankful my assistant is vigorously writing it all down because I have a different kind of negotiation afflicting my mind. I have a drawn-out countdown led by my heartbeat swimming through a suspended sea of tension until I hear her voice again. I won't be able to fully take in a deep breath until we speak.

I excuse myself, no longer able to wait and return to my corner office down the long hallway. I instinctively touch my chest to feel the key but it's gone. I don't dwell on the absence of my talisman and quickly fish inside my suit pocket for my phone. I sit comfortably in my oversized executive chair, but it feels wrong. I abandon my desk and relocate to the couch, and that feels wrong too. I look around my office with the New York City skyline wrapped around it like a postcard closing in on me from every direction and proceed to the windowless bathroom. I lock myself inside, but it's inane since I'm not sure who exactly I'm locking myself from.

I settle on the bench facing a mirrored wall and dial her number. She answers before the line even rings and I swear her voice is better than any painkiller I've ever taken.

"Hello."

"Hi Jeffery." The way she pronounces my name is indescribable.

"I don't remember where we left off," I lie. I could recite and transcribe our conversations verbatim.

"You enlightened me on why you drink sweet black coffee with a slice of lemon during the time you were coming into the city to be your future wife's guardian angel, and now I think you're about to tell me about your friend's sister."

Her perception of me being Jacky's protector reminds me of my wife's letter. She also believed I was her savior, but truly she was mine. I don't let myself get too philosophical and dive right back to the task at hand—the truth.

"During that time, I'd almost forgotten all about Eddie's

sister. I had so much on my mind that I didn't need to occupy space with a silly fantasy or some girl I knew practically nothing about. I'd started getting closer to Jacky, sitting next to her in all our shared classes, studying together like we did when we first met, hoping our proximity would force her to tell me about her condition, but she didn't. She kept it from everybody. Her silence drove me crazy and I felt lied to, I felt unimportant. I actually wished she had a real boyfriend she ran to on the weekends and not cancer, because another guy I could fight, but I couldn't fight cancer.

"Eddie hardly ever mentioned his family or his sister, and at that point, I hadn't spoken to her in months, but obviously, the curiosity was still there, buried under the harsh reality I'd found myself living with. The day after his sister's birthday, I questioned him about her as nonchalantly as I could. I remember him freaking out about forgetting to call and missing his sister's eighteenth birthday. He was worried that his parents had been too busy with their own bullshit and may have forgotten her birthday as well, and that he was the worst fucking brother on the planet. I felt awful. What if everybody had forgotten her birthday? Why didn't I call her? I remembered, and I had promised her I'd call. I wanted to call her, but I didn't have the time or the balls to hear the disappointment in her voice; after all, it was Friday evening and I was headed to the train station, right behind Jacky, to go into the city and make sure she was okay.

"It was Saturday and I was studying at the dilapidated place in New York I had called home every weekend when Eddie's sister actually called me. I never gave her my number or called her from my own phone, so I was surprised she had my number, but at the same time, excited to talk to her. She didn't say a word when I answered; she just hung up. But I knew who it was because I instantly recognized her phone number. I called her back and my heart broke when I heard her sad voice and realized how important my promise and I were to her. I had no intention of seeing her, but when I heard her crying, I couldn't pretend anymore that I didn't care or that she didn't matter. I didn't want to be that asshole responsible for breaking her heart. After she hung up on me, I decided to check up on her and make sure she was okay, and perhaps apologize for being a jerk and leading her on with my empty, foolish promises for years.

"I'd paid a visit to Eddie's folks' home on the Upper East Side and was greeted by his mom. Mrs. Klein was disoriented, drunk, and had no idea where her teenage daughter was, so I waited, and waited, and waited until I was ready to kill someone. I dialed her number countless times, but she wouldn't answer my calls. I had imagined dozens of scenarios—none of them good. I had this ache in my heart, reminding me that if something bad were to happen to my best friend's sister, I would be responsible. After waiting on her cold, stone steps and calling her for hours, she finally answered her fucking phone. I can recite that phone call in my sleep.

"She sounded out of breath when she answered. I'd asked where she was, afraid she would hang up on me again. *'Why do you care?'* she snapped back. If only she knew just how much I cared. I told her I'd been outside her house for hours. I told her that her mom had said she'd be back soon. Then I asked her if she was planning to come home at all that night. I was worried about her safety; it was late and she was only eighteen, still in high school.

"I was outraged, but it was nothing compared to how I felt when I heard a man's voice in the background say, *'What's wrong, baby? Who's calling you?'* I was ready to find and kill whoever had called her *'baby.'*

"In a state of rage, I yelled, *'WHO. THE. FUCK. ARE. YOU. WITH? Why did he just call you baby? Eddie said you don't have a boyfriend.'* I wasn't even drunk, and I was talking to her like she was mine, like I had a right to question someone calling her baby.

"But nothing could've prepared me for her next words. She said, '*Jeff, calm down. I'm with Phillip. He offered to fuck me at his place, and since you haven't made good on your promises, I'm taking him up on his offer.'* And then she hung up, leaving me to wait and suffer a slow, painful death at the hands of her words."

I close my eyes and let out a long breath as the image of Sara at eighteen bombards my brain—her puffy eyes and those sad, trembling lips.

"Do I even need to know what happened next?" Kali asks, ridicule and judgment coating each word.

"Yes, you should hear what happened next, because it was the beginning of what the rest of my life became—a lie and a truth, that even I couldn't tell apart anymore."

Kali

"Is This Love" by Whitesnake

I can't hold down the bile that keeps rising in my throat when he talks about him and other women. I lie on the rug in the middle of my room and listen to a story from the mouth of the person I know will affect my life, and in some ways, already has.

I know what he did. He slept with his friend's sister, and I'm afraid he did something horrible to her. I'm afraid he's about to tell me a heinous crime he committed. I may be his next victim. Psychopaths look like regular people, and in his case, they can even be very attractive. I shake my head at the nonsense that just entered it, because there is no way my grand-mère would've led me to my death.

There has to be more. I don't want to hear about the women he loved and slept with, but I asked for this, and now it's too late. I can't tell him to stop. I'm about to hear what he and some girl did and how it changed his life.

On the other end of the line, I hear him clear his throat and take a strained, deep breath. I can't see him, but I'm sure it can't be easy for him to talk about his wife and some girl.

"When she finally returned home that night in a cab—scared, sad and all alone, I realized exactly how important she was to me. I wasn't going to touch her, I wasn't going to kiss her, I wasn't going to do anything but talk to her. But we ended up doing everything. Until I held her in my arms, it was all just an innocent, safe fantasy, make-believe, an escape from feeling rejected. But that night, the instant we kissed in the backseat of that cab, my whole world shifted. I took her back to my shitty studio overlooking the hospital, and that's where I took her virginity and gave her my sanity. She was my pill, my drug of choice; I became an addict. When I touched her, nothing and no one else mattered. She would look at me like I was her world, and I wanted to be someone's world. I couldn't stop. I couldn't tell her that I had another world, so I kept both as far away from each other as I could.

"I never thought Jacky and I could have a future, not just because of her cancer, but because she didn't love me that way. She didn't look at me the way the innocent girl I spent every weekend with did. Most of the time, she would try to push me away. I'd spend the week in school allowing Jacqueline to pretend I didn't matter, and then I would spend the weekend with another girl and pretend Jacky didn't matter.

"After a year, nothing mattered anymore. I was waiting to finally graduate and start my life without my best friend being a constant reminder and a source of pain. I was tired of pretending, and I did love Eddie's sister very much. I was ready for school and Jacky to be over so I could start my new life with someone who wanted me in theirs."

He pauses. He sounds winded, as if physically reliving his actions.

"Did you tell your friend's sister you were sleeping with someone else?" I present a question I already know the answer to, but I need to hear his response. My question is meant to hurt him like he's hurting me right now.

"I told you that I kept them separated. One had nothing to do with the other. Jacky was a cactus that wouldn't allow me to get too close and love her completely. She would spend time with me and sleep with me, but our relationship was limited, guarded. There was a huge elephant in the room that she chose to ignore, and it infuriated me.

"I'd take the train into Manhattan every weekend for her, but she didn't know and I couldn't tell her. Not to mention, I was human; I needed to be loved and appreciated, and she didn't do either of those things for me. But the girl who waited at my apartment did. She loved me, she wanted me, and she appreciated my effort. I would touch her and all my problems would vanish and nothing else mattered. She was a portal, an escape, a make-believe world I created that would come to life at the end of every week. She was my reward and salvation. We talked about the kind of life we'd build together one day, and I couldn't wait to start a new chapter with only her once law school was done. I didn't need to tell her about Jacqueline; there was nothing to tell. We wouldn't be together anyway.

"I never in my wildest dreams thought that Jacky couldn't beat cancer. She was young and she had money to get the best treatment. Michelle kept hinting that she wasn't doing well, that life was unfair and she didn't know how she would go on without her best friend, but I didn't listen. My brain wasn't programmed to think of a world without Jacqueline in it.

"As we got closer to graduation, I spent less time with my so-called best friend. We didn't study together; we were too busy with finals, and it felt like a natural disconnect. Eddie's sister was accepted to Brown University. She was also following her family's footsteps to become an attorney, like her father and brother. I was going to get rid of that apartment and find a job around anywhere she was, but that's not what life had in store for us.

"I told you already that Jacqueline's father paid me a visit a month before I graduated and turned my life upside down. His daughter was dying and he wanted me to love her, marry her, and give her what every woman should have—a family. It was like a dream and nightmare wrapped into one. Her family had finally accepted me and I would get to marry the girl I always thought was unattainable, but she would be painfully taken away from me in a year. What was I suppose to do? Huh?"

I listen and realize he's asking me a question. "Jeff, are you asking me what I would do?"

"Yes, what would you do if you were me? Would you tell everybody the truth? Was I supposed to go back to New York and break that poor girl's heart?" The agitated sound of his voice tells me just how much he wishes he did tell the truth, but clearly he didn't.

"I would tell the truth. I would own my actions and consequences, even if it meant breaking someone's heart. C'est la vie." I hear him chuckle at my response.

"That's life, huh? Well, I'm sorry, I couldn't look her in the eyes and break her heart. I wasn't man enough to tell her that the place we'd made love and where she gave me her heart and her body was the same place I'd rented to watch over my sick best friend, who was my longtime lover, the one I was now going to marry. I didn't have the balls to tell her I came to the city almost every weekend to make sure Jacqueline was okay, and not just to see her. I was a negligent pretender, but I wasn't that kind of heartless monster … not yet. I couldn't witness her disappointment. So instead of doing the right thing and breaking up with her, I just did the cowardly thing and stopped going to the city to see her altogether. Like a child, I ignored her calls, texts, and emails. Nobody knew about us anyway, so it was easy to detox her out of my system like the addict I'd become.

"I couldn't feel guilty about my newly acquired predicament, because I had to concentrate on Jacky and whatever time she had left on this earth. That was my only job. Once again, I thought I had a plan, but I think the universe saw it and laughed. Then it showed me who the real life architect is."

"I'm scared to hear what happens next," I say out loud.

"What happened next is worse than you could ever imagine."

I swallow the acid and stop trying to predict his next move, and how or why Joella would have had anything to do with it. Our physical distance and his account of the past add another layer of separation between us, and with each new revelation, I travel a little further away from the idea of him.

"It was May first, and our last final was done. The whole gang was together at BlackGod celebrating, drinking as if tomorrow would never come. I drank to try to forget the girl I knew was waiting for me like a lost puppy back in New York. I drank to try to forget that my best friend was dying. I drank in an effort to pretend I wasn't a scared idiot who was about to propose to the love of his life that night. I drank and hoped I was anybody but me.

"I had Jacqueline's ring in my pocket when I went upstairs to the bathroom. I got to the top of the stairs and this woman, whom I'd never paid any attention to before, motioned for me to come closer. I was a bit buzzed, but I remember looking around. There was no one there except me.

"She said, '*Come, boy, I will give you a reading.*' But it was the way she'd whispered it with certainty that caught my attention. I said I wasn't interested, that I'd only gone upstairs to take a piss. I hadn't gone up there for a reading. I told her I didn't even believe in fortunetellers anyway. I'd always believed that you make your own fortune—you know what I mean? But upon closer inspection, the smiling woman looked familiar to me. I had to have seen her before, maybe sitting at the top of those stairs on another occasion I had gone up to use the bathroom. I mean, after all, we did frequent that bar no less than twice a week.

"I remember her saying, '*Your eyes ... two different colors. You're one in a million, boy.*' She stood with difficulty and drew back the black velvet curtains, and beckoned me to enter the small, hidden room at the top of the stairs, right across from the men's room. I can't explain what compelled me to accept her invitation. I can't decide if I was intoxicated, or perhaps hoping she'd actually know my future since my reality at the time took an unforeseeable turn.

"Her lips came together in a knowing grin as she said, '*Show me your hands, Godfrey.*' I corrected her and told her that my name is Jeffery, not Godfrey. I thought maybe she'd mistaken me for someone else. But before I could stop her, she'd taken hold of both my wrists. I sat down and listened, completely startled. Although, it was her next words that had me frozen in place. She said, '*Those eyes ... I've seen them countless times, boy. Don't you worry about your name, just pay attention to what an old woman has to say.*' I looked down at her wrinkled hands, which had given away her advanced age, and watched as she began to trace a line from my index finger down my palm and to my wrist. She stopped at my wrist, and then we both looked up in sync.

"She raised three fingers and smiled before saying, '*Three children will come from you—a king and two queens. But you will be lost without her. Your life collided with pain and suffering that won't end until you find her. Only the girl with the biblical name will save your broken heart, Godfrey. She will heal you and you will heal her. When she grows up, you will be lost no more, my boy, and your life will be filled with music and begin again.*' I removed my hands from her grip as if her prophecy had burned me. She had no way of knowing about *her*. She had no right telling me such crap. Who did she think she was? The girl she spoke of … it was over between us. I hadn't seen or called Eddie's sister in weeks. This stranger knew nothing. I was going to marry Jacqueline, end of story.

"I was never the same after I spoke and looked into your grandmother's eyes. She was the reason I went back to New

York to see the girl I had cowardly abandoned. I went back to try and explain, try to end things with her like a man and let us both move on. I had every intention to never see her again, especially since I was getting married. She had her whole life ahead of her, she was practically a baby who just graduated high school, and I was a new attorney, fresh out of school, who would be moving to New York to try and build a career. Jacqueline was my future, not her. But seeing the girl I couldn't stop thinking about, coupled with the gypsy's taunting words, became my ruin. She planted the seed, but I watered it with empty promises and I willed it to life. I lived a life of sin because I thought I knew my absolute future and what it held, but I knew nothing."

I hear him crying, but I'm too busy pacing my room in circles while methodically compartmentalizing his words. I struggle in my efforts to decode Joella's reading to him and try not to go crazy with all the information I finally have. I rewind and play back her prophecy over and over. She said his name, she knew who he was, in a way, and it must've been him she waited for all those years. She could've sold this bar thousands of times, but she never did, and he has a key. He had to have been the reason she kept this place and why she remained here waiting for him to come back. *But why?*

It dawns on me that I don't know Eddie's little sister's name. I don't recall Jeff mentioning or saying her name once in his storytelling. *But why?* I need to know her name, now!

My phone is suddenly quiet as I look down at my screen to see that it's completely black, *dead,* and Jeff and his story are gone.

Out of frustration I fling my phone across my bed, and just as quickly, go after it to find it and plug it in. I place my hand under the covers to try and fetch it but I can't seem to locate it. I dig further under the covers until my hand grazes over and comes in contact with a key.

Jeffery

"Didn't We Almost Have It All" by Whitney Houston

I did what I promised, I told her the prophecy, the nonsensical prediction of her old, senile grandmother, and she hung up on me, as I knew she would. Now I need to get as far away from the memories as my head will allow me, without undergoing a lobotomy. It's the first time I've actually regurgitated my life to someone out loud, and I don't particularly like myself very much. I sound like a lying pig that cheated on his sick girlfriend, fiancée, and then wife with a young, innocent girl, and I haven't even told her the whole story. I snicker with disgust. At least I won't be adding Kali to my reckless body count.

I don't care about understanding or knowing why that old woman presumably waited just for me. I rub my chest to try and find my key, but again I'm reminded I don't have it anymore. I left it under Kali's pillow. That key doesn't belong to me. Her grandmother would want her to have it. It doesn't matter anymore why she said what she said, and I don't care about her perfect granddaughter, either. *Lies, lies, lies.*

I splash water on my face and readjust my favorite green tie tightly around my neck before I brace myself to step back out into my life. I need to get back to work and look forward to seeing Emily and her family tonight. Hopefully she'll give me good news about Sara and her slow recovery. I'll also hand over the key to the apartment in the village I once called my home with Sara. I'll have Emily and Louis speak to Sara and William about it and decide to do with it as they see fit. I have no reason to ever go back there, just like Sara, that place was never really my home. My kids are my only home.

I glance outside at the heavy rain accompanied by an ominous thick, dark fog that has suddenly engulfed the city. The steady sound of water coming from the sky silences my mind. I look down at my phone, still clutched tight in my hand, and scroll to Kali's selfie. I have my finger on the delete button, but I can't bring myself to erase her face from my phone or my mind. I decide to keep her forever immortalized behind the glass screen to safely torture myself.

It's time to bury my life in work and my kids, and help Sara get back the life she deserves. I will no longer be a selfish prick creating heartache with false promises. Jacky, Sara, and now Kali have helped me grow up and accept my actions and their consequences.

My kids are ecstatic they get to meet and play with Emily and Louis' children tonight. It's one of our first family outings since Jacky passed away. We have a constant swarm of friends and family come visit us, but this is the first time in over six months that we're physically going somewhere.

The Bruels live within walking distance to our house, and since the rain from this afternoon has stopped, I've decided to walk rather than drive to their home.

I knock on the door using the big-ass knocker that looks as

if it were stolen from Versailles, and knowing a thing or two about Louis Bruel, I don't doubt that at all. I haven't cracked a smile all day, and this stupid doorknocker makes me and the kids giggle like a bunch of maniacs.

Emily opens the door with a small blond boy at her side. He looks like Louis' carbon copy with the bluest eyes I've ever seen. He looks a bit younger than my kids, but that doesn't stop Juliet from walking in and taking his hand, leading the way like the boss that she is. *She's my little Sara to a T.* Emily and I smile as I lift Jacob, who's more reserved than his no-nonsense sister, and walk in. Emily's older daughter approaches and introduces herself as Rose. She's stunning, just like her mother.

Jacob goes off with Rose, giving me one last look, to go see a promised playroom as I'm left standing in the middle of Sara's best friend's foyer. I feel like an intruder, an imposter, as if I got lost in someone else's story. Maybe this wasn't a good idea. I hope that Emily inviting me over doesn't make Sara even more upset with me. She hasn't answered any of my calls or texts. William said she's not ready to talk to me—I don't blame her. I get all my information either from Emily or Eddie, but I long to talk to her and make sure she knows how sorry I am. She needs to know that her children will always be here waiting for her, if she ever wants to be a physical part of their lives. I will never stand in her way of knowing her babies.

"Don't worry about the kids—they'll be fine. There are plenty of babysitters downstairs watching over them." Emily tries to put me at ease, but I feel wrong about being here.

I lie and say, "Not worried at all. Thank you for inviting us. It's nice for the kids to get out, and I know Sara would be pleased to have her kids meet yours." I recall Sara's excitement years ago at Louis and Emily starting a family, no doubt hoping to one day have a family of her own.

Emily leads us toward her living room, and busies herself making me a drink by the corner drink cart. Moments later, she hands me a glass full of amber liquid.

"Did Sara ever tell you how we became friends?" she inquires without taking her eyes off me.

"I recall her mentioning that your mothers went to school together."

She giggles, nodding her head. "Yes, our mothers are college friends, but Sara and I didn't really like each other when we were little. I was shy and Sara, well, Sara was never shy about anything. I suspect she didn't like being my friend because she constantly ended up punished when our mothers forced us to play together. I desperately wanted Sara to like me. I used to go to all her ballet recitals, but she was too cool to hang out with me. My mom always used to say that Sara would come around, that kids are mean, sometimes unintentionally, but that she was sure Sara loved me."

I listen to every word coming out of Emily's mouth as if a holy sermon; after all, she is one of the only links I have left to Sara.

"Everything changed once we got into sixth grade. I entered a silly talent show and chose to sing 'Wind Beneath My Wings' by Bette Midler. My parents couldn't come to the actual show, they had an out of town medical lecture that my mom was giving, so Sara's folks were supposed to come and support me instead. Sara's parents never showed up, but Sara still came by herself. She found me after the embarrassing performance and I can't remember being away from her from that point on. We were inseparable. She slept over at my house almost every weekend. We even invented our own '80s language to make sure nobody understood us. I thought I knew everything about her. I mean, I never believed half the things she said she did without me, but I was her best friend, and it was my job to listen. She shaped my life and taught me everything I know about friendship, boys, love, and sex." Emily snorts out a giggle. "I've done nothing for her. I just want to be a better friend. I owe her that."

I nod, happy at the prospect of Emily Bruel, public enemy number one, welcoming me into her home and sharing a part of Sara with me.

"Sara's here," Emily announces to me. Her words aren't making sense, as if far-fetched.

"Where?" I look around. The house seems empty. I haven't even seen Louis.

"She's downstairs in the playroom with the kids. She wanted to meet them and introduce herself to her children without you. She's not strong enough to see you and them together, not yet. But I think her finally meeting them will help her heal and get better."

I'm now standing with my back toward Emily, not wanting her to see my tears fall.

"Jeff, I hope you're not mad at me. She's been talking about them and missing them. She just wanted to meet them."

She doesn't need to explain herself for Sara wanting to see Juliet and Jacob to me. "I'm not mad, I'm happy. Jacqueline told the kids about their guardian angel named Sara, and they've been asking me to go find her ever since." I wipe the tears now fully running down my cheeks with the back of my hand and turn to face Emily.

She takes a TV remote and punches in a code. A huge oil painting above the fireplace disappears and is replaced with a big screen with a live camera feed of what appears to be the Bruel playroom. I instantly spot Sara sitting on the floor surrounded by pillows, talking to Juliet and fixing her hair.

Emily turns the volume up, walks over to me, and hands me the remote. She whispers, "Thank you for saving her life." Then she walks out of the room, leaving me spellbound as I watch and listen to the scene I've imagined and dreamt about for eight years. It's my Sara, who's not mine anymore, meeting her children for the first time.

Kali

"Like A Prayer" by Madonna

I walk into the bar and without Lauren or any of the staff members noticing me, I run upstairs, painfully clutching the key in my hand. I don't know who I'm trying to hide from. I own this place and have every right to be in Joella's private rooms just as much as Joella herself. I'm in a hyperaware state of anxiety, noticing things around me that I've never before registered, as the desire to feel close to someone without having to explain what's happening inside my mind suffocates me.

It's early in the day and the bar is still quiet. I look around to make sure I'm the only one upstairs as I draw the black curtains at the top of the staircase. I insert the old key Jeff left under my pillow and open the hidden door that only a handful of people know about, one of those people being the complex man I can't remove from my thoughts.

My decision to not call him back after my phone died was one of the hardest choices I've ever had to make, but I require time to digest and try to make sense of the things I now know, since logic and reason haven't been on my team ever since I met him. How can a perfect stranger make me feel everything all at once? He was married for fourteen years, he has children with his wife, who died of cancer, and I now know that his friend's sister played a damaging role in his life. But everything I've collected and learned about him makes no difference. He was right, nothing makes sense and I can't help him. Joella's reading means very little to me and I still don't know this other girl's name or what exactly happened between them once he got married. Did he use Joella's words as a crutch to justify his actions? And who's to say that my grand-mère's prophecy won't still happen? Why does he harbor such anger toward Joella if his life is not yet over?

He and Eddie's little sister may still have a future, if perhaps she's the girl with the biblical name Joella saw in his future—unless, of course, something happened to her, too. The thought of him with this nameless girl stings more than I care to admit, but it shouldn't, because he's not mine. I have no answers for him, I can't help him interpret my grand-mère's words, and therefore it only makes sense I stay away and let his life fall back into place. I was certain that once I heard the fortune, I'd know exactly why Joella chose him, but I'm just as much lost about their interaction as he is.

I slip the warm key, that hasn't left my hand, into the door and say a silent prayer before I enter my portal. As soon as I cross the threshold of the hidden apartment my grand-mère and my maman once called home, the scent of roses seeps in and neutralizes every part of me. The sweet familiar scent regenerates and clears my mind as if by magic. The last time I was here, I had Jeff with me, but it's time for me to face my ghosts on my own. I will get through this, with or without him.

I pass the room with the circular table at its center and carefully open the door leading to Joella's private apartment. It feels as if I'm walking into a museum or a frozen time capsule. It's the first time I'm here alone and I better not faint, because no one will catch me or find me this time. The dark living room reminds me of my tiny dollhouses my papa and I built back in Cassis.

There isn't a centimeter of wall space that isn't covered in my maman's pictures, who is still the most exquisite creature in the world. I pass by a mirror hanging between the hundreds of photographs, and when I catch my refection, I see what everybody else sees—my maman staring back at me. If I stand still, my reflection looks to be another one of her old photos hanging. Her eyes in every frame follow me, comfort me, as I walk around the room taking each morsel of the past in. A delicate, see-through, glass armoire on the far left side of the room stands full of vibrant colorful scarves. I can't contain myself; they call to me. I pry open the rusted glass doors and choose a green and brown floral wool shawl to cover my body and soothe my soul.

The fact that I'll need to go through all of Joella's belongings before selling this building cripples me. I don't want to be alone and I don't want to feel alone anymore, and this place reminds me of just how alone I really am. I don't regret coming here and spending time with the matriarch and last relative left to my maman, but now that she's gone too, I need to find a place that feels like home. The man with two colored eyes felt like home. It was only one night, but he still tasted like home should. I sigh, he is home; it's just that in this case, he's someone else's home.

I shake Jeff and his eyes from my mind and advance deeper inside. The last time I was here with him, I was hyperventilating and in shock. I didn't have a chance to inspect and touch this suspended encapsulated past that was left to me. I fainted but seeing it all now still seems familiar. I lightly push a half opened door and cringe at the awful shrieking sound it makes before I find myself inside the room that was once Joella's bedroom. Again, as if being slapped in the face with his memory, I experience something I have no right to feel for a stranger I can't stop thinking about.

I throw myself on a bed that's covered in white sheets and let out a cry that seems to come from somewhere too deep to name. No one can hear me and I make sure to let it all out. A good honest cry is sometimes the only answer. My cathartic sob finally subsides, followed by hiccups, and I can't help but take out my phone to look at the picture of his eyes again. I'm a horrible person for wanting someone who clearly doesn't belong to me. I lured him to kiss me. I orchestrated and forced our attraction. If I didn't come on to him in this room, we'd just sit like two regular adults and exchange words and nothing else. He was weak. He'd just lost his wife and I attacked him because he mentioned a piece of my past.

I won't ever call him again.

I've done enough.

I wipe my tears and sit up, inspecting the charming, feminine bedroom my grand-mère once slept in. The draped ceiling and the soft lighting make this room feel like a honeymoon suite at some overpriced boutique hotel somewhere in the south of France. I smile at the graceful statue of the dark-skinned saint that's placed prominently at the center of the room against the wall, adorned in dried flowers and melted candles.

After my maman's accident, and after her funeral, my papa and I haven't once visited a church—God couldn't help us, she was gone, and we had to live without her. We both felt responsible for her death in our own silly ways. But as I sit here on my own, surrounded by memories full of heartbreak, the urge to touch the patron saint of my people feels almost unbearable. I remove the relic from its chosen display and bring it close to my chest. I say another silent prayer and question the silence around me as to why I wasn't in the car that day with her? I ask for only one thing, I ask for guidance to help me find a place to call home, wherever that may be. I close my eyes, clutching the black Madonna to my heart, and the craving for sleep wins over my weary body. In my dreams I'm never alone.

I feel my phone vibrating under me as I wake up disoriented in a sunless room. I have no idea where I am as consciousness manifests. I adjust my eyes to the bright phone display and Lauren's chubby familiar face fills my screen.

"Hello," I whisper in a hackneyed voice that sounds as if I'm sick.

"Where have you been all day? I went up to your place twice already. Should I be calling the police to track you down?" I smile. Perhaps I'm not alone after all. If I went missing, someone would notice. Lauren would find me.

"You won't believe it, but I'm upstairs on the second floor. I fell asleep in Joella's bed." I hear her gasp even with the loud music and yelling in the background.

"Frenchy! How in the world did you get inside? Wait! Did you find a key?"

I touch Jeff's key that now hangs around my neck. His eyes materialize before me without warning and a stupid smile highjacks my lips against my better judgment.

"That guy that came asking about her a few nights ago—Jeff—he had a key. He left it to me before he ran away." I don't mean to sound disappointed, but I also can't mask how I feel. It will take everything I have to not call him back, but I have no choice. I need to leave him alone and not escalate our mistake—and him not calling me back confirms that.

"Why do I feel like you're not telling me something?"

"Nothing to tell, he's not important," I hiss out.

"Okay, whatever you say, Frenchy. That definitely sounds like nothing to me," she adds with a snort at the end of her sarcastic comment.

"I'm ready to sell the bar and I've decided that you and your mom should own it," I declare without warning, just having come up with my brilliant plan. I always knew that Lauren and her mother would be the only people I would ever consider entrusting this place to, and I don't need any money from them. I just want them to run it like they always have.

"Shut the fuck up. You know I don't have the dough to buy

this place from you. The building alone is worth millions." She giggles as if I just told her a joke.

"Lauren, I don't need any more dough. Joella and my maman left me enough of that. I just want peace of mind knowing this place stays in the family. The last couple of days it became clear I can't stay here; I don't belong. I feel alone without her here. There must be a place in the world where my heart will feel whole again." I continue rubbing the key as if a genie may pop out and grant me three wishes. No genie, no wishes, just a land of questions and a sea full of sorrow.

"Frenchy, Frenchy, haven't Joella and your mom taught you anything? Running away won't fill your heart. Your mom ran away to France but she never left. You first need to find all the scattered pieces of your heart for it to feel whole, and then no matter where you are in the world, you'll feel complete. Home is not a place, it's a state of mind. You had no intentions of leaving Rhode Island or this bar a few days ago and now you're ready to jump ship … tell me what happened with that good-looking bathroom creep!"

I have no idea how to explain Jeff to Lauren. I haven't been able to explain him to myself. Everything my eyes land on feels touched by him. But I shake my head and my hopes of Jeffery Rossi, until his image disintegrates and disappears. He's not my future; he's just a roadblock—an obstacle in my mind right now. I smile as hard as I can to tip my emotional scale and deny myself the urge to cry again. He belongs to someone else, he gave his heart away, and I don't need a man without a heart.

"There's nothing to tell. He was kind enough to tell me what Joella once told him fourteen years ago on the night they met, and I was lucky enough to get to hear it. It's that simple." My face begins to ache from the fake smile plastered on it.

"So you two didn't sleep together?"

Fuck! Is it that obvious?

"Why would you think we slept together?" I didn't say anything to Lauren or anybody else about him.

"I saw him leave through your staircase the next morning. I could be off, but I believe he was wearing the same clothes—I did get a good look at him and his attire when he first came in, just in case I needed to describe him to authorities. And another interesting little tidbit I picked up was the way he couldn't quite bring himself to leave and drive away. He just stood by his car, looking up at your window. It was very Romeo of him. It seemed as if he kept waiting for you to come running after him or something. And you seem different—blue, sad, very Juliet-ish. I don't know, I may have an overactive imagination and I may be overanalyzing your suspicious absence around here in the last few days, or perhaps I just put two and two together."

I hear the smile in her voice, and she's spot on. I'm an amateur. I wear my stupid feelings on the outside for the world to see and I can't fool anyone, especially her.

"He's no Romeo and I'm definitely not his Juliet. Yes, fine, we did sleep together. Which was a mistake, but at least now I have the key and Joella's words to him, so something good came out of him coming into my life and turning everything upside down." I'm all worked up when I have no right to expect anything of him. "Lauren, trust me, I made a mistake and so did he. We had no business touching each other. I just got carried away with his storytelling. It will never happen again. It was what you Americans call a one-night stand." I hate that saying, *one-night stand*. That term doesn't even make sense; we didn't do much standing on that one reckless night. And once again I'm drowning in thoughts of us naked together. I feel my face flush and heat quickly spread down the rest of me. Will I ever be able to think back to him and not feel anything? Will I ever be able to forget his eyes?

"So you're going after him?"

As soon as I hear Lauren's remark I begin to laugh out loud. "Really? After what I just told you, that's what you came up with? Am I going to find him?" Maybe she doesn't know me at all. "I'm doing the opposite of going after him. I'm running the other way."

"Why? Does he have a girlfriend? Is he married? Does he have kids? Is he one of those emotionally fucked-up dudes?"

Maybe Lauren is the fortuneteller. She just nailed each point and described Jeffery Rossi as if she were the one with him.

"Yes, to all of the above. This guy is bad news, and like I said before, we made a mistake. I got carried away with the serendipitous notion that Joella gave a random, handsome stranger a reading, and this so-called stranger actually came back. But I learned my lesson."

"Married with children and a girlfriend? Yeah, I'm with you, Frenchy. Run!" I sigh at her final assessment. "Do you want me to come up and get you?"

"No, I'll be okay. I think I'd like to spend more time here and look through some of the things she left behind. I'll leave this place unlocked and you can have whatever you and your mom would like. The rest we can donate to Goodwill or just dispose of."

I sit up and look around the cozy place that was once someone's home. Someone that is no longer of the same world as me, someone that once loved and lost, and I realize that life goes on with or without us. I spend the remainder of the day inside my grand-mère's sanctuary. I collect all the old pictures I can find, photos that I've never seen before. I find an ancient looking suitcase and begin to gather into it the things I don't want anyone else to have. I have enough shawls to open a store and enough photographs to fill twenty albums. Joella was such a simple woman. She had an abundance of wealth at her disposable and yet she had only a handful of trinkets that I suspect have more sentimental value than anything else. She didn't even own a television, just books, records and cassette tapes that are without a doubt my maman's. When I spy an accordion that I recall Joella telling me was my maman's first instrument, I clutch it to my heart as if it's alive.

Everything around me is a mess, including my crumbling life. It looks as if this apartment was turned upside down while robbed, and in a way, it was. I stripped it emotionally by removing its beating heart and leaving behind a stack of nothingness.

It's well past midnight as I force myself to leave the memory nest I've been lost in today. I carry down my heavy suitcase and that's when it hits me—I am a gypsy, it's in my blood. I have no mother to love me, no country to call my own, just a dream in my hungry heart of what love used to taste like and a longing to belong somewhere.

Six Months Later

Jeffery

"I Still Haven't Found What I'm Looking For[43]" by U2

When a person you meet once in your life, stays in your mind and strangely helps you get up and face the world each day, that person was sent to you for a reason and must mean something. I've gone to sleep and woken up every day for the past six months since meeting Kali with her image in front of me. Neither Jacky nor Sara have visited me in my dreams in many months, which strangely has helped me move on with my life and not soak in a pool of guilt. I wonder if I'll ever talk to Kali again. Besides looking at the few photos of her that inhabit my phone, I haven't done a thing to try and make contact with her. I don't have her last name—I'm sure it's not Gitanos, since that was her maternal grandmother's last name. I could do research and find out, but I won't. I know that if she wanted to speak to me she'd have called me by now; therefore, it's safe to say she got what she needed from our relationship, if you can even call it that, and walked away like the smart girl that she is.

I'm busy at the firm like never before. I haven't had any time to communicate socially with any of my old friends. My only free time I dedicate exclusively to my children. I'm a different man than I was a year ago—heck, I'm a different man than I was yesterday. The only person I make time to talk to besides Emily is William Knight. If a year ago someone told me that the person I would look forward to speaking with almost every day would be William fucking Knight, I'd have pissed in my pants laughing. At first, he just texted to let me know how Sara was feeling after the surgery, about her recovery, but with time, we've moved on and now we actually talk on the phone about regular shit like two guys who don't hate each other. I can't hate him knowing how good he is to her. I wish I could've been that good to her but I never was. A man who loves the mother of my children as much as I know he does can't be hated, just admired.

I have casually mentioned Kali to Will, unable to hold my feelings inside because some days I want to explode. I also thought it was important for him to know that I have feelings for someone who's not Sara. I was hoping to prove to him that he will never need to worry about me coming between them, ever again—I owe them both that. It's the strangest thing in the world, us talking to each other and confiding in one another like we have, but it's natural and it's clear that we no longer play for opposing teams. We have the same cause and many things in common—the most important being Sara Klein. I want her happy and smiling, and I will do anything for that.

Juliet and Jacob have been spending lots of time with Sara and William, as of lately. Sara has enrolled Juliet into a ballet program and takes her to class twice a week. The kids no longer refer to Sara as their guardian angel, like they did at first; they now just say that she's their best friend, Sara. The two of us haven't spoken about that night at The Pierre when she lost her baby, or anything else that happened before or after that moment. We haven't spent any alone time. She's been distant and reserved around me. Most of our communications go through William—or Liam, as she calls him—and I won't pretend that it's not painful for me, but I understand and accept it.

Will mentioned this morning that he and Sara will not be moving back to London like they had originally planned at the end of this year. Their decision to stay in New York and be close to our kids makes me thankful beyond words. It's the best news I've received in what seems like years. Children can't be fooled—they know when someone genuinely cares about them and isn't just being polite. They feel how much Sara loves them without anyone having to explain who and what she really is to them. One day, they'll know the whole story.

I've told Will about my impulsive road trip to Rhode Island six months ago. I vividly described to him how I acted like a lunatic trying to find some old fortuneteller, who has died, to demand answers for her silly words. I halfheartedly confessed how, instead, I found and foolishly slept with her granddaughter, whom I can't stop thinking about. He should be the last person in the world I speak to about this, but he's the closest thing I have to a real friend these days. He keeps urging me to take a chance and call her, find her, go after her. But I'm pretty sure she hasn't thought about me or our night together even once in the last six months.

Will, too, confided in me a few weeks ago that he's been trying, unsuccessfully, to get Sara to commit and set a new date for them to get married. But she's refused and he believes it has to do with her fear of not being able to carry a baby in her womb after her near fatal miscarriage. I hope to God for them to be able to have a baby. Seeing her with Juliet and Jacob only confirms what kind of amazing mother she would be, if given the chance. I understand her pain and I pray she finds comfort in knowing that Juliet and Jacob will always be hers, whether she has more children or not.

I have also taken the kids to visit their mother's grave a few times, attempting to explain to them as best I can how Mommy is in heaven waiting for us to one day all be together, but for now, she will be watching over us and keeping us safe. Juliet is convinced that the red robin that sits and sometimes knocks on her bedroom window every morning is her mommy waking her up for school. After witnessing the bird for myself more than once, I have started to believe that as well.

I'm going to make you proud, Jacky.

It's Saturday night, and the kids are spending the weekend with their grandparents; therefore, it's just me and my memories as I sit by myself in my big empty house wishing I didn't feel alone. My phone pings to life with a text. For a moment I wonder if it's Kali, but it never is.

-Are you busy?-

The moment I see her number, which hasn't changed in over fifteen years, I sit up. It's Sara, which forces my heart into my throat.

-I'm not busy- I type back as fast as my finger will allow me.

-Can we talk?-

I've waited to talk to her every day since she regained consciousness.

-Yes, of course-

I hold my breath for her lead, to find out if she'll call me, or want me to call her, or perhaps continue to text, when I hear a knock at my front door.

I drop the phone and run toward the door, knowing it's her but not quite believing she's actually here. I open the door without a moment of hesitation. She fills my doorway, and I never in my life imagined her here, in my house, about to come in.

"I hope it's okay that I've just invited myself over, but I know the kids are away this weekend and I'd like us to talk, alone, if that's okay?"

I'm afraid to make a sound and say anything, out of fear she may disappear. I step aside and watch her move cautiously past me. Her hair is back to its natural dirty-blond color, and the way she floats in you'd think I was dreaming. She looks around and smiles before returning her eyes back to mine.

"Nice place. Jacqueline had amazing taste."

I nod, still refusing to speak and chance the possibility of ruining this dream. She spies a project that Jacob brought home from school yesterday, which I've proudly placed on the kitchen counter. It's a picture he painted of his family tree with different color leaves applied to the branches with names and pictures attached to them. One of the leaves clearly says Sara with a photo I've supplied, and I can tell she just noticed her name by the genuine smile that bloomed and materialized on her pretty face, lighting up her eyes.

I think she's on the verge of crying as she clears her throat and half whispers, "If I didn't have Juliet and Jacob—my JJ in my life, I don't know how I'd continue living. They're my reason for waking up every morning, and I just want to give them the world. I never want them to feel alone, unloved or unwanted, because I love them and want them with every fiber of my being."

She can't stop herself and starts to cry anyway. I'm mustering all my strength to not cry with her. I take a few steps and come close to her. I should hug her and tell her how much she and the kids mean to me, but I promised her, the universe, and myself, that I'd never touch her again.

She closes the gap between us and wraps her hands around my waist as she allows herself to cry even harder into my chest. I let out a breath and wrap this strong, admirable girl as close to my heart as physically possible.

I finally find my strangled voice to tell her just how much our children mean to me, too. "I made so many mistakes with you since the first night we met. I led us down the wrong path, and I almost lost you, too. You're an amazing woman, Sara, and what you've been forced to live through makes you invincible. Juliet, Jacob, and I are the luckiest people in the world for knowing you. I promise you and William will get a happily ever after, and I will be the happiest person in the world for you. You deserve everything and you will have everything, don't ever doubt it. I will never be the one to stand in your way of happiness, ever again. We created two perfect kids and you will forever be a part of their lives. They love you."

She pulls herself away from me, catching her breath while wiping her tears and goes to sit in the living room. Without looking at me, she begins talking with that signature sarcastic smirk on her lips.

"I can't believe that you've told Liam things that you've never mentioned to me."

"Oh yeah, what kind of things?" I am a lawyer, I don't give away information unless absolutely necessary.

"Don't answer a question with a question, and don't try to deflect from the fact that you and Liam have become BFFs."

She's also a lawyer, so I may not be able to use my techniques on her.

"My pompous fiancé is very pleased with himself at how much he now knows about my ex—I mean, former … I don't even know who you are to me anymore." She covers her eyes with her hand as she lowers her head with a sigh.

I sit by her side. I'm not sure how to explain us and what we had, either. I can't say she's my affair, because that sounds dirty, and what we had wasn't dirty—our children are the biggest proof of that.

She looks up with the same eyes I get to see every day in our kids. "I know that we aren't the love of each other's lives. Jacqueline was the love of your life and I now know that Liam is mine. But I did love you. I still love you. I can't *un*-love you because that would mean un-loving our babies, and I'm beyond grateful for them. If it hadn't been for you and Jacqueline, those perfect little people wouldn't be in my life. I wouldn't have a life without them." She takes my hand and laces our fingers together and turns her body toward me. She reaches her other hand and caresses my cheek, making me feel human for a moment. "Thank you for saving my life, Jeffery. I know if I were alone that day I'd have bled to death and died. You and the children have kept me alive, and I promise to be here for you guys. I want you happy too, and I know your happiness doesn't lie with me. Now, tell me about this fortuneteller. Liam is being tight-lipped."

I laugh at the idea of telling Sara about Joella Gitanos. She'll think I'm a moron. And the moment I think about Joella, Kali's striking features fill my mind and a dull familiar pain begins to radiate inside. I've kept Joella's words tucked away for over fourteen years, but I already let them out once and they no longer have a hold on me.

"Do you remember when I stopped coming into the city to meet you?" She nods, of course she remembers. "I decided that it wasn't right for me to keep seeing you after I agreed to marry Jacky. I just didn't have the heart to tell you in person—like a man. I needed to end things with us and be with Jacky and give her one hundred percent of myself for as long as her disease would let me. So I just stopped calling and coming to see you. I thought that was the right thing to do, not get you involved in the mess that became my life. But then on the night I had planned to propose to Jacky, I got hammered at our local college bar. I went upstairs to pee and this old woman who always sat at the top of the stairs by the window called me over. At first, I was going to ignore her, but I couldn't. There was no one there but us. She offered me a reading, like at a carnival freak show, and of course I refused, but then she uttered a rendition of my name, which finally got my attention. It's weird. It just happened, and next thing I knew she was holding my hands, reading my palms."

"What did she say?" I hear the excitement in her voice.

Sara and I are still holding hands when I let go of her fingers and expose my palm. "She said that my life has collided with pain and suffering, but that once the girl with the biblical name grows up she will heal me and my life will be filled with music." I look at her as I let the fortuneteller's words penetrate and settle in her mind.

"Did you think she was referring to me?" She looks confused.

I smirk. "Yes, you're the only girl with the biblical name that I knew and you speak lyrics, so who else could it be? After her so-called prophecy, I had to come back and see you. In my stupid head it was a sign that you and I would ultimately end up together. We all knew that Jacky was very sick and the doctors gave her a horrific prognosis. I just wanted to come back and tell you that I'm sorry for hurting you, lying to you, and to explain to you that we couldn't be together for now, but one day, you and I would have a future. When I saw you, I couldn't just let you be. When I touched you, everything stopped hurting. I was afraid some guy would fall in love with you and take you away from me while I took care of Jacky. I imprisoned you with my promises and used this old woman's words as the key to justify my crime. She was wrong. She lied to me. I bought her lies and you bought my promises." I clench my fists and look away from Sara and the pity in her eyes.

"You didn't imprison me, you navigated my life toward the man I was destined for. Almost every choice I've made was because of you. Even if her words were false, what you and I created is true. I did grow up and I will try and heal you and our children after you've lost Jacqueline. Juliet will play the violin, Jacob will play the piano, I hear Liam can play a mean drum, Emily and I can sing some corny '80s songs … how much more music can you ask for?"

We both burst into laughter while the image of our Brady Bunch band comes into focus. Talking to her and seeing her laugh in my presence is nothing short of a miracle. It's one of the most splendid dreams I've ever witnessed come to life.

"I want you to smile like this from now on," I say in all seriousness.

"How about you? You can't keep beating yourself up over our past. It's over, and here we are together raising our kids. I don't know if you'll ever find another soul mate like Jacqueline, but I hope you'll let another love inside. I want you happy, too."

I crack a smile. "You're healthy, the kids are happy … what else could I ask for?"

"So, you gonna go after that girl, you know, the fortuneteller's hot granddaughter?" Sara gives me the side eye and her signature smirk.

I shake my head, rolling my eyes. "Did Will really rat me out like that? What a wanker you found yourself. I thought he and I were BFFs and now I feel violated." I laugh as my Sara cracks up, giggling by my side.

"He can't keep secrets, he blabs everything," she offers in her man's defense.

"Good, no more secrets." I stop smiling, ashamed of all the lies that once lived around us. I kiss her forehead and conceal the melancholy look off my face. I need to stay in the moment and be grateful for her role in our lives.

"Don't punish yourself, Jeffery. We've paid for our sins. Just find what makes you happy and go after it. You deserve to be happy, too."

I nod and accept her advice. Maybe one day I'll find another piece of my heart, another kind of love, but right now, I have

Sara, JJ, and the memory of Jacky, which is all the happiness I need.

Jeffery

"Twilight Zone" by Golden Earring

"I get the blue room for myself, right, Daddy?" Jacob asks me in the elevator before Juliet stomps her foot and yells back at him.

"Sara said we're sharing that room, so stop acting like a baby," Miss Bossy Pants adds, which will escalate this situation in 3, 2 … 1.

"Daddy, she called me a baby."

Here we go. I roll my eyes and try to shush them. The elevator attendant fails to hold back a giggle and I'm pretty sure this is the worst idea ever. The elevator comes to a stop on the 41st floor as my kids shoot out just in time to fly right into Sara's arms.

I'm not sure who's more excited about this sleepover, Sara or them. They're all squealing and jumping and there's a good chance Will and Sara will be asked to vacate their penthouse at The Pierre hotel after this visit.

"Is this wise?" I question Sara, but I doubt she can hear me with the screaming happening all around her.

"It's wise, now off you go," Will says half jokingly and grabs the small suitcase from my hands before escorting me back toward the door.

I really don't think I should be leaving them and running back to Rhode Island to go find some girl who clearly wants nothing to do with me—or my issues.

"Why you still here, mate? You need to go on about fetching your little buttercup while I attempt to bribe the neighbors from phoning the authorities on this beastly bunch."

Just as he says that, I hear a massive, ear-piercing shriek come from the living room as we both look up to see Juliet and Jacob attack what looks to be a fluffy little fur ball.

"You fucking got them a dog? I'll kill you. I'm not taking that animal back home with me, just so you know. I have enough animals I need to keep alive." I'm only half joking.

"Nope, don't look at me. She and Emily each brought home a bloody puppy last week. Apparently, Louis doesn't have much of a say in his household, either." He looks less pleased than me.

I smile with pleasure at the sound of the pure joy and excitement coming from my kids. "Thank you for doing this. I'm almost certain she'll tell me to hit the road, but at least I won't have to wonder *what if.*" I defend my daft move to go see Kali again.

"Exactly, but who knows, she might welcome you with open arms." Will winks at me as I leave my kids in the best possible hands and go quickly before I change my mind again.

It only took me four hours to make it back to Providence. Traffic and weather cooperated and my nervousness did a great job keeping me company. I've practiced repeatedly what I plan to say to Kali when I finally see her face to face and how I intend to beg her to give me another chance.

It's insanely busy tonight at BlackGod bar—I got lucky and found a spot across the street from the bar to leave my car. Mobs of college students fill every inch of space since it is Friday night, and this is obviously still the place to be. I walk in, or push in to be more exact, to look around and try to spot Kali or that blond bartender who really took a liking to me, I think sarcastically to myself. That same hesitant feeling that I had about leaving JJ with Sara and Will this weekend resurfaces.

I shove my way toward the bar and order a beer. I can't see a single even remotely familiar face behind the marble counter. Maybe I never actually met Kali. Maybe it was all a daydream? I take a few swigs at my beer and the ridiculousness of me coming all the way here without first attempting to call her or text her begins to clearly manifest.

I'm a fucking shmuck.

I finish my beer, still failing to identify anyone I could ask about Kali, which makes me question everything. I spot a waitress and ask her anyway.

"Hi, could you tell me where Kali might be?"

She motions to her ear, indicating she can't hear me, so I repeat myself twice until I give up and walk away.

I contemplate texting her and seeing how she's doing, but I chicken out and go upstairs to piss instead. The moment I reach the top of the stairs, I notice that the black curtains are gone. The door that was always hidden and locked is now wide open and seems to lead into a cozy restaurant.

I walk in to be greeted by a hostess.

"Good evening and welcome to Joella's. Do you have a reservation?"

I feel like an alien visiting another planet when I hear her questioning me again about some fucking reservation.

"Is there a girl—I mean, a woman—named Kali that works here?"

The short plump hostess that can't be old enough to drink

gives me a puzzled *beats-me* kind of look.

"No, sorry—no Kali here. Is that who you spoke to for your reservation, sir?"

I shake my head and look around before slowly walking out. What the fuck is going on here? Where is Kali?

I take my phone out and find Kali's number. I need to text her, and after ten minutes I come up with a very elaborate sentence.

-Hi-

I walk back down, deciding that I didn't come all this way to text her a fucking "Hi." I came here to see her pretty face and ask her out on a real date that doesn't include either of us talking about our pasts.

I exit the noisy bar and take a left, finding her private entrance, and follow the stairs that lead to the third floor and her apartment. I get to the top of the stairs, knock, and wait. My heart is beating in my stomach as I knock again, putting my ear against the door. I keep knocking until I finally hear movement. I brace myself for what's waiting for me on the other side of this door. She could be with another guy, or she could be alone and just tell me to go fuck myself.

The door swings open and the dark-skinned blond hair bartender who hates my guts fills the entrance. She's wearing a robe and has her hair up, which looks like a bird's nest, clearly not expecting company. She gives me the look of death and places her hand on her hip in obvious annoyance.

Great, this is what I need to deal with now. I should at least be happy that I found a person I actually met almost seven months ago, and that meeting Kali wasn't a figment of my imagination, but by the look on her face, there's nothing for me to be happy about. This woman despises me.

"Hello, sorry to barge in on you but I'm here to see Kali," I say as politely as I can, employing my so-called charm.

"Who?" she practically barks back.

"Kali, you know, the girl who owns this place."

She laughs at me, which infuriates me.

"I own this place, and I don't know who Kali is."

I smile at her because she's clearly not going to help me find Kali. Kali is probably inside having a laugh at this rib-tickling situation.

I figure I don't have much to lose as I push the door open further and yell into the apartment. "Kali, I know you're here. I don't want anything. I just want to apologize and talk to you. I'd like to start over. I can't stop thinking about you. I look at your pictures all the time and I just want a redo, a chance to get to know you from this point on," I yell, hoping my words reach her.

The highly-bleached blond is amused at my theatrical performance and adds, "O Romeo, Romeo! Wherefore art thou Romeo? There's no one here but me, asshole."

Is this really happening? Does the universe really hate me this much? I gently move the blond to the side and enter uninvited. I will find and talk to Kali if it's the last thing I do, and this woman or any other woman will not stand in my way. If Kali wants me to leave, that's exactly what I'll do, but I won't leave without her throwing me out herself.

"I know you're a big shot lawyer from New York City, but I can still kick your white ass," the lovely, welcoming Tasmanian devil informs me.

I look around Kali's apartment, and it's like I've invented everything. There are no instruments littering the living room. There's an actual couch with a big TV. I look around and nothing I recall from spending time with her is actually here. *What in the fucking fuck?* Maybe I'm in the wrong apartment.

"I told you it's just me," she further taunts me, pleased with my devastating state of disbelief.

I turn around, still in shock and I'm not sure how to get this horrible woman to tell me where Kali is. She couldn't just vanish. This was her grandmother's place, wasn't it?

"Wow! Your eyes are super freaky," she adds and all I want to do is scream.

"Can you ask Kali to call me, please?" I beg her.

"I told you, there is nobody named Kali here."

Her comment belittles and infuriates me to the point of rage.

"The girl I met when I was here six months ago—Joella Gitanos' granddaughter. Could you please let her know I was here and I'd like to speak to her."

She shakes her head.

This bitch makes zero attempts to acknowledge anything I say. I take one last look around to convince my disbelieving mind that Kali is, in fact, not here. I walk through the door, and without another word close it behind me. I drag my feet down the stairs and fumble into my car, completely disenchanted with my latest failure.

I can't stop wondering what happened to Kali. Maybe she moved to a different apartment or left altogether. *I waited too long.* Maybe she found a nice guy and he whisked her off to paradise. I smirk as I think that maybe she was just a figment of my imagination after all, and perhaps, I'm in need of some good ol' fashioned psychiatric help. If Jacky wouldn't have mentioned in her letter overhearing the old gypsy talk to me, I'd have concluded that to be a hallucination as well.

I take out my phone and find Kali's selfie that proves her existence outside my mind. It feels as if I just left her upstairs, and yet more than half a year has passed since we met. Looking at those eyes and lips, she seems too familiar to just be some girl—a rebound. I didn't even get a chance to tell her about JJ. If I never see or talk to her again, she will never know the full story that slowly stopped being shameful. I wish I could tell her I'm no longer upset with Joella, and that I stopped punishing myself for my past choices. I think, in a way, I even understand her prophecy, and she was right—I'm living my future. If only I could tell her this and hear her voice again.

I dial her number without thinking or analyzing what I'm doing. Less thinking, more doing, that's my new M.O. The phone rings three times before going to her voicemail, which doesn't even have her voice anymore but just a robotic "please leave your message after the beep." I hang up, and then before I get a chance to bail out, I call again. I wait for the message and begin recording. I have nothing to lose. I can't be ignored more than I have been thus far.

"Kali, this is Jeffery. I'm here at BlackGod and I'd like to see you more than I can express over the phone. I miss you and I want us to start over, see you again without bringing up the past. I want a chance to get to know you. I don't even know your last name, for God's sake. I want to hear you play all those instruments. I can't stop thinking about you. I—"

"If you're satisfied with your message, press one to send, two to delete, three to rerecord or four to continue recording."

I press four on my phone and keep yapping to a phantom robotic answering system. "Please call me back. I'll sleep in the car outside the bar waiting and hoping you get this message. Let's start over. I'm Jeffery Rossi, my wife Jacqueline died a year ago, I have two beautiful children—Juliet and Jacob—I met an incredible girl six months ago, and I haven't been the same ever since. I didn't sleep with anyone for two years before we made love on that night. I want a chance with you. I can't stop thinking about you. There are no other women in my life besides you. I know I have lots of issues, but I'd like a chance to explain face to—"

"You've reached the maximum recording time. Please press one to send."

I press one and send the message, and pray that Kali gets it.

"Tap, tap, tap."

I jump up, feeling my age the second I pry my eyes open. Every joint and muscle in my body aches. I squint my eyes, shielding the sun with my arm. I lower my window, not at all happy with my morning wakeup call.

"Meet me inside in ten minutes. I'm Lauren, by the way, and I still don't like you," the bartender declares in case I thought she suddenly fell in love with me.

"Top of the morning to you, too, Lauren." I rub my face and my neck, cursing my decision to spend a night in my car. I could've found a fucking motel. I'm not a kid anymore. But I was hoping Kali, and not sergeant Lauren, would come find me.

I check my phone; perhaps miraculously Kali texted me back.

I see a text from Will with dozens of pictures of Jacob and Juliet behaving silly and eating pizza. My favorite picture is of them fast asleep with the white puppy sleeping between them. I smile, wishing I was there right now instead of waking up in my car about to head in and talk to Lauren A.K.A. my biggest fan.

It's eight AM and the bar is obviously closed. I knock on the door and Lauren very graciously lets me in after making me wait for a good five minutes. I wonder if she plans on poisoning me, beating me with a bat, or just mentally abusing me?

"I got your message last night," she begins the abuse.

"Oh yeah? What message is that?" I'm genuinely interested in her sudden epiphany. She didn't seem to recognize me or Kali last night.

"I have her phone. She didn't need it where she went," she explains matter-of-factly.

I won't breathe until she says more.

"I got your voice message and I feel a little sorry for you. I still think you're an asshole, but I feel marginally bad for what you've been going through. I'm here to throw you a bone," she offers nicely but still sounds evil.

I nod because all I heard is that Kali is gone and this woman now has her phone and lives in her apartment. Something smells rotten. Should I be calling the cops?

"Where is she?" That's all I want to know. I need to know that she's safe.

"She's far away from here." Her answer does nothing to make me feel better.

"Is she okay? Did she leave the country? Can you give me her new number?" Lauren gets behind the bar and pulls a bottle of white wine from a locked cabinet. She expertly removes the cork and begins to fill two glasses of wine, as if she's a master sommelier. She hands me one glass, lifts hers in the air, and says, "Tchin-tchin."

I look at her confused, I guess I was correct—she plans to poison me.

She savors her wine, swirling it and sniffing it, lifting the glass to the light to inspect its color.

"Are you all sorted with your wife, girlfriend, and kids situation?" she questions. Obviously Kali has spoken to her about the things I've told her privately.

"It's none of your fucking business. Should I call the police and find out what you did with Kali?" This makes her spit out her wine and laugh maniacally.

"Yes, please call and try to explain to the police who this mysterious girl is you keep talking about—Kali, is that what you call her? Does Kali have a last name?" This girl may have a point.

"Can you just stop this bullshit? I didn't come here to drink wine or play detective games. Just tell me where she is." My voice betrays my confidence and reveals my desperation.

Before I can fire more questions, Lauren continues. "She gifted my mom and me the bar and left. I have no idea where she is physically. I believe she's purposely lost." Her response has a bittersweet ring to it.

She starts again with her stupid wine, inspecting the label as if all of life's answers are written on the damn bottle.

"I have no idea where she could've gone. She could be anywhere, but if I were a betting woman, which I'm not, I'd first go back to look for her where she probably got lost in the first place." She adds a wink to her sly smile, placing the bottle right in front of my face.

I inspect the label and see the name Château De LeBlanc, Cassis, France. And that's when the imaginary light bulb goes off. I smile and shake my head when I realize what Lauren is trying to do. I get up and walk behind the bar to give her a hug, whether she likes it or not. This Lauren girl, she may be all right after all.

"Is this necessary?" I hear her moan out in protest. "I don't like being touched. Listen, if you ever find her, if you mention me helping you, I'll come after you. You being a lawyer doesn't scare me." She can't keep a straight face with her futile warning.

"You have no idea what this means to me. I don't even know what do with myself, I have so much to tell her." I haven't felt this alive in twenty years.

Now I just need to find her.

Jeffery

"Hard To say I'm Sorry" By Peter Cetera

Sara and Will have become an integral part of my everyday life—they've become my lifesavers. Sara Klein has always been my physical form of therapy and escape. But Will, however, in my mind, was always my kryptonite until he became my most trusted friend and confidante. I wouldn't want to explain our out-of-the-box relationship to a stranger because I'd probably need to write them a book first, but here I am onboard Will's family jet, heading to Cassis, France, to go after the girl that I think and hope is indeed somehow a part of my future. You don't always need to have a long painful history with someone for them to earn a spot in your life. Sometimes strangers just come in and suddenly become everything all at once, and your subsistence begins to make sense. Life is a puzzle; we spend our youth collecting the pieces, and then we spend our adulthood trying to put all the pieces together to reveal the bigger picture.

I have no idea how I plan to find Kali in Cassis, if in fact that's where she is. But my gut is telling me to go find her and hold on to her hard with both hands. We may not have much of a past to anchor to, but we do have something in common: we shared a perfect night together and we were both lucky enough to have met Joella Gitanos.

I sit on the plane, hardly able to contain myself at the thought of finally seeing her again. The person I was before I met her wouldn't recognize this man who just spontaneously got on a plane to go follow a girl around the world. But ever since she entered my world, everything is different. *What if she doesn't want me?* The excitement begins to dissipate as reality comes to sit in the empty seat beside me. I have a crazy past that involves two women, two children, and enough chaos to merit any level-headed person to run. Why did she hang up on me? Why didn't I call her back? Could this all be a mistake? Mentally I try to convince myself that this is the right thing for both of us. She may not have chosen to collide with someone like me, but fate chose for her. *Leave her, go home,* the thought resonates in my head.

I look down at my hands, opening my palms. I see the place where Sara's name is tattooed on the inside of my ring finger. Do I deserve the love of another girl? I have my answer: she's a good girl, I'm a bad guy. I'm not getting off this plane when we land. I'm going back to my kids. I had enough adventures in my almost forty years on this earth that I'll be content just being Juliet and Jacob's dad for the rest of my life.

I close my eyes and will my brain not to summon the image of Kali sitting on the floor, wrapped in a floral scarf and passionately playing her violin soundlessly. If I try, I can almost hear the music, but some people like me never get to hear the harmony. I hope she finds someone good and fills his world with love that I can only dream about.

I send a text to Will.

-I've made a mistake. I shouldn't be pursuing her. When we land I'll make arrangement to come back home-

He calls me back almost immediately.

"What's this about? You were giddy as a pig last time we spoke and now you're running back home? You haven't even landed yet, mate." I can hear the disappointment in his voice, but I can't do this to her, it just isn't right.

"I was thinking about it."

"Well, there's your first problem, stop thinking. This has not a thing to do with what's proper or sane, this has to do with your heart. If people used their head when it came to love we'd all be single. If your heart can't leave her, then don't let your head talk you out of it. Listen to your heart, Jeffery. Everybody is cheering for you. We want you to find your happiness. If this girl makes you happy, go find her, don't wait, bloody tell her! It doesn't need to make sense for anyone but you. This is your future. It took you your whole bloody life to find her, and now you're running away from your destiny. I won't allow it."

I listen to the man, who was once my nemesis and is now my greatest ally, give me a pep talk, and he's right; as crazy as this seems, this woman has been a source of happiness that I never dreamed I'd find. I won't hurt her. I just need to find her safe and sound and beg to be allowed to love her.

"Jeffery Rossi, are you still bloody there?" I sigh, not offering any words, because I have none. "I know what you need." Will sounds hopeful. "You need your family by your side. You require all of us to hold your bloody hand and convince you that you are no villain. You hear me, mate?"

My eyes begin to tear and I'm thankful it's just me on this plane ride.

"You loved Jacqueline and took care of her for fourteen years. You loved Sara and did whatever you bloody could with the situation you were given. You love your children, and instead of being a shite arse and keeping them away from their biological mother, you allow them to spend time with her and help her heal. You saved her. She is my life, and I will make sure you find whatever piece of happiness was meant for you. You copy that?"

I can't actually speak with all the shit going on inside me. I just let the tears roll where they may, there's no stopping them now.

"Do the little monkeys have passports?" Will questions.

"What? Of course they have passports, why?" I hear him laughing and yelling Sara's name. What is that crazy Brit up to now?

"Sara, do you like Monte Carlo?" he asks her and I hear her say that she loves Monte Carlo. And then he adds, "Good, now call Emily and Louis and tell them we're going on a family holiday, immediately."

He gets back on the line and asks, "What's your little buttercup's full name, brother? Just so you're aware, between Louis and my dad, those two can locate an amoeba, if need be. Text me her name and I'll go tell the kids we're going on a trip. You're not getting lost on my watch. See you on the Cote D'Azur."

He hangs up without waiting for me to okay his outlandish plan, and I just sit there looking at my phone in a calm state of bewilderment as I realize that William, Sara, our kids, Emily, and Louis are about to meet me in the South of France.

Holy shit, is this real life?

Jeffery

"Hunting High and Low" by a-ha

I can't remember the last time I've been this happy. I look at the motley crew that clearly cares for me and has my back as we sail the Mediterranean waters on Louis and Emily's yacht "*La Vie en Rose*" headed toward the provincial seaside commune of Cassis. I don't let myself get too hopeful about the prospect of seeing Kali again, since nothing ever works out the way I imagine it. Right now I'm just going with the flow and allowing the hope and promise of tomorrow guide me.

Sara hasn't stopped smiling since we bordered this magnificent ship, while Will, Louis, and Eddie haven't ceased plotting like pirates. Whatever happens and whether or not we find the elusive Kali, which I still don't know her last name, the happiness I've already found will last me eternally.

Louis has informed us that he may have intelligence of Kali's whereabouts. Mr. Bruel has been able to track her down using the pictures I had saved on my phone. Louis, more so than anyone else, has been enthralled with her grandmother, Joella Gitanos, ever since he learned that she was one of the wealthiest inhabitants of Rhode Island, rivaling even the Newport royalty. He has been captivated by her anonymity and hasn't stopped telling us all the stories he's been able to find about her.

All I know from my conversations with Kali is that she was born and raised somewhere in Cassis, France, and therefore, we've decided to make that our first stop. I plan to go visit the Château de LeBlanc vineyard that Lauren so graciously pointed out to me, hoping perhaps they may know who Kali is. My quest for a girl that left her footprints on my soul has prompted a spur of the moment reunion that never in a million years would I have seen coming. I don't feel like the most hated man in the world by these people who've welcomed my kids and me with open arms and have made us feel loved. I see Sara and Will together and I'm no fool—she and I never shared what they have, and I long to one day be lucky enough to find that, too. Finally, I believe that faith has delivered Sara in the right hands. Watching all our kids play and interact is my greatest happiness, and I hope Jacky is looking down on us and can see the smiles on her children's faces.

"You nervous?" I look behind me to see Sara, wrapped in a blanket, approaching.

"Nope, not nervous. Ready." It's the truth.

"Tell me, what are you thinking?" Sara comes to stand by my side, with the wind blowing her hair off her face.

"I always trusted in what that fortuneteller told me. She waited for me at the top of those stairs because I was somehow a part of her path. Maybe she knew exactly when to tell me what she did. She could've spoken to me years before that, but she didn't. This is her doing—it was her job to implant a future in my mind in which both you and Jacky were part of. I get it now. You and I were never meant to stay together, we were just meant to collide and cause an explosion in order to bring about our true destiny. We all have roles in this world, and you and I created Juliet and Jacob. That was our purpose. You and Will are clearly perfect, and perhaps, I was destined to meet Kali." I look into the eyes that I love and realize that there are so many loves that make up a person, and each love is different, never the same love twice.

Sara smiles and laces her arm in mine. "Liam and I got married," she tells me.

I look at her and open my mouth in shock. She nods her head and I swear I can see the low perched moon illuminating with happiness in her bright eyes.

"Does everybody know?" I question with the biggest, most genuine smile plastered on my lips.

"No, I don't want to say anything to anyone until we get back home. We'll have a big party and announce it officially."

I engulf her in a hug and kiss the top of her head.

"Liam was going to tell you but I wanted it to be me. I hope you can be happy for us, despite our past or perhaps because of it," she explains with caution.

My heart beats out of my chest with happiness that feels like my own. Those two deserve every last drop of magic left in the world. I can actually feel my heart swell with pride and gratitude at having her tell me herself. I guess you never stop loving people. You just adjust your perspective and love them in different ways.

"I'm happy for you, you know that, right?"

She nods. "I know. I just want you to stop blaming yourself and feeling responsible for me. I'm not that fifteen-year-old girl you met on the dance floor. I'm not the eighteen-year-old you found shaking and crying in the backseat of that cab. I have made choices and you are not to be held accountable any longer. I'm lucky to have every single person on this boat shape my life—especially you and JJ. I wouldn't be here without you guys. If this Kali girl gives you a hard time, I'll beat some sense into her." She makes a fist and winks. "I have no doubt that if you care about her to come this far, she must be special. Now, tell me your plan, because if you listen to Louis, my brother, or especially Liam, you may be charged with kidnapping."

We both laugh at her accurate assessment of "Operation Find Kali."

"I'm the lucky one. What would I do without you?" The thought of a world devoid of Sara squeezes my insides.

"You'll never have to find out."

She gives me a tight hug before leaving me standing by myself on a dark deck to watch the waves bring me closer to the girl I can't stop hallucinating about. I feel invincible with this bunch adamant on me finding the woman I've somehow convinced my heart should be mine, the old gypsy's alluring granddaughter, of all people. I think, in a way, each and every one on this boat has found their other half and they want me to have what they have. I had that once with Jacqueline but it was tainted by constant fear, pain, and our lies. I hope I get another chance at happiness—a chance to do it right.

I continue to stand on deck and inhale the crisp night air, allowing the Mediterranean Sea to remind me of Kali and her sweet scent. I take out my phone and find her picture. Her features have become incredibly comforting and more familiar than my own. I sometimes think I'd probably be able to find her based on touch alone.

Lauren gave me back the key I'd left that night for Kali under her pillow all those months ago. I've carried it around with me at all times until we meet again and she becomes my talisman.

Tomorrow morning I will be in Cassis, her Cassis, onboard the fucking Love Boat. Tomorrow can't come soon enough.

I wake up to Juliet and Jacob both jumping on my bed like the little monkeys they are. They're excited that the boat has stopped, screaming and shouting for me to look out the window. I grab them in each hand and lift them in my arms to go look outside. The picturesque scenery sooths me as dozens upon dozens of little fishing boats all around us dance on the crystal blue waters. I gasp at the proximity of the hills and the cascading buildings surrounding the harbor; it all looks painted, surreal. I put my kids down and walk out on the balcony to inhale the fruity aroma in the air. It's as if she's standing right there. It's early, but the city up ahead in the distance seems alive with movement, making my heart drum with purpose once again.

The kids run off to play with their friends—they're all calling each other cousins, which the women find adorable. Emily and Sara have already married Jacob off to Rose and Juliet to Eric, which is quite amusing but a bit premature. I stand stone-like, not fully trusting where I am, who I'm with, and who I'm here to find. Perhaps this is just a dream, *a beautiful dream.*

I turn when I hear a knock on my door and see Will pop his head inside my cabin.

He looks worried, as if he hasn't slept all night—a bit jitterier than his usually calm, carefree self. "You're okay? You look seasick." I'm hoping Sara is feeling fine, I don't want her or anyone else to suffer while on this boat because of me.

He shakes his head and tries to avoid looking me straight on. "Bad news, mate, I don't think she's here," he announces stoically. "My dad rang earlier and a reputable source of his confirmed that there's a good probability we won't find her … I mean here—we won't find her here. I'm sorry," he adds with panicked red-rimmed eyes that divulge him probably keeping something away from me.

And the bad news begins. I sigh and roll my eyes. Did I really expect this to be a smooth sailing kind of trip?

"Don't be cross, we'll still spend the day here and then continue sailing," he declares with a hint of defeat. In an attempt to keep the morale up he then offers, "The kids are having a blast, this holiday was exactly what we all needed."

I nod, *yeah, no big deal, just a minor setback.* "Sounds good. Can you and Sara handle Juliet and Jacob today? I'd like to go into town on my own and visit a local vineyard, maybe find someone who knows her." I can't let this curveball discourage me.

"Sure thing. Take your time. We'll go walk around the village and see what Cassis has to offer. Maybe we'll take the kids fishing or to the beach." I can tell he's trying hard to sound excited.

I thank Will and begin my day getting better acquainted with Kali's hometown. I recall her telling me she hated the sea, which must've been hard for her growing up around here, since everything seems to be centered around water.

The Bruels' massive yacht is anchored ten minutes' boat ride away from the harbor of Cassis. I disembark the yacht into a small boat waiting to taxi me to Port Miou. The long-winding port is encompassed with white limestone cliffs that are overgrown with emerald-colored pine trees and the clear turquoise waters glisten around me like glass. I can't get over how breathtaking this town is.

I thank my skipper as I'm immediately greeted at the port by my driver for the day. Louis has arranged for him to bring me to the address I was able to find printed on the wine bottle Lauren so graciously gifted me. I look around as we drive through town, leaving the sea and climbing the hills inland. Everything that meets my eyes is vivid and alive with this town's infamous black currents sold and depicted everywhere.

I'm peacefully withdrawn when I realize the driver stopped the vehicle, bringing us to the gates of what looks to be a grand estate. I slowly get out of the car and soak in the indescribable landscape. If I'd grown up here, I'd never leave.

White limestone amphitheater cliffs surround the vineyard in front of me, which leads my eyes right down to the clear azure waters of the bay below. The name 'Château Kali de LeBlanc' is beautifully written on one of the stone pillars, which hold the slightly ajar wrought iron gates, lined on both sides with olive trees.

My eyes are transfixed on her name printed on stone confirming her existence. This is where Kali is from. Lauren didn't just direct me to some vineyard in Cassis; she led me right to the place Kali was born. I have no doubt that this is the place where she grew up and spent her whole life until she moved to Providence, Rhode Island five years ago when she decided to go live and get to know Joella Gitanos. The knowledge that I'm standing at the gates of her home, the place where she was raised, affects me in an indescribable way. I feel as if I belong here.

I touch her name on the metal plaque, pretending for a minute it's her my fingers are caressing. I push open the gates and walk down a pebbled road leading to a white Mediterranean style estate. An older man stands at the door with his hands in his pockets, assessing me as I approach.

"Bonjour," I offer in my best French accent.

"Hello," he answers.

"Do you speak English?" I'm hoping he does because my French sucks.

"I speak English, not worse than you speak French," he retorts with a slight French accent.

I smile and nod. Just as I'm about to come closer and properly introduce myself, he raises his hand in the air for me to halt.

"This is not one of the tasting vineyards open to tourists, and I'm afraid I won't sell you any of our wine, so please don't misuse your time." His words clearly tell me to leave.

I nod, a bit surprised by his unwelcoming comment. I ignore his warning and proceed to try and reason with him. I remove my glasses and state, "I'm here to find a girl—I mean, I'm here for Kali," I correct myself, but I've already messed up. I can see the way he reacted to me saying her name. His face pales and his eyes enlarge. It's clear I just fucked up and dug my own grave. I may as well hand him the gun.

I apologize, not sure for what, but if this man, who I suspect may be Kali's father, wanted to throw me out before, he's most definitely about to kick me off his property for coming looking after his daughter.

"Are you a friend of Kali's from America?"

I nod. Yeah, one could say we're friends, in an overly friendly kind of way.

"She's gone. It's best if you leave." He turns around and begins to walk away, forsaking me to stand outside like a stray dog.

I wonder how he would feel if I told him how much I care for his daughter and that I can't think about anything but her. What if I told him that I once met his mother-in-law and that I think it's his daughter I'm destined to be with?

I decide to say exactly what I feel. I don't need his approval to go find Kali, but I want him to know my intentions and that he can't just send me away by telling me she's gone.

"I came to Cassis to make sure Kali was okay since she left the States without much warning. I was hoping to see her and speak to her. I care very much for her," I admit honestly. However, by the look on his face, it's clear he doesn't care much for my honesty. He turns to face me before he will most likely close the door in my face, sporting the look of death.

He tilts his head to the side and smirks. "You are a bit confused. I don't believe you care for Kali because you haven't had the pleasure of knowing her." He walks inside, and to my surprise leaves the door open.

I follow him without an invitation. Infuriated at his dismissive assessment of my feelings towards Kali. I know how I feel—I care about her more than he knows. I can't stop dreaming or thinking about her. She isn't just some girl; she's important to me and I need to talk to her.

Inside the house, I feel as if I'm nine years old instead of thirty-nine and about to tell the principal why I kissed a girl in the playground. He proceeds deeper into his impressive home, silently choosing a chair overlooking the lush vineyard and the blue sea. He takes a wine glass from the side table and motions for me to sit on a chair across from him.

"My daughter wasn't herself when she returned from America a few months ago. I'm not *stupide*, I didn't expect her not to change, and after all, I never even dreamed she would come back here after meeting her grand-mama. You always know when your kids change. I had a feeling she was running away from something, or in this case, *someone*. She mentioned you, when she had no choice," he adds reluctantly.

A tiny smile of hope finds residence on my lips, a smile that I should probably wipe off, but I can't because I just heard him say that Kali mentioned me. I try my hardest to school my features and look serious, but it's impossible.

"Sir, I have things I need to tell her. She doesn't know everything, yet. I need to make things right and tell Kali that I love her." The words fall effortlessly from my mouth because they're the truth.

I've never said out loud that I love her, but I feel exultant in unburdening my feelings and uttering them to her father.

His eyes enlarge as he makes an animated, shocked expression and then starts laughing at me—a full-blown, loud, need-to-put-the-glass-down, body-shaking kind of laugh. I hold my breath because if he tells me I'm too late and she's with someone else, or that he doesn't want someone like me for his daughter, I may have a heart attack and start crying like the nine-year-old boy he makes me feel.

"I, too, would like another chance to tell Kali that I love her, but I don't think she can hear me," he states, no longer laughing.

I'm beyond puzzled at his reply. I'm at a total loss of how

to answer him back. Why can't she hear him, does he not have her number?

"Godfrey." He calls me by the name Joella once did with certainty. "Kali is dead."

Wait, I don't understand, she's dead? As in not alive ... no, she can't be dead!

"Dead?"

When those words resonate and echo in my head, I feel as if someone pressed a button to stop my heart and eject all the air out of my body. Saliva goes down the wrong pipe and my attempt to breathe quickly morphs into violent choking. Tears run down my face as I cough for air and for someone, anyone, to make him take back his words. I'm now ready to wake up and for this bad dream to end. It can't be that everything I love gets taken away from me.

He looks away from me and I have no doubt he will continue to rip my life apart with more words. He gets up and walks over to a table covered with fruits and beverages expertly arranged. He pours water into a tall glass in what feels like slow motion. He approaches and hands me the glass, but I refuse; I want to choke to death, I don't need his water.

"Kali, my beautiful wife … she died in a car crash close to fourteen years ago, on the same day that was also her birthday. I thought she didn't come home because she was upset with me for pretending to forget her birthday that morning. We had a big surprise for her but she never knew. She was the daughter of the legendary Joella Gitanos of Providence, Rhode Island—you may have heard of her," he says with a lascivious smile. "My friend, a local fisherman, the same one I'd buy fish from, found her car at the bottom of the sea. She was covered in water, just like her mère predicted and wrote. But it's not Kali you came here for … it's our daughter, Sarah, that I believe you claim to love," he says, finishing me off for good.

No, no, this can't be right. I must've choked to death and now I'm hearing things.

"What did you say her name was?" I need to make sure this is real life. I refuse to believe my head; it's deceived me before.

"Her name is Sarah LeBlanc. She was named after her mama's and grand-mama's favorite saint, Sarah La Kali, to help keep her safe. Sarah La Kali is the patron saint of the gypsies; she's the black Madonna. I remember my wife would sometimes call our baby 'La Kali' when she was a little girl." His words and tears come out at the same time when he recalls his wife.

Sometimes in life, everything stops. Everything you thought you knew becomes illuminated and retold in a different light. This man has just ruined me with a few sentences, and simultaneously set my entire existence back on its axis, stopping it from spinning out of control.

Sarah?

Sarah?

Sarah?

It takes me a few minutes to reteach myself how to breathe and speak again. Oxygen is reaching my brain at über slow speed because life will never be the same after this moment.

"Why did she tell me her name was Kali? Why didn't she just say her real name?" I question him with misplaced anger, as if he knows or is at fault for his daughter keeping her real name away from me.

He blinks away the tears. "You'll have to ask her. She mentioned to me that Joella frequently addressed her as Kali in the last few years. She was old; she may have imagined that Sarah was her lost daughter, Kali. Sarah does look very much like her beautiful mama once did. The eyes, the hair…" He closes his eyes, traveling back in time.

I don't have a choice but to accept his explanation and scream inwardly at everything unfolding before me.

"I'm sorry about your wife. Your daughter told me about her. I … I need to go find Kali—I mean, Sarah." I trip over my own words. It's the first time I say the name *Sarah* and it means something completely different in my life. In my head, she's still Kali while I attempt to wrap my brain around the fact that Kali's real name is Sarah. I hear Joella's prophecy on constant loop, replaying in my head like a broken record. How could she have known this? Could her words actually come to be? Is the girl with the biblical name, the one that was meant to save me, could she be Sarah LeBlanc and not Sara Klein? Did I get it all wrong? The proverbial rug is being pulled from under my so-called life, but suddenly, for the first time since that day Joella spoke to me over fourteen years ago, I am able to see my future with lucid clarity.

"My name is Victor LeBlanc. I am the surviving husband of Kali Gitanos and the father of Sarah LeBlanc. It's good to meet the man who claims to love my daughter after only meeting her once, I believe. But I am no hypocrite. I fell for her mama before she even said hello to me. Did my daughter tell you why her mama left America to come live with me in France?"

I shake my head. I know it had to do with Joella and something she may have said about her future, but we didn't get that far.

He sighs and offers a defeated grin. Placing his hands in his pockets, he turns his back on me to gaze toward the blue waters in the distance. "Joella Gitanos would go to great distances to make certain her heirs do not ever suffer. But she's not God, and her gift can't change the future. All she can do is see small parts of it and then try to piece it together, which is in itself a curse. To know, but not be able to do a damn thing about it except try and help her loved ones suffer less, that's all she can do. Growing up, my wife wasn't allowed to go anywhere near a body of water. No baths, no pools, no rivers, no bays, no seas, and no oceans. Joella wouldn't even permit her daughter to fly over water—crazy woman.

"Thirty years ago, I came for a visit, and when my family

and I stopped at a local historical pub that sold our vin rouge for years, it didn't take me long to fall madly in love with the striking American girl behind the counter. I have never seen anybody like her. My family returned to Bordeaux, but I stayed; I couldn't leave after meeting her. I enrolled in university and continued courting the most breathtaking girl in the world to try and convince her to give a good-looking French boy the time of day.

"I would come to the pub every evening to keep an eye on the young girl I knew would one day be my wife. One night, I went up the stairs to use the lavatories when an elegant gypsy woman, dressed in rich, vibrant robes and adorned in gold chains, called upon me for a reading. I laughed and couldn't help but become captivated by the theatrics of it all. She took hold of my hands and my life changed forever. She traced my lines and told me I would have one daughter but that my happy life wouldn't last because the sea is jealous. She said my life was about to collide with pain and suffering, but perhaps, I could change my future by staying away from the sea. Perhaps I fell in love with the wrong girl, she said. I remember looking at her and wondering what kind of horrible fortuneteller she was. Shouldn't she say good things to me? Isn't that what people pay her money to do? I removed my hands from her grip and was about to leave when she said that if I leave and go back to where I came from, I could escape this horrible fate and perhaps have a new one with someone else and spare the poor girl from being surrounded by water and dying too young."

I look at this man, disbelieving my ears once again. His encounter with Joella has a familiar ring to it. Why would she play with our lives like that? Why would she try and navigate him away from his destiny with her reading? Didn't she want her daughter happy and in love?

"Do you understand what she tried to do? She wanted to run me out of town, thinking she would save her daughter because she saw me in her future. Thinking that by me leaving, Kali would be safe and away from water. I was a fool. I didn't believe a word she said and I decided to stay in spite of her cruel words, because I was in love and I couldn't see a life without the most beautiful girl in the world.

"I told Kali about this horrible woman I met at the top of stairs—not the prophecy, just our encounter, which she later informed me was her mère. She was very upset with her for giving me a palm reading. She said she's never seen her read anyone's hands. I wasn't going to tell Kali the gypsy's forewarning prediction. Joella, too, wouldn't tell her daughter what she had read on my hand. There was a great big argument between them with lots of crying, words and threats being thrown around. Kali had found one of her maman's journals, and after reading it, decided she needed to leave Rhode Island, her home, her friends, and outrun her maman's predictions. She wanted not a thing to do with Joella, and even refused her inheritance. The only object she couldn't part with was her beloved violin.

"The two of us ended up leaving America and came to build a life in Cassis. Before you ask why Cassis and not Bordeaux, I will tell you that Kali only agreed to leave if I took her to a place her mère would never find her, a place surrounded by water. Joella knew my family and our wineries in Bordeaux, but she had no knowledge of Cassis.

"Kali and I—we were children and she just wanted a new start. We wanted to be together and live our lives and run away from the silly prophecy that I was told and she had read. But you see … that old, retched woman knew how her own daughter would die, and she couldn't do a damn thing about it. Maybe if she didn't say what she said to me that night, maybe Kali wouldn't have found her journal and read about her own death, and maybe we would have stayed and lived in America and Kali wouldn't have ended up at the bottom of the Mediterranean Sea. But everything she tried to do brought us to our fate—almost as if her mission was to send us away toward our destiny." He closes his eyes and smiles as if in pain, probably holding back more tears. It reminds me of how his daughter also tries to smile while chasing tears away. I imagine he must be thinking how everything in life only makes sense and becomes clear after it happens, and sometimes, it's too late.

He continues talking with his eyes shut. "Joella told my wife the night before we left Rhode Island that she knew she would never see her again, but that she would not leave this world until her only granddaughter was set on the right path. Kali refused to believe in her own maman's visions, calling her evil and crazy. She wouldn't even tell people she was a Gitan or, as you Americans call it, a gypsy. As an only child to a single parent, Kali vowed we would have ten kids, but Joella knew there would only be one, sweet, talented little girl, who looked just like her mama and loved to play her violin.

"The last thing Joella told her daughter was that she couldn't follow her while she tries to run away from her destiny, because her job was to wait for a boy named Godfrey. A boy with two different eye colors and two different lives to find her granddaughter with the key that she will give him. I know who you are, Godfrey. I knew exactly who you were when my daughter came back home and spoke about losing her heart to a complicated man. I've been waiting for you for thirty years."

Every word from his mouth leaves me in a complete and total state of marvel. But it also brings me a step closer to Sarah—his daughter Sarah, the gypsy's granddaughter … my Sarah. I need to go. I need to run. I need to tell her who I am and what she is to me. I impatiently get up, not able to wait another second. I'm speechless. He must know that I have to go find his daughter immediately or I'll disintegrate.

"Saintes-Maries-de-la-Mer is where you'll find your promised future, Godfrey. Be good to her, she's all I have left," he adds as I nod my head, frantically understanding what I was born to do and run out the door.

The driver brings me back to the harbor in a flash. My mind hasn't stopped racing in a hundred different directions since I ran out of her father's vineyard. I run toward the place where all the little boats are docked, but they're all empty. I look around for anyone who could bring me back to the yacht, but there's no one in sight; it must be lunchtime. I get impatient and decide to row myself back to the ship and have someone bring the boat back later. I can see the Bruel yacht docked prominently in the distance—how hard could this be?

I jump in an empty moored vessel, and after untying the rope, begin to row like a lunatic, like a possessed animal, like a man who just stole a boat. I need to get back and find Kali, I mean, Sarah.

The strong sun reflecting off the white limestone Calanques lining the port is literally burning my skin. I stop rowing to catch my breath and let go of the oars to unbutton my shirt, contemplating whether I should jump into the calm Mediterranean Sea to cool off. I sit still in my stolen boat and allow my reality to filter through the manic haze around me. *How can all this be happening?* I lie down, breathing in and out slowly to prevent the inevitable panic assault, and that's when I realize just how emotionally and physically tired I am. And then it dawns on me that I need to tell Sara Knight that we are halfway around the world looking for another Sarah.

"You mean to tell me she's bloody alive?" Will questions again for the third time as if he can't believe that the girl we've been searching for could actually be alive. Since getting word from Will's father last night, they were all under the impression that Kali passed away and were trying to figure out gentle ways to tell me she was dead.

I look around the table at everyone's faces, and they mirror my own baffled state of mind. I have just finished recapping my fucked-up life to the six people I've known for a very long time; the same group of people who know my life and the choices I've made. They've seen the struggles I've lived through and the heartaches I've caused and survived. However, I direct my speech mostly to one person—Sara, who quietly listens to me tell the same story she already heard before about a gypsy fortuneteller changing my life. But now she is no longer the girl with the biblical name at the center of my world that will save me, and I desperately want to know what's going on inside her complicated mind.

Without any announcements, Will, Eddie, Michelle, Louis, and Emily all get up and leave the table simultaneously. It's just Sara and me, the last two people left in the world staring one another down.

"Say something," I beg her.

The wind has picked up since we set sail for Saintes-Maries-de-la-Mer, blowing Sara's light hair toward her face, shielding her eyes from me.

"Jeffery, I hope you don't think we were a mistake?" she states in a small voice laced in worry and fear.

"No! Never! I wouldn't change a thing, even knowing what I know now, I would still do it all the same. You are one of the best decisions I have ever made, and Jacob and Juliet are all the evidence I'll ever need to know we were meant to be in each other's lives. I have to believe that Joella deliberately intercepted my life, which greatly affected your life, and that's what brought you to Will and me here."

She looks out toward the distance at the glistening water surrounding us.

"Jeffery, that's not why I'm upset; I know all of that. I don't doubt our purpose or regret the choices that have gotten us to this point in our lives. I just don't want you to move JJ away from me. I may not be your salvation, but they're mine," she begs with tears streaming down her cheeks.

I gasp at her words and her fears. I get up and walk over to her and kneel at her feet. I make her a promise right here and now. "I will never move away. I will never take your kids away from you. I will never hurt you or them, ever again. I've done enough hurting to last me two lifetimes. You will always be a part of my heart and my soul. I will make sure you are always loved and that you have the most excellent life; the kind I promised you, but could never give you because it wasn't me you were created for."

She wraps her arms around my neck, sobbing loudly into my shoulder. We stay huddled together like two lost children as the universe reveals itself with yet another piece of the puzzle.

"I can't believe that your Kali is actually your Sarah. Wait here," she announces and runs inside, leaving me on deck alone.

She returns with a pen in hand a few minutes later. She takes hold of my left hand and turns it to inspect my open palm. She finds with her fingers the faded place where I had her named tattooed under my wedding band fifteen years ago and writes S A R A H over it with her pen.

"I'll always be your first Sara, but I hope that she'll be your last. Our kids will have both of us guarding them and you from now on, just like their mother promised them."

I nod and smile at her heartening comment.

Sarah LeBlanc has no idea how many people she's about to inherit, but I bet Joella Gitanos knew.

Sarah AKA Kali

"Alone" by Heart

I've lived in Cassis for most of my life, and I never knew that one of the reasons my maman and my papa chose to live here was because of its proximity to Saintes-Maries-de-la-Mer. I sit in the place my parents visited over twenty-five years ago after they got married to ask the black Madonna—Sarah la Kali—for guidance and protection. My papa told me a few weeks ago that my maman vowed to name her first daughter after her beloved saint as a token of her love and devotion. I now realize that all the women in my life, in their own way, are connected to this patron saint of the Gitan people, which I am proud to be a descendent of.

With my papa's blessing, I have decided that I must join this pilgrimage for my soul that somehow got lost between here and there. This grand festival to honor Saint Sarah only takes place once a year, and I'm fortunate to be here on this magical, warm day in May.

I have spent over four hours standing in this crypt below the church of Saint Michael with the statue of Saint Sarah watching over me. I have told her about everything and everyone that lives inside my heart, both dead and alive, and I hope she will hear and answer my prayers like only she can.

The sense of loneliness that wouldn't let me stay in Rhode Island has greatly diminished since I came back to my place of birth. I now get to carry the matriarch of my family with me everywhere I go, tucked inside my heart, never again allowing myself to feel alone. I kiss the locket dangling around my neck with the solace of knowing the women I've lost will always guide me. I have transported and hidden all of Joella's journals just as she left them—unopened, un-violated—except one. The saint I was named after, the same glorious daughter of God that I now sit at her feet, graced the leather covers of the one journal that was meant for me to find and read. My grand-mère has been writing my book since before I was born, moving all the pieces necessary to help the stars align. I have vowed to my papa to never read beyond the point I am at right now or how my life will one day end, but I have read enough to know that I am in the right place and on the right path.

As hard as I've tried, I haven't been able to stop thinking about him once from our one night together over a half a year ago. I don't feel bitter for having met and touched him, and with the new direction my heart has swung, I accept my destiny and his contribution to it. He will forever be etched in my past, and I will forever be grateful to my grand-mère for bringing a mysterious stranger named Jeffery Rossi into my life, even if for one night.

I smile as I realize that he will never understand what I now know, and perhaps that, too, is for the best. My chest aches as I recite Joella's words to him in my mind. She wrote in her journal that Godfrey will come carrying the key to my future, and he did. I think back to how clear and simple my grand-mère's words to him were. She was describing me in her prophecy—I am the girl with the biblical name, it was my hands that create the music she spoke of, but Jeff has no idea. He believes Joella made a mistake, but she never made a mistake, and he will never have the privilege of knowing.

In a positive mindset, I recognize the role I was meant to play in his life, in his moment of weakness, and I'm indebted for the role he played in mine. I try to not think or imagine him outside our short, fated interaction, because it's senseless and still painful. I'm certain he went back to that young girl he always loved—Eddie's little sister, now that his wife has passed away and fate no longer stands in their way. I'm sure they found each other—as lovers always do. I don't wish him mal, and I truthfully hope they finally have a happy life together. I will do my best to have a beautiful life as well.

I enfold my arms around my own waist for a much-needed hug. *All will be fine,* I promise myself. I have grown up in the past six months, more than I had in six years. My existence now has priorities that are not based on juvenile impulses and curiosity. I ceased wishing for silly, unimportant things, such as for him to call, text, or come find me. I now only have one wish to be the strong person I need for myself, and never require more than what God gave me in order to feel whole.

I have brought my beloved violin that once belonged to my maman—and before that, to Joella and her mère—and I've been joining in accompaniment of the divine melody emanating from dozens of guitars played by other gypsies that have come to honor this female deity almost all day. The hymns that fill this crypt have completely restored my aching soul, making me postulate that maybe I've been here hundreds of times before, and perhaps, in a way, my soul has.

I inhale the scent of burning candles that light the prominent shrine, causing a sense of suspended euphoric reality; an enchanting environment. I would never be able to recap or explain to another person this feeling unless they came and stood next to me and witnessed her spirit for themselves.

I stand on the long line to re-enter the underground shrine after taking a quick break to give my fingers and legs a rest.

"This is amazing."

I hear someone speak English and look up immediately. The Provençal festival of St. Sarah has been known to bring thousands of tourists to this little seaside town, and I'm not at all surprised that a few Americans have found their way to the crypt. Two women stand in line directly in front of me, and it's obvious they can't contain their delight at the visual feast taking place a few feet away from them.

I try to continue my peaceful meditation and absorb all the positive energy dancing around me, but I can't help but listen in on their conversation, excited at being able to understand them.

"Is it weird that we're here?" The blonder woman asks the taller girl.

"They don't know we're Jewish. You look like a shiksa anyway."

They both snort out an infectious kind of laugh that I can't help but smile and silently join in on. By their comfort and ease, they seem as if they've known each other for years, perhaps they're even sisters. As an only child growing up on a secluded vineyard without a mama and fearing the sea, I didn't have many friends besides my musical instruments. I unintentionally become extremely envious when I see female friendships that someone like me can only dream about.

"Do you think he'll ever find her?" The shorter blond asks her friend—or sister.

"I hope so. I'm afraid his heart can't take any more pain … similar to how I was when Liam found me in London."

I look up to see the two women huddled together, resting their heads and drawing comfort in one another.

"I was worried you'd be hurt by all this. He meant so much to you for so long that I couldn't imagine the two of you moving on together like this."

A burst of adrenaline fuels my interests as I feel like a spy listening in on a conversation not meant for my ears, but these two women have completely captivated me, and now I can't concentrate on anything but their tête-à-tête. I close my eyes as if praying, but really, I'm just eavesdropping.

"Being loved by Liam and starting a life with him is beyond anything I've ever imagined for myself, but as happy as I was, there was still a piece of me that was missing. JJ and Jeffery … they'll always be a part of me, and I need to be a part of them for my life to feel complete. We've both come to the conclusion that I don't love him the way I love Liam, and he doesn't love me the way he loved his wife, and that's okay. Look at our children—they were the reason we came together. I want him to be a happy person and the perfect father I've watched him be from a distance, and for that, he needs another person to remind him that he's human. He thinks he's a villain, but he's not. He's just a good guy who got lost. He needs one woman and one life, a kind of life he doesn't need an escape from. I'm not that woman—I never was, but I think she is. He needs to find her, I feel it in my bones. Our relationship reminds me of that song, *'Making Love Out of Nothing At All'* by Air Supply."

I'm pretty sure I stopped breathing when the taller American mentioned the name Jeffery. I'm not sure if I've even heard her correctly, or if I'm just hearing what I want to hear. I haven't uttered his name since I told Lauren about him, and hearing his name now feels illusory. I summon all my will to stay put and not bother these two American women. I want to ask the taller one if it's Jeffery Rossi she's referring to, and if by chance, she happens to be Eddie's little sister? But that would be preposterous. There is zero way they could possibly know my Jeffery—well, he's not mine in a physical sense, but he was mine for a short moment in time, and he will always be mine to me.

Panic quickly spreads down my body and I suddenly can't find enough air to breathe, as if the hundreds of lit candles around me are using up all the oxygen left in this tiny space. The concave walls around me unexpectedly begin to cause a claustrophobic anxiety that I've never before experienced.

I step out from my place in the line, making more noise than I should, and begin to push myself out. I need to get out of here now! I'm a bit disoriented as dark spots smudge my vision. *Which way is the exit?* Sweat forms around my lips and I strain to ventilate my lungs, but there isn't enough air here. I need to go outside.

In my imagination, I hear one of the women—the one who spoke his name—call after me. In my mind, she yells "excuse me, miss" over and over, but it's safe to say I have an overactive imagination, and I just need to get out of this overcrowded space fast, or I'll faint.

Where did all the air go?

Jeffery

"All Out of Love" by Air Supply

I clutch a fragile violin that I'm afraid might crumble in my hands by the look of its age. I doubt this old artifact can even produce any music; it looks as if it may dissolve if someone attempts to play it. Sara and Emily have given up trying to pursue the girl they claim this violin belongs to. If it weren't for the fact that I saw Sarah play a violin that morning on the floor in her apartment before I left her to go back to my children, I'd think nothing of this ancient-stringed instrument, but this can't be a coincidence, it must be hers. I have no doubt that Emily and Sara were at the right place at the right time.

We've been scattered in a military style deployment throughout this little village of Saintes-Maries-de-la-Mer in the worst possible time to be here. There are way too many tourists and caravans everywhere with some kind of gypsy festival taking place in the next two days. After I gave my A-team Kali's real name, we were able to received confirmation from Will's father that the driver brought Kali—I mean, Sarah—to a small boutique hotel. I was there at the little hotel waiting in the lobby and knocking on her door for hours without any luck. Louis and Will spent all day driving Emily and Sara around town to try and maybe spot her on the avenues, which is useless with the amount of people wandering the streets. Thank God Eddie and Michelle had been entertaining all our children or we'd get nowhere.

The sun has already set and we're all back onboard sharing our findings, or in my case, lack of. I didn't think it would be this hard to locate her, but I've had no prospects whatsoever. The only semi-interesting discoveries from our fruitless quest have come from the women. Emily has told us about some church she and Sara were told to go and investigate—being the number one tourist destination in Saintes-Maries-de-la-Mer. They somehow made it to the basement of said church after waiting in line for hours. They found out it was a very holy gathering place for gypsies who come from around the world to honor Saint Sarah, which I have deduced is the same place that Mr. LeBlanc had named and described to me. Emily goes on to tell us about the big crowds and the dimly candlelit crypt, how it was very loud, and men were playing guitars and singing songs. Emily produces a black Madonna statue, which she purchased, and announces that she will now be adding this unusual yet powerful relic to her long list of non-Jewish holiday paraphernalia, to which Louis promises that he'll kill her if she observes one more fucking holiday that she has no business celebrating. But it's clear that Emily will do whatever her heart wants, whether Louis approves or not, and he will love her for it.

Emily then continues to narrate their emotional experience at the church. How they were ready to leave and then heard a loud sound behind them. It's Sara who noticed this violin on the floor, and picked it up before it was trampled over. Sara then tells us how a dark-haired girl running out toward the door caught her attention, and that the two of them tried to catch up to her. When asked if the violin was theirs, all the other people shook their heads; therefore, they concluded that the instrument had to belong to the girl who ran out. They assumed she must've dropped it without realizing. Long story short—by the time they made their way above ground, the girl was gone, swallowed by the crowd surrounding the church, and they were left holding on to this violin which they now don't know what to do with, or who to return it to.

It has to be her violin.

"What's your next move, mate?" Will comes over and hands me a beer.

"I'm gonna go back to the hotel where they confirmed she checked in yesterday, and hopefully, she'll be back in her room by now." I haven't let go of the violin, because in my heart, I know it's hers and I wish it were her I was holding onto and protecting right now instead of this wooden apparatus. "I can't imagine it being very safe to be out alone this late." I unconsciously tighten my grip as I feel one of the strings from the violin loosening from under my fingers. I look down and an overwhelming sense of fear blooms inside. What if something were to happen to her? What if someone tries to hurt her? What if we can't find her? What if I never see her again?

Will, probably reading my doomed facial expressions, puts his hand on my shoulder and says reassuringly, "Jeff, stop imagining the worse. She'll be ace until you find her. And you *will* find her. The whole bloody universe is conspiring to bring you two together. It's gonna bloody happen, mate."

I smile, because he's right. I need to stay optimistic and believe that things will work out. We didn't come this far to fail.

I pat his hand, still on my shoulder, and say, "Congratulations. I heard you're somebody's husband." I joke around with the only man that deserves to be her husband.

"I was itching to tell you, but she made me promise to keep a tight lid until she had the chance to speak to you first. I'm going to make up for all the rubbish we had to endure up to now, I want to give her the stars," he vows, looking up at the clear, star-littered sky. I'm convinced that there is no man alive who could love Sara more than Will.

We engulf each other in a man hug, and this is definitely not how I envisioned my life, but I couldn't be happier for them and the good life I know they'll have, content that, in a small way, the children and I will be a part of it.

"Go fetch your little buttercup, mate. We need to meet this Sarah of yours." He winks.

I'm already walking toward the stairs to take a ride back to the hotel I spent most of the day scouting for her in, and hopefully, she's back in her room, safe.

"I promise I won't come back without her," I call out from the steps.

"That's the spirit!" I hear him yell back at me.

She better be back at the hotel, or this may prove to be a very long, hard night for me. I was serious about not coming back without her, or at least news of her. Fate has to step in and help me find my Sarah.

Sarah

"Thief of Hearts" by Melissa Manchester

It's almost midnight, and I should go back to my hotel and not be here alone this late. I'm supposed to act like an adult and take care of myself because no one else will. In my delusional state of mind, I ran out like a madwoman upon overhearing his name, and as luck would have it, I somehow lost my beloved violin. I went back to the church twice already, but I haven't been able to find it, or anybody who's seen it. I've been assured that nobody returned a lost violin. How could I have dropped one of my most precious possessions? How could I have been so careless? I wonder if perhaps someone may have found it on the floor and just decided to keep it as a toy or souvenir? Or maybe it was stepped over, crushed, and reduced to dust—like me.

My tears won't end as they run down my cheeks, and I'm beyond the point of hysteria. All I have left of my violin is the bow, which I've held onto for dear life. I have one of Joella's floral scarves wrapped around my shoulders, but I'm still numb and frozen to the bone. The reality that I will never be able to replace the violin that was once played by the lost generation of women I will never again see is absolutely crushing.

I feel myself start to violently shake, and all I hear is my heart thumping out of control while my teeth uncontrollably knock against each other. The devastating sense of loss and regret cripple me as I sit on a cold rock, watching the black waves crushing down against the shore, over and over. I haven't been this close to the sea in over a decade, afraid of its power, but it can't do more damage than I've already done. Here I am, sitting by the same waters that once took my maman, and pray to somehow have her precious violin returned to me. It's all I have left of them. Perhaps the black sea will listen to my plea as I promise to never ask for anything ever again, just as long as their violin lives somewhere unharmed.

My emotions have completely depleted me to the point of exhaustion. My neck can no longer hold my head up as my brain begs my lids to close and put an end to this nightmare. I begin to drift off to the land of unconsciousness where I'm never alone and he always comes back for me.

I'm cocooned under a down blanket and the distinct spicy scent of the man I won't dare mention ever again surrounds me. I recognize this dream; my psyché visits him in his home frequently. I open my eyes, and of course, my dear violin and bow are lying right beside me. I'll hate waking up from this paradise where I have everything, even the tiny piece of his heart he left with me six months ago. I close my eyes again in the chance of delaying the unavoidable consciousness that will take it all away shortly. I never want to wake up. This is where I want to belong.

I feel myself rocking back and forth with the sound of the sea lolling my aching soul. I touch my chest and feel not just my locket, but also the key that is once again around my neck as I greedily place my other hand on the violin. Perhaps I'll be able to pluck them both out of my dream and into my grim reality. I caress the strings gently, and instantly sense a slack string under my fingers. I'm about to wake up—that's how my dreams usually end, with pragmatic fragments of reality penetrating my idyllic fantasy world.

"Sarah."

I've never heard him say my name, my *real* name. I knew it would be too painful recalling how it sounded coming from his lips.

"Sarah, are you up?"

My name sounds perfect from his lips.

I feel his soft hands moving my hair away from my face, grazing my cheek and forehead as if he's done it millions of times before. God, I hope he never stops touching me. How do I stay here?

"Why are you so beautiful? How could I have left you?"

Those are the words I put in his mouth. Those are the words that every woman wants to hear. To be loved, cherished, missed. This is what I imagine he says to me when he comes back to find me.

"I've watched you all day, and I know you still need to rest, but I want you to get up. We need to talk. I have so much I need to tell you."

I smile and allow his gentle touch and loving words to soothe me from the inside out. Perhaps I'll be allowed to stay in this dream and never again wake up.

Jeffery

"That's What Friends Are For" by Dionne Warwick

The doctor has checked on her twice since Will returned, clutching her lax body in his arms. He's assured me that all her vitals are good despite her body working overtime, but it's nothing a little rest and nutrition can't restore. She goes in and out of sleep like she hasn't slept in weeks. Sometimes, it's as if she knows I'm here and she talks to me, responds to my touch. Tired, cried out, and dirty from sleeping on the beach, this girl is still one of the most beautiful things I've ever seen, almost too beautiful.

Thank God Will and Sara found her. If it wasn't for them, I'd still be at her stupid hotel waiting like a fool, and she would never show up. My heart breaks thinking of this fragile young woman crying, alone on a cold beach in the middle of the night. The last place I would have imagined finding her was by the sea, knowing the story of her mother's death. Women have a sixth sense to know where to look, and Emily and Sara did enough research on the Romani pilgrims at the Camargue to understand the symbolic importance of the sea and why their people come to witness the plaster statue of Sarah La Kali being submerged in the water and blessing all those around her. Women make the best detectives.

Will and Louis drove Emily and Sara back to the church to inquire if anyone had lost a violin, which in fact, they had. They told them of a young woman who played the violin at the crypt for hours, that she was in tears looking for her priceless instrument. They left all their information and the coordinates of where the yacht is docked in hopes of the young woman returning. Emily and Louis came back to the ship to wait in case someone showed up, while Sara and Will continued on foot from the church following the flower-covered path down the coastline to the seashore.

Everything makes sense; her father mentioned that Sarah La Kali was her mother's favorite saint, and they have named their only daughter in honor of her. Sarah LeBlanc came here to celebrate her culture on the holiest day of the year for the gypsy community. It's the one day where her people, dispersed around the globe, come together here at Saintes-Maries-de-la-Mer to take their beloved Saint Sarah la Kali, adorned in flowers and engulfed by layers of bright-colored robes, down to the sea. It's a time of celebration, forgiveness and rebirth, a place where thousands come to ask for miracles. I hope that this fragile, yet strong woman, who I finally get to hold again, gets whatever her soul came here to ask for.

"Jeff."

I turn as Emily stands in the doorway of my room that has now been allocated for Sarah while she comes to her senses. The Bruel generosity is beyond words, and I'm thankful to be on the receiving end of it, whether I feel deserving or not. Having friends who drop everything and come to your rescue is a blessing only few get to experience. *I'm blessed.*

"Dinner is still waiting for you; they've warmed it up twice already. You've been in here all day, and the doctor said she's okay … she just needs to rest. I think you should get something to eat," Emily offers in her motherly tone. "Sara is giving JJ a bath and then she'll put them to bed, so stop worrying. Everything is going to work out—it has to."

Emily is right; I should let our obliviously unconscious guest sleep and go refuel myself before I too pass out. I follow Emily out, giving Sarah one last look before I close the door behind me. It's hard to wrap my brain around her presence, in my bed no less, and our current predicament. I hope that when she does finally wake up, she won't be mad at me, and that she'll want to talk to me and let me explain. But ultimately, I pray it's not too late for us to start over.

I walk up the stairs toward the dining room on deck and hear my daughter's laughter coming from inside the room where Sara is bathing her and her brother. I can't help but smile. All the things I love are within arm's reach, and the warmth circulating inside me is nothing short of incredible. I wish I could stop time this instant and enjoy how all the pieces of my life have begun to fall into place and make sense.

Sarah

"Eyes Without a Face" by Billy Idol

The sound of a violin wakes me as if from the dead. I sit up in pain as my sore muscles come to life and my unfamiliar surroundings knock the wind out of me. *Where. The. Hell. Am. I?* I'm in a small, dimly lit room that feels like a jail cell without any windows, just a porthole. *I'm abducted,* is the first coherent thought that enters my mind.

"Hi."

I jump up as I hear a little voice coming from the left of me. I turn and come face to face with a blue-eyed little girl with hair almost as dark as mine. She looks to be maybe seven or eight years old. She's sitting on the bed beside me with her damp hair cascading down her shoulders, and she appears to be in a kind of nightgown. I notice that she has my violin clutched tightly in her small arms, but that can't be right, because my violin is gone—lost forever.

"Do you speak English?" The little girl vigorously nods her head. "Where did you get that violin?" I ask, sounding overly accusatory for no good reason.

"I found it on the pillow next to you. Is it yours?" she asks, while handing me back my past.

I take the violin from her outstretched hands, and a half cry escapes my lips as I recognize my best friend. There is no doubt it's indeed mine. How could it be here? How did it get here? How did I get here? Where am I?

"What's your name? I'm Juliet, and if you'd like, I could teach you how to play. I'm very good," she proclaims with such confidence I can only smirk with admiration.

"Hello, Juliet. I'm Sarah. I would love to hear you play, and if you have time, I would be honored to be your student." I attempt to keep a straight face as I answer the sweet child wholeheartedly.

Her mouth opens, revealing two missing teeth as her eyes light up with joy. Her smile is infectious, and for a split second, looks familiar. She tries to contain her excitement but fails and claps her hands in pleasure at my response.

"Yes, oh my God, Sarah, you have the perfect name. I have a best friend named Sara, and now I'll have two Sarahs." She's deliriously pleased.

I can't help but mimic her happiness before I'm reminded that I don't have any idea where I am, but perhaps, Juliet knows where we are and who's in charge.

"Where are we?" I question in a conspiring whisper.

"We're on a boat, silly. It's called 'La Vie en Rose.' This is Eric and Rose's boat—they are my cousins. I think I'm going to marry Eric when he grows up," the little girl declares, employing a remarkable French accent while naming an Édith Piaf song. Maybe I've been captured by some strange cousin-marrying cult.

"How old is your cousin, Eric?" It's all too bizarre; I may simply be in a mental institution.

"Eric is five and Rose is ten," she affirms with a smirk.

I've been abducted on a luxury yacht owned by children, it seems. Perhaps Peter Pan will come to visit me soon, too.

"Where are your parents?" I ask, needing something to add up and make sense in my head. But the way the light in her eyes just dimmed, I regret asking her anything.

"My mommy left to a place called heaven. It's nice there; I don't think she's coming back. My brother doesn't believe the red robin that comes to visit me every morning in my window is her coming back to see if I'm okay." The sad little child, who reminds me of myself, continues to break my heart. "Mommy said that Daddy will find a guardian angel named Sarah to help us after she leaves for heaven. Are you an angel?" the sweet girl asks me.

I look at her, at a total loss for words. I see his features materialize on her face one by one, as if a puzzle revealing and displaying a whole picture right before my eyes. I can feel his gaze on me—peering into my essence. I know whose child she is; there's no denying it. I have an overwhelming urge to give this little person a hug and promise her that all will be well one day. I don't know how I know, but I just do.

"Can you play for me?" I circle back to a safe topic. "You know this violin is very old. It is over one hundred years old and it's been around the world like a well-traveled gypsy." She smiles at my description of my inanimate best friend, and the light that was extinguished earlier returns, illuminating her steel-blue eyes.

She nods her head while I restring the loose cord on my beloved violin. I quickly tune and hand the instrument back to Juliet as I watch her expertly place it on her left shoulder. She then takes the bow, positioning her delicate fingers elegantly, ready to begin her solo concert.

She stops to think and then adds, "My brother usually accompanies me on the piano, but he's sleeping and we don't have a piano here, so just pretend you can hear a piano." She waits for my reaction.

I nod; I can't wait to hear my violin come to life at her command. "What song will you play for me, maestro?" I inquire before she starts.

"It was my mommy's favorite song. Jacob and I were preparing it for her birthday, but she had to go to heaven before she heard it. Daddy says she can hear it from heaven and that she's yelling bravo." She swallows hard before continuing to kill me with her words. "It's called 'Where Do I Begin' or Daddy sometimes just calls it 'Love Story.'"

The child begins to play a melody that I myself have played hundreds of times. My maman, too, used to love and play this song when she would teach me to play the violin, when I was a child not much older than Juliet. I lie down and close my eyes as the lovely, smooth sound brings back thousands of long-forgotten memories. I can hear my maman's voice sing the lyrics in my head as I drift back home. This is a dream—a beautiful, sad, vivid dream.

"What are you doing here?"

I open my eyes and sit up at once to a woman standing over my bed, directing her question at Juliet.

Juliet smiles, gets off the bed, and goes to stand next to the woman, who to my delight is an adult and may have a reasonable explanation for all this. Juliet hugs the woman, who upon closer inspection could be her mother; they do look a bit alike. Maybe I just imagined she was his daughter.

"Sara, this is also Sarah. I'm teaching her how to play the violin. I think she's our guardian angel, too."

We both smirk at Juliet's introduction. When she mentioned knowing another Sara, I thought she was referring to a friend her own age, not an adult.

"You should be in bed and not bothering anybody this late, your father will be mad if he finds you here." Her other friend Sara reprimands her more like a mother than a friend.

"She's no bother. It was a treat to hear her play," I offer in defense of my new little violin teacher.

The woman lifts her gaze and smiles my way while hugging Juliet to her side. It's impossible to be mad at this sweet little giggling person with two front teeth missing.

"Hello, sorry for this. I'm Sara Klein by the way. No!—I mean Knight, my name is Sara Knight. I am the one who found your violin at the crypt when you dropped it yesterday. My girlfriend and I ran after you, but we couldn't find you outside the church."

This must be the tall American girl I overheard speaking about him. I begin to power blink, because her last name sounds familiar, and she could be, she may be … oh God she is.

"Juliet, please go back to bed quietly and let me talk to your new friend."

The little girl nods, waves goodbye my way, and then leaves me alone with Sara Klein or Knight or whatever her name is. I've made the connection—I know exactly who she is.

"Eddie Klein's little sister," I say out loud before my brain can censor my mouth.

"Yeah, Eddie is my brother. Liam and I found you on the beach last night. We tried waking you but you seemed disoriented. The way Jeffery described you, I knew it was you immediately. I saw your bright scarf a mile away. When we couldn't wake you, we called Jeff, and he made sure we didn't leave you on that cold beach alone. It honestly wasn't safe for you to be sleeping there with the herds of people congregating, and in your condition, so we brought you here, where a doctor was waiting to examine you. This is my friend, Emily, and her husband, Louis', yacht," the attractive woman explains, shining light on how I got to my surroundings and alleviating the overwhelmed expression on my face.

I recall him talking to someone named Emily on the phone, which at the time, I thought might have been Eddie's little sister, but this is Eddie's little sister—the woman he loves. I still don't understand what they're doing here in France in the first place. She could've just left the violin at the church. They didn't need to go through all this trouble for me.

"Was that Jeff's daughter?" I question, but I already know the answer.

"Yes, she looks just like him, doesn't she?" Her eyes brighten up.

I nod and continue firing questions in an attempt to understand. "Why did you bring me here?" It still makes no sense.

"Jeffery has been looking for you. We're all here to help him find you," she answers as if it should be obvious.

"Why? He wasn't looking for me before." It's the truth. He never called me back. He clearly wanted nothing to do with me. Once he unburdened himself to me with Joella's words, our business together was over.

"You'll have to ask him that, but we're here to support him," she says sternly, in no rush to give me too much information.

I know this is none of my business, but I'm going to ask her anyway, because I'm on a yacht that I didn't ask to be on with people I've never met. "Are you the girl he loves? He told me about having a relationship with you before and maybe after he got married." I look right into her eyes, and what I really ought to be asking is if she and Jeffery are now together.

"What Jeffery and I share is complicated. We've known each other for a very long time. We will forever be a part of each other's life because of the choices we've made, which neither of us regret. He told me about your grandmother—the fortuneteller, and the reading she gave him back in college. And he also hasn't been able to stop talking about you. If you're worried about us being together, don't. We're not meant to be together. We've never been good for each other. I knew a long time ago that he and I weren't destined for a happily ever after the way we envisioned in our youth, but it wasn't until he met you that he accepted that reality as well. You can't force a love that isn't intended. I'm now married to a man who has put all my past relationships into perspective, and perhaps, that's what your interaction did for Jeffery. Believe me … he's not the bad guy. He makes himself out to be, but he's not. He made choices as best he could based on his circumstances."

"So you're not together?" I ask, still confused because maybe I missed something. My heart is beating way past what I'm sure is considered normal, and I can't decide how I feel about this woman or the things she's telling me.

"Right. I also have a feeling that you still don't know about a very important aspect of his life, which I'm sure he would like to be the one to tell you about. But you should know that I will always love him and the kids, and I plan to be around to watch and help them grow. He is the man who has navigated me—good or bad—to where I am today, and for that, I will always be thankful."

I nod and continue to power blink, absorbing all the farfetched information this woman is sharing with me. She clearly cares about him and his children, which is odd being that she said she's married to someone else. I want to yell with frustration and simultaneously hide at the prospect of inevitably coming face to face with the eyes I see every single minute in my mind. I stop pretending to understand and be okay with my current situation, and close my eyes to try and calm myself down from the storm heading toward my heart.

"I'll let Jeffery know you're awake, and I'll go make sure Juliet is in bed. It's nice to finally meet you … Sarah," I hear Sara Knight say. "You should know that in all the years we've been together, he never once came after me—trying to find me. Only true love refuses to be stopped by obstacles—distance, reason and logic."

By the time I open my eyes to look at her, she has already left the room. I'm alone on Emily and Louis's, or whatever their names are, boat. I quietly recap my crazy situation in my head. I just met his daughter and his ex-girlfriend and I have my most precious possession back in my arms—unharmed—but perhaps the most important thing I've learned so far is that Jeff Rossi came halfway around the world to look for me, *me!* And he brought his friends and family along with him.

Jeffery

"Glory of Love" by Peter Cetera

"Why are you still not sleeping?" I proceed to tuck my little hooligan princess in. Jacob is passed out on his stomach, blissfully snoring, while his sister is a ball of energy ready to bounce off the walls. I'm staying in the kids' room tonight, since I have Sarah situated and resting in my room.

"Daddy, I don't want to sleep. I'm not tired. I just met a really, really, really, nice girl, and she said I could teach her to play the violin. Her name is also Sarah, and I know that I was the one that found her and not you, but I still think she could be our angel, just like Mommy said."

I can hardly swallow after hearing her words.

"You met Sarah, the girl sleeping in my room?" I query with trepidation.

She nods with more excitement than I've seen in a long time. I sigh, taking a deep breath. Things never happen the way we envision. Juliet wasn't supposed to see Sarah before I had a chance to explain everything. I smile, trying to picture their encounter. I wish I could've been there when she ambushed Sarah. I need to tuck this little menace in and go see my daughter's new friend. She must be dazed and confused, and if Juliet got to her, she may be overwhelmed as well.

"Will you try and go to sleep while I go and talk to your new friend? I'll let you know if she's our angel or not." But I already know she is.

She lunges herself at me, wrapping her arms around my neck, and kisses my cheek with little pecks over and over. I hug my little baby as close to me as I can. She is the sum of everything I love—she's my soul. She lets go of me and gets under the covers next to her brother and pretends she's fast asleep. *Silly girl, I love them both so much.*

I leave the twins and walk in the direction of my cabin. I see Sara leave the room and walk toward me in the hall. *Great!* It seems that all the people I love have already met my angel.

"Sara," I cautiously pronounce her name, which may sound like a greeting, but it's actually a question.

"Jeffery," she responds with a side smile that begins to answer my silent interrogation. "She's beyond scared. You should go talk to her ASAP. She just woke up on a freaking yacht with a bunch of strangers and got a violin lesson from a seven-year-old. I'm not sure what you told her, but she was under the impression that you and I, or 'Eddie's little sister' as she put it, were together. I want you to be responsible and explain us and JJ to this woman before anybody gets hurt; it's imperative that you do. You need to make it right with her. She shouldn't feel alone in her state. I could actually feel her loneliness when we found her on that beach."

I stand and listen to Sara direct her worry and frustration at me, and all I can think about is my Sarah, who was once Kali, only a few steps away from me feeling scared and overwhelmed. I don't want her to feel any of the things Sara is describing.

I nod and give Sara a quick kiss on the forehead, anxiously compelled to see the woman who's hijacked my life. "I'll make it right," I promise as I prepare to walk toward my future. "I won't hurt any more people by keeping away the truth," I declare as I proceed to knock on her door.

I'm about to hear her voice for the first time since she hung up on me over six months ago. I've waited to hear her voice every time I picked up my goddamn phone. I take a deep breath and walk in after she calls out for me to come in.

This is it! This is what I've crossed continents for—to see her.

Our eyes lock the second I'm inside the small room. I had a million things to say to her, and now, I just stand silently watching her, letting our eyes become reacquainted. I can't believe we actually found her, I can't believe she's really here, and I can't believe Sarah and I were fated to be together long before we ever met.

"Forgive me."

"Pardonne-moi."

We both say at the same time.

What can she possibly be sorry about? "Why are you sorry?" I hope my question doesn't sound harsh or cold.

"I should've called you back and let you tell me the rest of your story after my phone died. I was selfish. I didn't want to hear that you and your friend's sister were getting back together. It was just one night between us and it was my fault. You never called me back, which confirmed everything in my head." She whispers the last part, sounding ashamed.

"I thought you hung up on me. I figured you heard enough. I was a mess and I couldn't drag you deeper into my fucked-up world. Why would a young girl like you need the baggage that an old man like me comes with? I'm sorry it took me this long to figure everything out. I need for you to know that I haven't stopped thinking about you for one second since that night. I can't turn off everything you brought back to life. Whether you knew it or not, because of you, I was able to get up every single day and face the world. I miss you, Sarah." I call her by her real name to her face for the first time, wanting to shout it from the rooftops. *How did I stay away from her for this long?*

Her lower lip trembles ever so slightly while her eyes enlarge, as if in disbelief. Does she not feel what I feel? I can't look away from her. The pictures on my phone don't do her justice. I forgot how magnificent she is in real life, the most exotic being I've ever witnessed. I wait for her to say something, anything, because I need to know she'll allow me to be next to her, get to know her, prove my feelings, and be a part of her life.

I continue to stand with my back against the door, too afraid to move closer to her. There are words that need to be spoken, and if she won't say anything, then I will. "When will our daughter be born?" I ask her without warning as I drop my gaze to where her hands are resting protectively.

She lowers her eyes to her growing belly, and once again, remains silent. She probably wants nothing to do with me, but I know that's my child growing inside her, and I deserve at least a conversation.

"Please talk to me. I don't know what you're thinking, and I don't want to lose you because you somehow think I don't care about you or our baby."

"How do you know it's yours?" she spits out with anger coating each word.

Why is she angry with me? I didn't know she was pregnant. Is she angry it took me this long to come after her? Is she angry because she thought I was with Sara? Is she angry with me because she assumed she'd have to raise our child without me? Did she have any intention of ever telling me? So many questions fire off in my mind simultaneously, and it makes it hard for me to stay focused. I remind myself that she's finally within my reach and not alone somewhere, lost in the world.

"Your grandmother told me it was my daughter fourteen years ago. Your grandmother moved heaven and Earth to make sure I find you. Don't push me away. I know I'm not perfect, and I'm not good enough for you, but I love you and I will love our baby, too. I want a future with you. I waited my whole life for you to grow up … you are the promised music I've been waiting for. Please tell me I'm not crazy," I yell. She needs to say something!

"September first," I hear her say. "Our daughter will be born en Septembre. But I don't want you to think that you owe me a thing. I swear to you, I can provide very well for her without you. You don't need to feel obligated to me," she mumbles foolishly without looking at me.

I take a few strides toward this woman who has affected every cell inside me and kneel by her side. "I set out to find you and tell you that I can't function without you. I didn't know about the baby. I didn't even know if you still remembered me. I just had to see this spectacular woman named Kali who has turned everything upside down, the same girl I couldn't imagine not seeing again. On the way to find you, I also found myself. Coming after you set everything on the right path and life started to make sense again. You are my Sarah! Joella Gitanos didn't lie, she didn't make a mistake, it was always you. I just wasn't ready for you and you still needed to grow up." I take hold of both her hands together in mine and kiss them. She must know how important she is to me.

"I met your daughter." I can sense the smile in her voice without having to look at her. "I think she likes me and my name, and especially my violin. Unlike her papa," she adds sarcastically.

I look up into her eyes. "I love you, and your name, and especially your violin. It helped me find you." If she only knew how much I want to kiss those lips.

"I also met the woman you love—your original Sara. She was very gracious to me. She cares about you and your enfants very much." Her voice changes, no longer carefree.

"Sara and I have been involved since before I got married, I've told you that. She was always there for me. Instead of taking drugs to ease the pain, I would get a dose of Sara. We lived in limbo for years. I should've stopped going to see her, stopped making promises, because I had a wife that I loved very much and would never leave, but I was a coward. I was scared I'd be alone once Jacqueline's disease caught up. Sara Klein was the egg donor—the biological mother of my children. I always thought she and I would end up together, and having us be parents was the only promise I could give her to ensure we had a future. It was our secret and the one thing that kept us together for years." I feel her withdraw her hands from my grip and lie back down. She shifts on her side, turning away from me. This is the reaction I was afraid of, the reaction I dreaded. But she needs to know everything. I want her to understand.

"Three years ago, Sara met William Knight in a hotel in New York after she got evicted by her ex-husband. She was married for a few years, mostly for appearances sake; it wasn't a real marriage. I walked in on her and William in that hotel, and the second I saw them together, I knew that we'd never have a future. You could taste their chemistry—she and I, we never had that. After that fated collision, all our secrets became everybody's business. She rightfully fell in love with him and ceased having any kind of relationship with me. She was granted legal rights and guardianship of our twins, but ultimately, she left New York. She and William eventually found one another again, as true love always does, and they were supposed to get married twelve months ago.

"I hadn't seen Sara for two years, until a year ago when I asked her to come back to New York after Jacqueline passed away. When I went to her hotel room to talk to her, something horrible happened." I close my eyes, remembering that horrific day.

"What happened?" Sarah turns and awaits my answer.

"I was asking her for another chance, for the sake of our children. In my mind, I have always held onto your grandmother's words as a divine promise. She was the girl with the biblical name that would be my salvation. But she told me how much she loves William and how she never loved me the way she loves him and that they're having a baby—she was pregnant. We finally had the conversation we should've had years ago, finally letting each other go, saying goodbye. One of Will's security guards walked in, scaring her and me, and she fell to the floor, bleeding, and almost died in my arms." I hear a loud gasp and notice Sarah grabbing her belly.

"Did she lose the baby?" Her eyes are beyond expressive.

"Yes, she lost the baby—not because of me or because she fell. She had an ectopic pregnancy and was bleeding from the inside, but thank God she's still here. It's a good thing I was there because Sara has a specific, rare kind of blood type, and the two of us are a perfect match. I still give blood regularly, just in case."

She sits up, listening.

"When you and I met, and after we spent a night together, things began to fall into place. My love for you is different from the love I felt for Jacky and Sara. I can't explain it, but it's important to me that you understand you're not a second choice or a consolation prize. What I feel for you transcends my past relationships, but only makes sense because of them. I long for your presence, and for the first time in my life, the unexplained void that was always there feels full when I think of you, and *us*; the questions that have plagued me are answered and I never want to be without you. I am the sum of all my choices, all my mistakes, all my experiences—they've all brought me to you." I've been talking to her belly and finally chance a glance up.

She has tears coating her stormy eyes.

"Please don't cry, and don't be upset with me. If you want nothing to do with me, I'll walk away and let you go, but I don't want to. I want you and the baby and Juliet and Jacob; I want us to be a family. I want to try and make you happy. I can't imagine a life with anyone but you. You need to know that before you send me away," I beg and plead with the woman that holds my future and the fate of my unborn child in her hands.

I hear her slowly inhale and then loudly exhale before she locks her bright eyes with mine, ready to deliver my verdict.

Sarah

"Will You Still Love Me" by Chicago

The only man I have ever loved, besides my papa, is begging for me to give him a chance as I sit propped up on the bed, unable to move or speak, afraid this is all a deceitful illusion. I've now learned things about him that are causing my head to spin and my heart to shut down, but they still haven't changed the way I care for him or his meaning in my life. He's under the impression that I don't want him because of our age difference and his messy past, but that couldn't be further from the truth. I thought it was me he didn't want. Jeffery Rossi is on his knees, pleading for me to be a part of his family and sounds as if he has every intention of raising his unborn baby, the one I assumed he'd never know about or meet.

I look away from my stomach and into his worried eyes. I have to tell him how I feel. I must wipe that unsure look from his turbulent eyes if he feels even half of what I feel for him.

"I have prayed for you to come back to me every day since you left that morning. I waited to hear something, anything, from you. I asked whoever would listen up above, to grant me even the smallest piece of you, but I accepted that I couldn't have you because your heart was already taken. When I found out I was pregnant, I took that as the only piece of you I was allowed to have. It was a small seed of hope growing inside of me, the one you and I created before I understood why we had no right to be together.

"You see … I had a remarkable childhood in Cassis before my maman died. It was full of love and laughter—all I remember is warmth. I wanted to give the only part of you that you unknowingly left with me, a beautiful life too. That was the best I could do for her and me—I came back to the place I was happiest. I understand you didn't choose to be with me or have a baby with me, and I wasn't going to add to your troubles," I say to try and explain to him that I'm not some horrible woman who wanted to keep a child away from a devoted papa. He was never an option and I wasn't interested in becoming a burden.

He doesn't say a word and continues to look at me with a penetrating, unyielding stare. He slowly gets up, towering over me like a giant. I hear him remove and discard his shoes on the floor by the bed, and without losing eye contact or saying a single word, he climbs into bed behind me. I feel his hands pull me into him with the type of ownership I've craved and dreamed about. His touch is the silent answer sending a welcomed tremor throughout my body. I've felt the warmth and safety of his arms before, only to later lose them to a harsh reality. I must play it safe and think not just about myself but about a child who should only know love and acceptance.

"You and the baby are not a problem, you are the solution. You are my happiness and my reason for waking up. You are my family, Sarah." The warmth of his words warms both the nape of my neck and my heart. "I want to be your home, the place you always feel safe and happy." His words echo in my head like a kind of déjà vu. I suddenly don't just feel Jeff, but I feel my maman's and grand-mère's warm embrace as well.

I turn inside his hold with my protruding belly between us as I face him nose to nose. I look into his dual-colored eyes, which are the only eyes I want to lose myself in for the rest of my life, and in this moment, I do feel safe. I feel full—I don't feel alone.

"You know I'm never letting you go?" is the last thing he says before I close my eyes and feel his lips make contact with mine. How can a set of lips be able to heal everything all at once?

He begins to kiss me, softly, patiently, almost too cautiously. I let a sigh of relief escape into his mouth when it finally dawns on me that he's really here. Jeff and I are in bed together, and we both want the very same thing. He hasn't forgotten about me, he hasn't forsaken me—he came after me. My half moan is the signal he needs to deepen his guarded kiss. His tongue enters my mouth, filling it eagerly as I let go of my reserve and kiss him back the way I've dreamed and fantasized about thousands of times since that first kiss in my kitchen. I'm not sure if I want to cry or laugh, but all I want is to never stop kissing him.

"You feel that?" He mirrors the words I once asked him.

"Yes," I answer with a wide smile.

"Good, I plan to do something about it. I plan to make you feel that every day for the rest of my life, Sarah."

Hearing my name leave his lips is a kind of luxury I never thought I'd get to enjoy.

"I never thought I'd hear you say my name," I cry, but this is the happiest I've ever been.

Jeff wipes my tears, allowing me to inhale his scent and calm my weary heart. He lifts my chin to align my eyes with his penetrating glare and smiles before speaking again.

"I have been saying your name before I even knew it belong to you. You were written into my future decades before I could even understand what love was. I've been lost navigating through this life, not understanding what I've been searching for, not knowing I had to find you. Whatever you feel, I feel it, too. I will never let you go—I will never hurt you, Sarah." His voice cracks when uttering my name. It's just my name, but from his lips, it feels like a promise—a solemn swear.

"What now?" I hold my breath for his answer.

"Now we press play and let the music begin. Sarah LeBlanc, will you be our guardian angel?"

His smile is my life. I outline his eyes with my fingers before touching his lips and whispering, "Only if you be mine…"

St. Lucia

One Year Later

Jeffery

The weather has cooperated beautifully thus far, and it seems that Crown Affairs will be able to execute the entire ceremony on the beach as planned. We're all barefoot, standing on the beach, lining a gate made up of two wooden doors covered in flowers. I look at the sandy beach and all the assembled guests filling every single seat on both sides of the flower canopy. I catch my stunning wife playing with Jolene, attempting to pin a flower in her nonexistent hair, which our daughter is determined on ripping out and eating.

I look away from my slice of heaven and notice a blond-haired woman in the distance. She's not part of our wedding party, and I'm certain I've never seen her before. The stranger occupies a lone lounge chair in the middle of an empty sandy beach. She's close enough for me to make out a stack of papers in her lap and pen in hand. She smiles while watching us and then continues to write vigorously. I wonder who she is. I was under the impression Will closed down their family resort just for friends and family in honor of his wedding. I turn back to look at the woman on the beach, but she's gone …

Emily pops her head out from inside the hotel, giving us the thumbs up that her best friend is ready to go. The orchestra begins to play a slow stirring melody, and a moment later, a lump forms in my heart at the sight of Juliet and Jacob holding hands, as the flower girl and ring bearer, while the guests begin to clap and cheer. Our babies take their places at the podium with Juliet clutching my wife's old violin and Jacob at the piano. Sara doesn't know about this surprise as the kids begin to play her favorite '80s song: "When I See You Smile" by Bad English with the help of the twenty piece orchestra joining in. Then, like a dream, Sara materializes, clad in white, casting a spell of awe on the crowd. She wears a smile bright enough to light New York City and you could touch her happiness from a mile away. She's never looked more striking. The entire bridal party—Emily, Louis, Eddie, and myself included, like the audio fools that we are, begin to sing out loud the lyrics to our friend's favorite ballad as she walks down the aisle crying. I look over at Will—the man on the receiving end of that smile—as he lowers his head to hide his tears. These two finally get to share with the world the happy ending they've spent their whole lives searching for. I swallow my emotion and thank the universe for granting me this view.

I suddenly see the blonde writer from before walking away, turning back to look at us from time to time until she disappears from view. *Who is she?* I shake my head to see if anyone else noticed her, but they're all focused on the bride and groom. I slowly scan all the different souls that comprise my world, zeroing in on my wife, Sarah, and all our beautiful children, and that's when I'm finally able to appreciate how life doesn't always make sense when we're living it, but in rewind, it's all crystal clear.

And they all lived happily ever after

© *Rhys Ulich*

Did I just finish my 3rd book? This is my third letter of thanks so it must be! Thank you for spending your time and money reading my novels and agreeing to let me take you on the Audio Fools journey in rewind. I am grateful to every single person from all corners of this earth that has allowed me the opportunity to entertain him or her with my words.

I've said it before, and I'll say it again; I am blessed and fortunate to have so many beautiful souls guide me in this life. My family is a Godsend. I wouldn't be able to choose kinder, smarter, more loving humans if I tried. My husband is a perfect partner and has granted me freedom to chase my crazy dreams, and I hope one day to make him proud of the road I've chosen. My children have obviously never read my books, but I hope they too will one day admire their mama and understand her passion. The women in my family have physically, emotionally and mentally picked me up off the floor and held me up when my own strength refused to. I bow down to you and I love you more than any words written in black and white could ever convey. My friends have had the misfortune of dealing with the turmoil and chaos the publishing world entails. I'm sorry if I wasn't an attentive friend and I thank you for not forsaking me when I needed you most.

My sister from another mister and my guiding light is not just my friend but also happens to be one of my biggest supporters and kickass publicist, Irene Myers. I love you and all that you do for me. Thank you for slaying my imaginary insecurities once a day and twice on Tuesdays. If you didn't push and believe in me, I'd have given up long ago. As you read this, I hope you imagine us onboard you know what, with you know whom, raising a toast to all our hard work.

I couldn't be the writer that I am today without my amazing editors, Kristen Clark Switzer, and Lori Sabin. Thank you for your intuition and guidance in shaping LOST IN REWIND. You have helped me grow as a storyteller, and your input was instrumental in sculpting the conclusion of this series. A huge thank you to the person who works hard to make my words look pretty: Julie at JT Formatting. I am very grateful to my good friend and fellow writer, Mara White, for giving LOST IN REWIND one last polish.

The cover of LOST IN REWIND perfectly depicts Jeffery Rossi with the help of model Adam Cowie, shot by the very talented Chris Davis AKA Specular. This cover has been patiently waiting for me, and I hope my storytelling will do it justice. Thank you to Perfect Pear Creative for pulling everything together and bringing it to life.

In today's crazy ruthless world of publishing, an author like me can't be seen or get into the hands of readers without the tireless work of book bloggers, bookstagrammers, other writers and of course loyal readers. I write and my books get read because of your continued help. Your likes, follows, tweets, emails, reviews, and posts are what keeps me hanging on. I thank you and hope that you will stay with me on this crazy, wild, magical ride, which I never want to end.

Thank you to Emily, Louis, Sara, William, Jeffery and Kali for choosing to talk to me and trusting me to write their stories… next stop happily ever after.

xx Tali

Tali Alexander is a Jill-of-all-trades—married mother of three, doctor of pharmacy by day and romance novelist by night. Tali has fulfilled her passion of writing with her debut romance novel **LOVE IN REWIND** (first book in the Audio Fools trilogy). Since its debut, fans have embraced the unconventional love story of Emily and Louis Bruel making **LOVE IN REWIND** #1 on Amazon Kindle charts (September 2014). With an increasing demand from her fan base for the next installment, Tali has released the next story in the Audio Fools trilogy, **LIES IN REWIND.** Tali's fans finally get their third and final book in the series titled. **LOST IN REWIND,** out now!!!

Goodreads
https://www.goodreads.com/book/show/20804287-love-in-rewind

Twitter
https://twitter.com/Tali_Alexander

Pinterest
http://www.pinterest.com/talialexanderbo/

Facebook
https://www.facebook.com/TaliAlexanderAuthor

Instagram
http://instagram.com/talialexander

e-Mail
Tali@TaliAlexander.com

Other Titles by Tali Alexander

WWW.TALIALEXANDER.COM

Love in Rewind
Lies in Rewind
Lost in Rewind

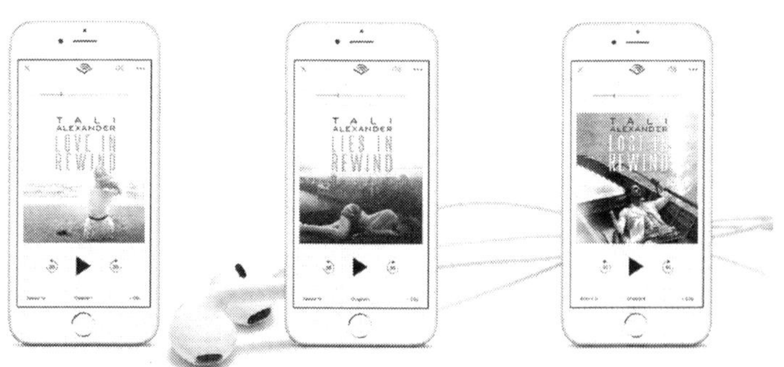

Look for the Audio Fools series in audiobook
available where audiobooks are sold.

Made in the USA
San Bernardino, CA
17 March 2017